JANET PYWELL

Ellie Bravo

An Unusual Love Story

Contents

About Ellie Bravo

Across the Lough started as a writing exercise when I was studying for my MA in Creative Writing at the Seamus Heany Centre, Queen's University, Belfast, Northern Ireland. The task that I set myself was to write 500 words a week so that in 100 weeks I would have 50,000 words - enough for a novella.

I immersed myself in this project, as well as writing my first novel - *The Golden Icon* and various short stories that turned into *Red Shoes and Other Short Stories* and — the blog grew. To make it fun, I added images of Ireland and places that my protagonist Ellie Bravo visited, recipes that she cooked and also things that interested this intelligent and dynamic, young woman.

After finishing the original version of the blog, I approached Silke Bader, Publisher & CEO of Curve Magazine and LOTL Magazine in Australia. She offered me the opportunity to contribute to the Romantic Fiction category, where I began again to serialise my story. On these blogs I published the first few chapters of the first draft of the *Ellie Bravo* novel under the title: *Across the Lough*.

The novel has changed dramatically from the first draft that I posted weekly and, I believe the essence of the characters and the plot-line has been enhanced through many revised versions and feedback.

Due to the growing popularity of *Ellie Bravo* and following the publication of *Someone Else's Dream,* another contemporary love story, I have revisited this novel to revise and edit further. I have also very slightly, changed the ending.

I do hope you enjoy *Ellie Bravo* and if you do — please leave a review.

To see more about Ellie Bravo please visit: http://ellybravo.blogspot.co.uk/

Happy reading ;-)) Janet

Chapter One

I straighten my blouse, push my cropped blond hair behind my ears and smile expectantly at Mr Gower. He is balding and bespectacled with an upper class accent.

"We've given it a lot of thought, Ellie," he says.

I tilt my head, hold my breath and smile in anticipation, I've worked hard for the new role of Marketing Director.

"Peter is getting the new position."

I blink and exhale in a gasp.

He holds several sheets of A4 that he seems intent on lining up with his immaculately manicured fingers. "I understand all the effort you have put in and recognise your ability in this area but I must think of the company. It is important that our staff act with the utmost decorum and discretion and unfortunately it seems—"

I bang my hand on his desk, lean forward and I speak quickly,"I have put this new project together single-handedly. Peter has only played a nominal role. He won't have the ability to implement all my ideas. He doesn't have the—"

Mr Gower holds up his hand. "The decision has been made. Peter Morgan will be the new Marketing Director. I'm sorry."

Breath explodes from my lungs and I stare at him as the silent truth bounces gently between us.

"It's Kat Small, isn't it? She's put you up to this, hasn't she?" I insist.

He focuses on a distant point over my shoulder — a view of Canary Wharf — we're on the eighth floor surrounded by glass windows. He coughs. "Proctor and Gower pride themselves on—"

"On what? That their marketing executives don't sleep with their clients? Kat told you, didn't she?" I lean across his table forcing him to look me in the eye but I am suddenly conscious of the glass dividing the other offices and the surreptitious eyes of my curious colleagues. It dawns on me — the whole office knows — Kat has spread the word.

There's no more that I can say to my boss, it would be futile, so with one sweeping hand I cast the neatly stacked files on his desk up into the air. He cries out as pages take flight, fluttering like paper planes, single pages of confetti, floating and hovering before crashing to the floor.

I stride from his office slamming the door behind me. I'm on a collision course from which I cannot hold back and in six strides I pass my watchful colleagues and fling open Kat's door.

"You told him. How could you?"

Her auburn hair is a curtain framing her oval face. Her green feline eyes watch me with caution as I approach her desk.

"Stop!" She holds up her hand. "Don't make things worse, Ellie."

"They couldn't possibly be any—"

"You brought it on yourself."

"Why?" I ask quietly. "Why did you tell him about my one night with Angela when you have been having an affair for the past three months?"

"Angela is a client."

"So?"

"So, it's bad for the company. It's against the rules."

"And since when did you care about the company, Kat? If you cared that much you wouldn't be giving this promotion to Peter. He will never be able to do the job and you know it."

Kat shrugs.

"You only care about yourself," I whisper, "And now you've ruined my career and my reputation. Why?"

There are footsteps behind me and when I turn around I see the burly security guard in his smart navy uniform.

"Frank?" I say.

"Come to escort you from the office, Ms Bravo. Mr Gower says he don't want no problems."

"What? With me?"

Kat stands up and over her shoulder Tower Bridge glistens in the watery, winter sky. "You're not as indispensable as you think you are," she says, "Besides, our personal life is not relevant here at work."

"We were lovers for two years, Kat. You've always been unfaithful and now, when you can't control me, you've turned my friends against me and you've taken my job. I never knew you were so spiteful."

"We all have a sell-by date Ellie and today, this is yours." She smiles.

* * *

Sun and showers, tears and tantrums, lovers and losers.

I'm leaving it all behind to start a new life.

Well, probably not the rain or the sleet or the snow. As the ferry boat sails up Belfast Lough, I wonder if the rainbow over the imposing yellow Harland and Wolff cranes that the locals call Samson and Goliath are an omen. Is it a symbol of my colourful past or a painter's canvas and the opportunity to obliterate the pain and shame of my previous life?

The skyline is interesting and the hills are covered in three day-old snow. I don't focus on the new Titanic Museum that stands like a beacon in honour of the infamous ship that sailed from here a hundred years ago on its fatal maiden voyage. I don't think about the Troubles that hit newspaper headlines every summer during the marching season and neither is my gaze distracted by the grey film studios where *The Game of Thrones* is made for television.

Instead, I stand on the deck with my shoulders hunched and my heart lodged in the dark cavern of my empty stomach like a heavy boulder in the Garden of Eden. Although I dip my chin into the collar of my biker's jacket, salt from the Irish Sea and a bitter March wind bites at my cheek. Snow flurries dance like fairies, lightly tickling and teasing my skin, so I turn from the voluptuous clouds that taunt me like heavy breasts and close my eyes feeling the icy crystals as they land on my face.

I am alone but worse than that I am lonely.

* * *

Auntie Annie's house is in Holywood a few miles east of Belfast city. From her living room window I look across Belfast Lough and, on the opposite shore, I recognise Belfast Castle nestled under the snow-capped hill they call Napoleon's Nose.

Farther along the coast is the church spire in Jordanstown and to the right are the white town houses and apartments built around the Carrickfergus marina.

From the kitchen come swirling rich aromas of cinnamon, turmeric, frying onions and garlic. Auntie Annie is tall and thin with teasing blue eyes. She has spent the past few days cajoling me into good humour but when she sees my face she says, "If you are going to be miserable you can take your Harley Davidson and your grumpy mood and go back to London."

"The lamb tagine smells delicious," I reply to quell her irritation with me.

"You're not still sulking about that job?" she says, "I hope you are not going to have this long face all during my lunch party? It's St. Patrick's Day, for heaven's sake!"

Auntie Annie doesn't know about my love life. She doesn't know I'm gay. It's my secret and one that I will keep guarded forever. It's easier to wear a mask than to tell the truth. And I will never let my sexual preferences get muddled up with my professional life again.

One night of passion with Angela Sheen, Proctor and Gower's favoured client and manager of an exclusive boutique hotel chain, and my life is in pieces. Kat made sure of that. She ruined our relationship and then my career.

Auntie Annie reaches for a saucepan and pushes me gently out of her way.

"I'll be the life and soul of your dreary St Patrick's Day lunch even if your guests are all boring and old." I add a charming smile to soften my black humour. "We can even play the Rigor Mortis game afterwards to see if they survive your cooking."

"Now that's much better. I feel as if my cheeky niece is back in the land of the living." Her blue eyes twinkle, and she smacks my bottom playfully as I walk past and, in spite of my bad mood, I laugh and swing my hips.

It's a long standing tradition, started by Uncle John when he was alive, to host a special Irish lunch so I wear a shamrock on the collar of my shirt and a green tie around my neck that says: "Kiss me, I'm Irish."

The guests are dreary apart from Simon and Louise Tavner who are my age. They are mid-thirties, tall, good-looking and filled with energy and enthusiasm.

"Ellie Bravo," I say, attempting a smile that stretches my cheeks but fails to crinkle my eyes.

Simon's handshake is firm. His soft grey eyes are intense. "Your Aunt has told me all about your incredible marketing skills. She's very proud of you."

I try but I can't stretch the smile so I shrug and take the hand of the next guest and I've already removed my green tie before lunch — after my fourth glass of wine.

Over our meal the academic and bearded Mike McGee talks incessantly about his tedious travels and his camping experiences as a student and a French girl who sexually exploited him. His bespectacled wife smiles indulgently and I sense that she will go home and try to compete with this girl's memory, embellished in Mike's imagination from forty years ago.

I cover a yawn with my hand.

The Morrisons are equally as dull. They have the same grey hair, grey voices and grey suits. The only difference between them is his grey moustache, but only just, she is working on hers.

After we've finished dessert I'm desperate to leave the dining table. Louise follows and sits beside me on the sofa, her leg touches mine and her cool fingers are on my skin as she asks about the inky star tattoos on my neck just under my ear.

I pull my short, roughly-cropped blond hair to one side and show them off.

I am relaxed after eating extra helpings of succulent lamb and after drinking copious amounts of red wine so I open my blouse to show her the wave of letters printed on my skin that run across my chest and undulate to my left shoulder.

"*Not all who wander are lost,*" she reads aloud. "Are you wandering Ellie? Or are you lost?" Her eyes are deep purple.

I am saved from replying by her husband, Simon, who leans forward and says to me, "You worked for Proctor and Gower in London. They're one of the best."

I am looking at Louise and listening to him but the wine has made my mind slow.

"My business is IT. We write specialist software for companies and provide online data storage and hosting as well as designing websites. Does that make sense?"

"I can barely work a mobile," I mumble.

Mike McGee begins a laborious story about how he lost his phone in Bulgaria. His wife produces a shiny new one from her bag as if giving evidence in a court room, and when he gets to the part about a sexy receptionist en route to the police station to report the loss, my eyes begin to close and thankfully his voice fades as I nod off.

"I don't think anyone noticed you snoring," Auntie Annie says as I help stack the dishwasher a few hours later. "Although it was a little noisy toward the end and the dribbling was a little off-putting."

"You were lucky Simon and Louise were there or my head would have fallen into my dinner." I am drying pots and stacking pans in the cupboard.

"Louise is a lovely girl. It's such a shame they can't have children. They are going for more fertility treatment. I think it's his problem not hers but he won't adopt a child. He's very stubborn and she's very upset…"

Annie pours us a nightcap and we settle companionably beside the open fire. I gaze out at the darkness and the shimmering lights across the Lough until she says, "I'm not sure of the reason you came over here but don't be in a hurry to move on. Think of this as your home. Stay as long as you like, Ellie."

Perhaps it is the warmth of the alcohol, the crackling logs, or because I feel guilty that I didn't make more effort at lunch but I am too scared to speak. I am too frightened that my lips will tremble, my tears will fall and my resolve will crumble. So I nod my thanks, press my lips together and focus on the burning fire. I cannot tell her how grateful I am.

* * *

The following day Simon telephones and to my surprise he offers me a job. A temporary job that Annie tells me will "get me out of myself".

I start on Monday morning but on my way to his office and it is lethally wet, a red Audi swerves right across my path and squeals to a stop in front of me. I'm almost killed.

I'm forced to brake the Harley and I skid. It takes all my skill and strength not to crash to the ground. My breathing is rapid and I'm furious. I pull off my helmet and I'm swearing loudly when the passenger door opens and a slim ankle followed by a long slender leg emerges gracefully from the car.

The body that unfolds is taut and straight. The woman has long dark hair and she stands on the pavement straightening her skirt before she turns her attention to the car's back window. A smile lingers on her lips and she tilts her head.

From the window two scrawny arms reach out and grab the woman around the neck. A child with a mop of brown hair and round glasses leans precariously from the car and the two heads meet in a brief kiss. The woman laughs showing a generous mouth with even white teeth and deep brown sparkling eyes.

A man's voice shouts from inside the car which then inches into the busy flow of traffic leaving the woman to duck from the tight embrace, slam the car door, and take several quick steps so as not to lose her balance.

Just in time.

The Audi accelerates narrowly missing a blue van before breaking hard at traffic lights only a few feet away. A smiling face with Harry Potter glasses appears in the back window. The young child with the mop of hair waves wildly and laughs. She sticks out her tongue holding two fingers like horns to her head.

In response the woman makes a fist with her fingers and places it on the end of her nose waggling slim fingers and her pink tongue.

I can't help but laugh aloud.

A dog barks, a bus chugs its smoky engine into life and from somewhere a baby cries.

I ruffle my damp spiky blond hair and wipe drops of water from the collar of my red-leather jacket. Droplets of rain splash onto my face and I brush them away without taking my eyes from the scene in front of me.

The lights turn green.

The car and the smile on the woman's face disappear and when she turns our eyes lock and I feel the heat of the stranger's deep dark eyes. We might have smiled at each other but instead we stare. Two awkward strangers. Two people drawn together in a moment of brief interest, a minor web of curiosity, each assessing our differences. The fraction of a second lasts longer, suspended in time then a cool breeze blows against my neck and a car horn toots. Our invisible bond is broken.

I am gripping the handlebars on my bike as rain settles on my eyelashes and when I brush the dampness away with the back of my hand, the woman has gone.

I secure the Harley in the street and pull crumpled directions from my leather pocket.

Here, in Northern Ireland, the streets feel more spacious than London. The buildings are certainly smaller, only two and three storeys high. In the Lisburn Road there are estate agencies, hairdressers, expensive boutiques, coffee shops, a tapas bar and several expensive art galleries. Above these retail premises are offices, beauty salons and agencies. Most have red brick and dark glass windows.

I follow the instructions to the main entrance tucked down a side street and I read the brass plaque: Bizweb Solutions. I take a deep breath and step inside the unknown where I know Simon Tavner is waiting for me.

Narrow stairs lead to the first floor where I am greeted by a pretty receptionist with dyed purple hair and a wide smile.

"Take a seat and I'll call Simon," she says cheerfully.

The floors are dark wood and the walls natural brick. I stand at the large window admiring the view of the street below and the park and gardens across the road. The snow has melted leaving puddles and debris in the gutter.

"Cranmore Park," Simon says, appearing beside me. "It's a great place in the summer to eat a sandwich at lunchtime."

After shaking hands he takes my arm and guides me through swing doors into a spacious room with rows of workbenches where six young people sit concentrating with the same intense scrutiny, in various poses, all gazing at screens. They barely look up at us.

"This is the hub of the company. It's where the geeks hang out," he explains. "Stuart and his team are the programmers who update and rewrite software. Then there's Liam and his team who update, manage and create websites, and they also look after the hosting and data storage."

Stuart is tall, pale and lanky like a basketball player and his face flushes red. Liam is handsome and wears and an expensive suit. He gives me a flirtatious Johnny Depp smile.

I raise a hand in greeting.

Simon guides me into a small office in the corner of the room. The sales manager, John McCarthy, is a stocky fifty year-old with a dour expression, a thick moustache and a damp handshake and I wonder who would buy anything from him.

"This is Ellie Bravo, marketing expert from Proctor and Gower," Simon says. "John has done a great job with our sales and marketing but we really need to get more accounts. The recession is kicking us hard, there's a lot of competition in our business, and the banks are knocking on the door."

"We're on track to get that new account," John speaks quickly, his accent is strong and I struggle to understand him.

"The one with ZenFitness?" Simon asks.

"It's in the bag. I'm sure of it. So you see our marketing hasn't been that bad." John tucks his shirt into the back of his trousers.

"We need to look at the greater picture. Ellie has a wealth of experience and she has personally won awards for marketing and innovation. She will be a great asset to the company."

"A hot-shot from London." John stares at me. "It's a different ball-game over here. It's about who you know."

"I'm sure I'll manage." I stand straighter so he has to look up to meet my gaze.

"I'll arrange a strategy meeting with Maria. She's our accounts and administration manager and…" Simon turns to John. "We'll need to sort out some computer training for Ellie."

"Stuart's too busy for training," John replies. "It not what he does."

Simon smiles and slaps John's shoulder amicably. "I'm sure you will sort something."

On the floor above the techie lab there is a kitchen, toilets, boardroom and three offices. Simon's office, my office and one for the accounts and administration manager. My office consists of a pine table, a black leather chair, two smaller chairs for visitors and a filing cabinet. On the desk is a MacBook. I try not to think about my last job; the luxury office in Canary Wharf with views of the Thames and planes flying overhead into Heathrow airport.

Simon leaves to see if Maria isn't too busy to meet me and when he closes the door I flop into a chair. I push my fingers into my eyes to quell my tears.

What am I doing here? How has everything gone so wrong?

I barely have time to wipe my cheek when the door opens.

Maria is tall with dark hair and velvet-brown eyes. She recognises me, as I do her, and instinctively I clutch my red leather jacket to my chest.

"My husband almost knocked you off your motorbike this morning," she says by way of greeting. Her voice is a lilting Irish brogue and her eyes are dark and wary.

"He drives like a bloody idiot," I reply.

"You should be more careful. You were going much too fast."

Chapter Two

The first few days drag past. The strategy meeting was dismal and my training with Stuart has been non-existent, so I sit flicking balled pieces of paper with an elastic band into my crash helmet balanced on the edge of the desk waiting for five o'clock. My paper-flicking skills are improving although I am developing red wheals on the back of my left hand.

A mop of brown hair and big round glasses appears at the door then disappears but I am distracted. The balled paper misses its target.

"Hey," I call softly. "You made me miss my target."

The figure moves back into my office. I recognise her from the back of the red Audi last Monday morning. She has the same sparkling brown eyes as her mother and a puzzled look on her face.

"Can you do this?" I ask demonstrating my skill.

She moves hesitantly around the desk to watch.

I guess she is about eight years-old. She is dressed in jeans and wears a *Hello Kitty* sweatshirt. I toss an elastic band across the table and push some paper balls toward her.

She studies what I do, takes aim and misses.

"Terrible," I say, "Not good enough! You need to practice."

We spend a few minutes indulging in my new hobby; balling,

rolling, flicking.

"Don't you have any work to do?" she asks.

I shake my head and take aim.

"No phone calls to make?"

I shrug.

"Mummy's always working."

"I know."

She moves to stand beside me. She closes one eye and pokes her tongue out of her mouth and she grins when she hits the target.

"Yey! You're improving!" I laugh.

We high-five.

She frowns. "What's your name?"

"Ellie."

"Mine's Lily."

I nod.

"I'm waiting for mummy. We are going to the butcher's to buy dinner for Sunday."

I don't say anything.

"It's for Easter dinner," she explains.

"What? How awful! No chocolate eggs?" I nudge her playfully and she giggles. "Do you know why we give each other Easter eggs?"

"Cos we like them?"

"We do, but it's an old Anglo-Saxon legend." I lower my voice and she leans towards me watching my mouth intently. "Once upon a time, a Saxon Goddess called Eostre found a wounded bird in the forest so she gathered it in her gentle hands and transformed it into a hare…"

"Why?"

"So that it could survive the winter, but the hare found that it could lay eggs."

She giggles and I continue, "So it decorated the eggs each spring and left them as offerings like a gift, to say thank you to the Goddess."

I roll and flick a ball. I hit the target. I know she is studying me and thinking. She picks up her elastic band and we take turns flicking. She leans against my arm and I smell lemon shampoo from her hair and I think of my two nephews Matt and Jake in London whom I miss. She flicks a paper-ball and scores.

"Great shot!"

We are cheering and giggling when Maria appears in the doorway.

"Lily? Put your coat on it's time to go."

Maria doesn't look at me and Lily frowns.

They both leave without speaking and I call out to their retreating backs, "Happy Easter, Lily."

She turns and waves, and as they go downstairs I hear her say, "Mummy, do you know why we give Easter eggs...?"

* * *

Easter is finished and it's after work when I swing my leg over my Harley and I'm conscious of a man standing beside me. I pause with my helmet in my hands.

"Nice bike," he says. He's good looking, broad shouldered, late thirties with long greying hair. His fingers caress the chrome work. "You look after it well. The chrome looks good."

I nod and smile at the compliment.

"I had a Ducati - a long time ago. Italian bikes are fantastic.

It was a flying machine. I drove it around the Highlands one summer when I was a student."

"Ducati - that's a nice bike too."

"The best." His smile is wide and charming.

I go to put my helmet on my head but he continues speaking, "How are you getting on in there?" He nods at the door of Bizweb Solutions. "Have they eaten you up and spat you out yet?" he laughs.

I frown. "Have we met?"

"I'm Michael, Maria's husband."

I think of the red Audi on my first day.

He continues, "You must be Ellie Bravo. Maria has spoken about you and Lily seems to think you are pretty cool." He maintains eye contact with me. "John's a prat," he adds, and in spite of myself I laugh. "You think I'm joking. His wife was lovely but it's no wonder she left him. He has no personality and small-man syndrome."

"Small-man syndrome?"

"Yes, you know the type. He's puffed up on his own self-importance. Always hitching up his trousers. He needs a pair of braces."

I put on my helmet and secure the strap. Although I smile at his description of my colleague I'm not comfortable with Michael's over familiarity. He's too indiscreet and I want no part of it.

"You'll have to take me for a ride," he says. His hand, near mine, closes around the handlebar and I am momentarily caught off-guard. Flee or fight springs to mind and when I don't reply he moves away.

"I guess Maria is still working upstairs, is she? She's a workaholic. I don't know what she does in there all day. I have to drag her out sometimes. There's more to life than work, don't you think?" He raises an eyebrow.

"Definitely."

"Nice leather," he says. His fingers touch my jacket sleeve. "It suits you. A sexy woman on a beautiful bike, what more could a man ask for?"

I miss the rest of what he says because I gun the engine loudly and speed off.

* * *

"Where the bloody hell is she?" I hear John's voice as I run up the stairs. I throw my helmet and leather jacket on my desk, grab a pad and pen and head to the boardroom.

It is Wednesday morning. The weekly managers' meeting.

Simon stands at the window. John taps sheaves of papers at the table and Maria sips coffee with her hands wrapped around a mug. Their three faces stare at me.

"Hi," I say. I don't apologise for being late. Instead I sit down determined to focus on business but after ten minutes my attention wavers and I concentrate on suppressing yawns that rise like tidal waves from my lungs.

John's enthusiasm for an imminent deal dominates the conversation. "So with the ZenFitness account, we'll need to employ at least two extra programmers and install the hardware I've detailed in this report." John slaps the papers with his palm. "We need to host more websites. This is our future. This is where we belong and where the money is."

Simon's grey eyes are thoughtful. He doesn't appear convinced.

"Are we definitely getting the account with ZenFitness,

John?" Maria's eyebrows knit together in a frown.

He leans on the table. "It's in the bag. I'm sure of it."

"But we need to diversify." Simon drums his pencil. "We need to do something different."

John groans and Maria lifts her long hair onto her head into a bull-dog clip and rubs her bare neck. When she looks up our eyes meet and I turn quickly away.

Conscious that I am not involved in the discussion I wait for a break in their conversation and then I speak slowly, "Without a signed contract the ZenFitness deal is worth northing. There's no point in making any financial commitment, or recruiting more staff, or buying software if the deal isn't concrete. Besides there's so much self-hosting out there, we're better off concentrating on the company's positive strengths like writing new software and expanding on things like apps and games and at the markets that will increase our profits."

I look at each of them and Maria turns away.

"We can deliver to ZenFitness." John ignores me and his voice rises insistently, "And to other companies like them. This is the type of business we need—"

"Okay," interrupts Simon. "It's just a case of planning things properly, working out our priorities and, if necessary, a bit of reshuffling with our budget."

"Shuffling what? We haven't got the resources or budget to shuffle. Juggle more likely," Maria says, and John is the only one who laughs.

Simon's mobile vibrates on the table. He picks it up and listens before saying. "Yes, book seats for tomorrow." He hangs up sheepishly. "I have to go to a convention. Louise's father has a contact that he wants me to meet in Germany."

"Happy Days." John looks exasperated and leans back in his

chair.

"Well, let's leave it there." Simon looks at me. "Ellie, you look into some new ideas and solid plans we'll meet here next week. John you get the ZenFitness deal signed and Maria just keep juggling."

The meeting is over.

I pick up my pad and pen and when Maria stands up I deliberately walk from the room following in the wake of her musky perfume.

"That was a complete and utter waste of time," I say to her in the corridor. "Although I suppose it was a good lesson in how not to move a company forward."

"You don't know how we have all struggled to get this far. It hasn't been easy."

"Life is a struggle, Maria. Life is full of problems and hassles. This is just chicken-shit," I reply.

Maria looks at me and blinks her brown eyelashes. I smile warmly and disappear into the sanctuary of my office closing the door on her pretty O-shaped mouth.

* * *

I'm determined to make changes, so on Monday morning I'm first to arrive in the office, that is, before Maria. Sometimes I think the geeks downstairs stay all night. I venture into the kitchen and pour hot water over rich, dark coffee and into a new pot that I bought at the weekend. I heat milk. I only like Spanish coffee and I've decided I'm not drinking the instant crap that Maria makes continually.

Instead of the thick porcelain mugs I find china ones pushed to the back of the cupboard and I raise them aloft in triumph.

When I look up, Maria is staring at me through the long pane of glass in the door. She looks trapped like a rabbit in headlights so I smile and beckon her inside.

"Spanish coffee," I announce grandly, "and the croissants are a peace offering."

Her mouth smiles but her dark eyes are wary.

"It's time I stopped being an idiot and started to help," I say, "My behaviour hasn't been great and it's time I changed."

Maria's eyes widen and she raises a hand to her hair that is tied in a tortoiseshell clip. Small tendrils frame her face.

I continue speaking, "It must be lonely to be up here on your own."

"I don't really notice. I'm busy enough, doing all the accounts."

"Cooking the books?"

"There's not a lot to cook, believe me. And it will be tougher now since the ZenFitness deal fell through on Friday afternoon. We were relying on that deal to see us through the next few months."

"That's a shame. John must be so disappointed that it's fallen through?"

I place two mugs on the bistro table and sit down hoping she will join me.

She perches on a chair. "He's probably angry more than anything else. I'd also say he's embarrassed. He hates to be wrong and you were right about getting a contract signed."

I shrug.

"This is lovely coffee," she says, sipping appreciatively and her eyes begin to thaw.

"Everything tastes better when someone makes it for you." I smile.

She sighs and it makes me think I hit a nerve. "Do you like living here?" she asks. "Are you settling in?" Maria pulls a croissant apart with her fingers before placing a small amount in her mouth.

"I love Holywood. I'm staying with my Auntie Annie." I sip coffee and hesitate. "Auntie Annie and my mother are sisters. Their mother - my Grandma, was from Belfast but my mother left at eighteen and went to London where she met my father. He's Spanish and they're separated now. He's a doctor in Malaga."

"And your mother?"

"She's travelling around Asia with her current boyfriend." I don't know why I am telling her this.

"You have olive skin like a Spaniard."

"I know." I smile, relieved not to speak about my mother. "That's from my father's side."

"You don't have children? You never married?"

"Er, no."

"Well, marriage isn't for everyone." Maria refills her mug and stands up.

"Perhaps not, but I'd love a daughter like Lily though. She's very interesting."

"No, you wouldn't. She can be a little horror." This time her smile reaches her eyes and they dance in delight.

I return her grin but she changes the subject.

"Are you going to get computer classes from Stuart?"

I shake my head. "John says he's too busy."

"You should speak to Stuart. You'll learn a lot." She hesitates at the door and as an afterthought she adds, "Thanks for the coffee, and by the way, don't let John annoy you. He's like a soft puppy underneath that hard exterior."

"What, one with rabies?" I reply.

* * *

Later that afternoon Maria pops her head around my office door. "This is Michael, my husband," she says.

I recognise him immediately and I am about to say we have met when he reaches for my hand.

"Nice to meet you. I've heard a lot about you Ellie," he says. "And that's a nice Harley you have downstairs. You look after it well. You must take me for a ride one day." His smile is charming and he acts as if we've never met.

I'm surprised and I say nothing. We chat for a few minutes about motorcycles until Maria says, "We are going to see Lily in her ballet." She tugs on her husband's arm and he gives me a disarming smile.

"Family duties beckon." He laughs and then whispers, "Don't forget my spin on your bike."

I nod.

And, as they go downstairs, Michael turns and winks at me.

It's then I realise he has manipulated me and, by remaining silent about our previous meeting, I feel complicit in his lie.

Why did he not tell the truth?

And why did I not speak up?

* * *

A few days late my Harley is parked outside the office. It has a black low-slung leather seat and high handle bars. It is sleek and sexy. The past few days have been warm and spring-like and, after work, I have gone home and spent a few hours polishing the chrome. Now it glitters in the April sunshine.

Maud's coffee shop is on the main street and I go inside and order a bacon bagel and when I leave the cafe I see Maria turn down the side street just in front of me. The road is empty and when her pace slackens so does my own. She circles my Harley cautiously and slowly like a trained bullfighter circling its wary prey. Tentatively she reaches out and strokes the black leather seat and I imagine it is soft and warm from the sun. She stretches her arm to the handlebars. The chrome is shining; bright, inviting and alluring.

I stop and I try to imagine what she is thinking.

Can she feel the sensual power of the throbbing engine beneath her?

She strokes the front light, her hand caressing and caring. I see her chest heaving and her breath in short easy bursts. Her head turns so I duck quickly into the doorway of the estate agents and watch through the glass pane of the office window as she throws her handbag over her shoulder, bends her knee and swings her left leg over the seat.

She is astride my bike.

I smile and walk as though I have just turned the corner.

"Hey there, are you admiring my Harley?"

As I draw level she jumps off the bike. Her cheeks are flushed. She straightens her trousers and adjusts her handbag on her shoulder. I stand beside her on the pavement and smell the scent of fresh lemons coming from her long hair.

"S- Stuart said you took him out and it was fantastic to ride on the back," she stammers.

I'm happy that she's embarrassed. It makes me feel more confident.

"He loved it. Would you like to come for a ride with me?" I

deliberately make my voice throaty. I remove my sunglasses and place them on my head. I want to be teasing and tempting like my Harley but Maria refuses to be seduced.

Instead she straightens her back and challenges my direct look. "Why not?" Her voice is defiant. She stares at the bag in my hand from the coffee shop. "I hope you've got a croissant in there for me."

I laugh. "Now Maria, I do believe you are getting quite cheeky."

There are footsteps behind us and we both turn around.

"That's a death trap that bike." John has come down the stairs of the office. He pulls a cigarette from his jacket and lights it, sucking the butt and blowing out smoke greedily.

"That's rich coming from you with that in your mouth," Maria replies.

"This is a necessity. It's all the stress in there." He stabs the burning tip to the door. "Simon's cancelled the meeting again. I don't know what he's playing at. He's staying on in Germany for another week." He sucks hard and flicks ash to the ground. "He's said nothing about this mystery contact. It doesn't make sense. He should be concentrating on things here at home. I've been speaking to Liam about finding more leads but without some support…" His voice trails off and he looks at Maria but his gaze brushes mine.

Simon is an enigma, but I'm not going to say that to anyone. "I'd be happy to help," I say, "I just don't want to—"

"You're either a part of the team or you're not." He spits a sliver of tobacco onto the ground. "If you want to be involved you'd better start pulling your weight. We're not a charity."

* * *

Several days later Stuart's skinny frame is leaning across my desk and he's tapping at the keyboard. He presses a few buttons with knobby fingers and waits. He has a pale angular face, serious eyes and he smells of *Paco Rabanne* and I wonder if he notices I am wearing it too.

"It should only take a moment to download." He is staring intently at the screen. "I can't believe it got through our firewall." He has a puzzled look on his face.

"These things are done deliberately aren't they?" Maria stands beside us holding her coffee mug which has *Best Mum in the World* written on it.

He considers her question before answering. "Viruses or worms are often implanted by hackers who want to create havoc and make a name for themselves. It's often an ego thing done by someone who is looking for fame or to make money illegally, or sometimes they hack into the Ministry of Defence simply for the fun of it and because it is so easy."

"Fame, money and power," Maria says. "It's a heady mixture."

"So, did someone do this deliberately to my computer?" I ask.

"I don't think so. Normally our firewall is resilient to these types of viruses. I've never seen anything like it. I'll have to have a good look at it when I get time."

He stands over six feet tall running his hand across his flat stomach as if to press the creases from his faded black *Snow Patrol* T-shirt.

"Where did you learn all this?" I ask.

"I joined the company from Ulster Uni two years ago. I'm interested in programming but I enjoy site-hosting and development too. E-commerce and custom technology integration are great for establishing a company's web presence.

It's interesting and it's exciting and I like that it's all online marketing." He frowns. "But then you know all this Ellie, don't you? You're an expert. I Googled you and you're well-known for all this. You've got an amazing reputation."

From the corner of my eye I see Maria's eyes open wide in surprise.

"But what about writing software for games and apps," I insist. "Isn't that the future?"

"Yeah, I think it is…" He looks at Maria.

"That's what I think. Would you help me?" I add

"Er, I'm not sure. I won't have the time. I mean, John needs…"

"I understand, Stuart. It's not a problem." I say no more and we stand in silence watching the program run on the screen until Maria says,

"How's Siobhan?"

She is referring to the purple-haired receptionist with the cheeky smile. Maria winks at me and, for the first time, I see devilment in her eyes.

"She doesn't like geeks." Stuart blushes. "And she's saving money to go to London. She wants to be an actress."

"But there's nothing to stop her from going out with you while she's waiting to go to London, is there?"

"Well…" Stuart studies something invisible on the floor. "John's asked her out too."

"John? I know he separated recently but I don't think he should ask Siobhan out," Maria replies icily.

So I say, "I'm sure Siobhan can look after herself. Besides he's too old for her and he's far too boring."

"If John backs off, then there's only Liam to contend with although he seems to have enough girlfriends."

I punch him playfully on the shoulder. "You hang on in there. She won't be able to resist a handsome guy like you."

He smiles, his face flushes pink, and when he leaves the office it's like the spring has sprung back into his trainers.

"Will you say anything to John?" I ask Maria.

"I think I might. Siobhan's only been here a few months and she may be too embarrassed to say no. Besides it will liven up my day." Her brown eyes are like silk. "Although I would have thought Liam would have been more Siobhan's type. He's got the film star good looks, the Johnny Depp smile and he dresses much better."

"Nah, he's too smooth. I've seen her with Stuart and he makes her laugh. He's a friend and that's his secret weapon — that, and kindness. It's what most women want."

I am looking at Maria but she is busy studying the coffee at the bottom of her mug. She won't look up and she won't meet my gaze.

Chapter Three

It's quite late when Lily's face appears at my office door. "Ellie? Are you finished working? Mum's still on the phone. Can I wait in here with you?" She throws herself onto the chair. Her feet don't reach the floor.

"So what's the gossip on the street?" I lean across the desk. "How's school?" I ask.

"Well…" Her tongue reaches out to touch her top lip. "Charlie's Mum is getting married again and Charlie is really, really fed up," Lily replies. "So I want to get her something for her birthday."

"OK. You want to look with me on the internet?"

Her face lights up and we spend fifteen minutes leaning across the desk looking at the screen, discussing ideas until Lily says, "They were arguing again last night."

"Who?"

She sighs theatrically and lowers her voice, "Mummy and Daddy. They thought I was asleep but I could hear them downstairs. He was shouting all the time."

When I look closely at her pale skin I see she has dark circles under her eyes.

She traces her index finger against the inky outlines under my left ear lobe. "I love these stars," she says. "I want a tattoo like this."

* * *

On Monday morning, Maria is in her office. She is in deep concentration, surrounded by piles of invoices and numerous black folders.

"Coffee Break," I call. "Come on. Let's go. It's a beautiful day and there's a Harley waiting for us." I hold out a spare jacket and helmet.

Her eyes widen in surprise then she points at the mess on her desk. "I can't. Look at all this I must do."

"It's Monday morning. It will still be here when you come back and besides you have all week."

"Oh my God, Ellie, are you sure?" Her eyes are filled with fear, anticipation and excitement. "I'll probably be a terrible passenger."

"You can steer then just turn the handlebars in the direction you want to go. Come on, let's go." We are giggling like teenagers as we run down the stairs.

In the reception Siobhan's purple head looks up from the file she is reading. Stuart is beside her looking over her shoulder at the diagrams. He grins and raises a thumb. "Good luck, Maria."

"My turn next," Siobhan shouts.

In the street the bike gleams; tempting and dangerous.

Maria stands on the pavement as I adjust her helmet and, like Lily, she has dark circles around her eyes. I feel her quick warm breath on my cheeks and I dare not gaze too closely at her lips.

I gun the bike and it purrs into life.

"Swing your leg over and lean with me when we corner," I shout out. I turn to make sure she knows where to hold on to but she is distracted, staring up at the office window. I follow her gaze and John stands watching us from his office but he is not smiling. I ease the bike carefully into the traffic and Maria laughs loudly and waves a careless arm in John's direction.

The familiar thrill of excitement surges in my loins as we ride along the Lisburn Road. I turn left passing the impressive building of Queen's University and campus, then past the Botanic Gardens and the Ulster Museum and through Stranmillis toward the embankment of the Lagan. We follow the river heading toward Shaw's Bridge and once on the dual carriageway I open the throttle and the bike roars. Maria grips my waist and screams with delight.

We stop at traffic lights.

"Are you OK?" I shout.

"I LOVE IT!"

I turn the bike toward the Annadale Embankment and past the rowing crews on the slow moving river and, once over the bridge, we cruise through the residential area and I stop at a side entrance to Cranmore Park.

I dismount and remove my helmet.

Maria seems unsteady on her feet and I hold out a hand to support her.

"Are you okay?" I ask.

She is emotional following the rush of adrenaline. She blinks rapidly, tugs at the zip of the jacket and begins to laugh. "Wow! What a feeling. That's never happened to me before," she screams, pulling off her helmet and swinging it into the air. Her chest is heaving. "Lily would say that was sick. Now that's what I call *living!*"

I pull my hand from her grip, secure the bike on its stand then follow her dancing steps into the park and sit beside her on the bench.

Her face is tilted toward the sun. Her eyes are closed. She is deep in thought. Lost in a memory. Two joggers pass us and in the distance a cocker spaniel barks and chases a grey squirrel who disappears up a horse chestnut tree.

We sit silently, side by side, our shoulders almost touching and she sighs heavily. "You know that wasn't a one off?" She doesn't open her eyes. "You'll have to take me on the Harley again. I need to live, Ellie. I need to feel excitement. I need to feel alive."

I don't reply.

In the distance a car honks its horn.

"I want to be happy, Ellie." Her eyes remain closed and I watch a single tear slide down her cheek. She catches it with her index finger but not before another replaces it. "I *need* to be happy," she whispers.

Chapter Four

"Thanks for that newspaper cutting you left on my desk last week." I slide into the seat opposite Maria in the boardroom. "I think you might have saved my skin."

She bites into a digestive biscuit and pushes the crumbs absent-mindedly into a small heap on the table. "What happened?"

"We got it. OUT In Belfast. It's a new city magazine and they are launching a website, Facebook and Twitter account with us. Plus we are redesigning their existing website and hosting the site for the entire group of OUT magazines in all the major cities in the UK and Ireland."

Maria raises her coffee cup. "Congratulations. You've done well. Is the contract signed?"

"Most definitely." I return her smile. "I owe you a drink. I would never have seen it in the paper. I would not have known it was up for Tender."

Her brown eyes are warm and the smile stays on her face as John comes into the room panting and perspiring. He flops into the nearest chair and glares at me.

"Simon said, you got the contract signed with OUT magazines," he says. He reaches across the table for a chocolate cookie and takes a massive bite. When he eats, crumbs sprinkle down his shirt and he flicks at them with his stubby fingers. "I'm going to give Liam this account to look after."

"But it was Stuart who helped me to put the proposal together. He's familiar with the project."

"He can't do it. He's too busy. Anyway, I'm the one who manages the work schedules, so I'll decide who is looking after what accounts."

"But—"

"We need bigger companies, Ellie. We need to get bigger accounts. And to be honest I'm surprised someone as qualified as you, all the way from London, would bother with a small fry deal like this." He grunts as he stretches to fill a mug with coffee. He spills milk on to the table. "Still, I suppose, you got burnt out in London and you lost your mojo. You'd better make sure you don't get your fingers burnt over here now that would be painful."

"Burnt out?" I ask in astonishment.

Simon walks in unaware of the tension and animosity between us and tosses a red file on the table.

"As I see it," he says, "there are two possibilities. We can expand on our software programming and app game and development or we can buy a retail outlet and provide hardware components and sell to the public."

"Why don't we just carry on the way we are?" John asks.

"We'd be bankrupt in a year," Maria replies. "We haven't increased our sales in the past year, only our costs."

"We're overstaffed." John glares at me.

I lean my elbows on the table and speak quietly. "Selling hardware is not only a big risk but a huge investment. We will be up against major companies who sell high volumes on the internet or ones that have a major retail outlet already established. We cannot compete by diversifying in that direction. If you won't branch out into apps and games then it's back to basic online marketing. The only thing that makes financial sense is competing for tenders, targeting potential new companies, upgrading existing customers, networking…"

"I'd need staff if we expand," John interrupts. The buttons of his shirt are strained over his stomach.

"I agree. You need *trained* staff." I emphasise. It's about time I made a difference in this company. I match his stare.

"Liam and Stuart are well-trained," John blusters.

"I mean someone in sales. *Someone* who can *close* a deal."

"I sell - that's my job!" John slams his fist on the table.

"Yeah? Well, as I see it - you had the ZenFitness deal all lined up. It was in the bag, you said—"

"That's how we do business in Belfast," John raises his voice.

My eyes lock with his. My voice is low. "Then maybe that has to change. It's about target markets, implementing strategies and making sales."

Simon eyes are cast at my report in front of him. He is oblivious to the hostile atmosphere in the room. "I like your proposal Ellie, to expand on app development. Let's explore this further and discuss this again next week."

Simon's in a hurry. The meeting is over.

An hour later I'm behind my desk busy deleting four unanswered calls from Kat when Maria appears in the doorway of my office.

"Well, the sparks certainly flew in there. You caused quite a stir. The lion has finally roared — haven't you?"

"It's been waiting to happen. I'd prefer to know where I stand with John. I can't bear people saying one thing and meaning another. I went through that in my last job and I'm not doing it again. At least John and I both know now what's expected of us."

"Open warfare?"

"No. Not on my part. I don't want to fight with anyone. I'm only thinking of what's best for the company."

"Well, Simon is sending John on a sales course." she smiles.

"Not before time."

"So, how about celebrating? What about that drink you owe me? Michael's working all week in Dublin and he's not back until Saturday. We could go out Friday night. I could collect Lily from ballet and take her to my mother's and we could meet up for dinner in town?"

"Great" I'm beaming happily, desperately trying to arrange my features so that I don't look too pleased or too excited and all thoughts of John are now banished from my head.

* * *

On Friday evening I'm in a small bistro tucked in a side street near the Grand Opera House in the centre of Belfast. To my right are two grey-haired women on their second bottle of wine and on my left are a young couple who barely speak to each other.

Maria slides into the seat opposite me.

"Hi Ellie - sorry I'm late. My mother could be from Spain for the inquisition she gave me." The waiter appears wearing a long striped apron and he hands her a menu. I shake my head at her apology, it has only been a few minutes and she continues speaking, "She believes good Catholic girls don't go out without their husbands and, because I'm going for dinner with a girlfriend, she thinks I'm trawling bars looking for an extra-marital affair." Her laugh is warm and throaty.

I shake my head and tut. "Perish the thought!"

We take a few minutes to discuss the menu and order deep fried squid to start and steaks as a main course, then we sip red wine and chat about our families.

"Joe is my eldest brother," Maria says. "He has an apartment in the marina at Carrickfergus." I remember the white buildings that I can see across the Lough from Auntie Annie's house.

"Patricia is the youngest and although she is almost thirty she still lives at home. She can't afford to move out. She's always swapping jobs. She's a civil servant. Then my other brother Connor is married to Kate and they have two children. Michael and I usually go out with them but we don't go out that often now… in fact, we haven't been out for ages."

"This is a novelty for me too. I haven't been out to dinner since I arrived here."

"But you must be used to wining and dining in London."

"Yes, but I was in a relationship so there weren't many girls' night-outs either," I reply, reluctant to talk about my past.

The waiter brings us salted chilli squid to share so we lean across the table and dip the coated chopped tentacles into a honey sauce and then another dish with garlic mayonnaise.

She wipes her mouth with her napkin. Her hair is tied with a red ribbon and she wears a black open neck blouse. Gold bangles rattle on her wrists as she reaches for her wine.

"Michael and Connor play golf most Saturday afternoons and Kate often pops around to my house but she talks constantly about nappies and the kids' tantrums so I avoid meeting up with her as much as possible. It probably sounds awful but I make excuses not to spend too much time with her.

"The thing is, is that Michael is also a very plain eater and he isn't one for the theatre or the cinema. So we don't go out much at all. He isn't the most adventurous man in the world but he's a good father though," she adds quickly, and her cheeks flush.

She tells me Michael and Connor studied Engineering at Queens University and she followed them a few years later and studied accountancy. "When they graduated Connor worked for a builder then formed his own construction company and Michael worked for the government supervising buildings that were part of the regeneration process. Now Michael works with a company that builds roads and he's working on a bicycle path between Dublin and Galway. He's in the south of Ireland most of the time," she adds, "but he comes home at weekends."

We chat about different cities in Ireland; Dublin, Donegal and Derry.

The waiter removes our plates.

Maria sips her wine. "Michael and I never really dated each other. We were part of a group that went out together. You know, to the cinema or to a pub or to a party. He had a motorbike in those days and he would go off for weekends on his own. Then when Connor and Kate got married it seemed the most natural thing that we would too. It all happened pretty quickly. He sold his bike and Lily arrived a year later and the rest, as they say, is history."

Our rib-eye steaks are served on a bed of creamed spinach and the chips are presented in a small fryer. The waiter brings us another bottle of wine.

"When I saw you on your motorbike that first morning I

never realised we would be working together. Thank God, Michael didn't knock you off your Harley. I felt quite envious of you on your motorbike. You looked so confident almost regal like a gliding black swan." Her face turns serious and then she giggles. "I resented you. I think I was jealous."

I pause with a chip half way to my mouth and smile at the memory.

"I watched you get out of the car. Then you hugged Lily and you pulled faces at each other. You looked so happy. It made me smile even though I was cursing the driver."

She toys with the salt cellar. She has long slim fingers and pink nails.

"Why did you come to Belfast, Ellie? Please don't tell me you were attracted by the climate or the hint of danger in the troubled areas. Were you escaping a broken love affair?"

"Funnily enough," I pause with juicy steak on my fork.

"Oh, no. I was just guessing. I bet he was a handsome, a successful property developer in London or a wealthy stockbroker. Did he break your heart?" Her brown eyes widen in curiosity.

This is my opportunity to tell her the truth and to reveal my sexual preferences so I take a deep breath. I think about Kat and about Angela Sheen and the mess I made in England mixing my work and private life. I will not make that mistake again.

"We worked together," I say, knowing it isn't all entirely true, describing Kat. "He's one of the most inspirational sales-people in the UK. He's a high achiever and I was proud of him. We were driven by success. We were a good couple, motivated and invincible: Sales and Marketing. A happy balance. You know, like you and Michael, Yin and Yang, sun and moon, night and day - one without the other was nothing," I stop suddenly.

I have said too much but I still haven't told the truth. I cannot say three simple words and I am ashamed

I am gay.

* * *

Over the past few weeks Auntie Annie and I have fallen into a routine. She plays bridge on Friday nights, goes to Yoga on Wednesday evenings, plays golf on Monday afternoons then has dinner at the Club afterwards.

Meanwhile, I have joined a gym and I work out most mornings, when the gym opens at six, before I go to the office. This means that if it is sunny or dry I can go out after work for a walk or ride the Harley and explore the area.

I share a bottle of chilled Sauvignon Blanc with Auntie Annie while I fry diced chicken with sliced onions, chopped garlic and chilli flakes. When it is brown and tender I throw it over a rocket and cos lettuce with sweet-corn, ripe baby vine tomatoes and fresh spring onions. I add basil leaves for decoration and their aroma fill my senses and I inhale deeply as I place it on the table.

As we eat, Auntie Annie is telling me about her son Michael - my cousin - who has been working in Melbourne and her brother, my Uncle David who has lived with his family in Canada for thirty years.

"I spoke to Michael last night and he is leaving Australia tomorrow," she says. "He's going to live in Toronto near David." She spoons the chicken salad onto her plate.

I am distracted. I think of Maria's husband Michael and wish he would go to Canada. Today after work I walked along by the sea collecting shells, admiring rocks and seaweed that looked like like crocodile skins and listened to the gulls screeching. The fresh air cleared my head even though I kept surreptitiously glancing across the Lough wondering what Maria and Lily were doing.

"He's going to work in David's law firm," she adds. "He's your age. It's time he settled down and got a proper job instead of travelling around like an errant student."

"Maybe I should travel more." I look out of the window and stare across the Lough to where Maria lives. My eyes rest on the spire of Jordanstown church. Farther along the coast the white apartments in the port of Carrickfergus glisten in the evening sun and I think of Maria's brother Joe who lives there.

"David and Angela have been on at me for ages to go over and visit so I've decided to go for a few months in the summer. David and I used to be very close growing up. I was even bridesmaid at their wedding so it will be lovely to spend more time with them all. It's worked out perfectly and it'll save me flying to Australia to see Michael. I'll look at flights after dinner." She sips wine and regards me thoughtfully. "Perhaps you'd stay here Ellie and look after the house while I'm away. You seem to be settling in and you'll make friends in no time and there's always Louise and Simon..."

"Simon's rarely in the office."

"Umm. He's having a tough time with Louise. I think she has given him an ultimatum."

"Ultimatum?" I look up quickly.

"She wants to adopt a baby. She's desperate for a family."

"Maybe that explains his strange behaviour and long absences from the office."

* * *

Later in the evening I'm stacking the dishwasher when my sister Skypes me. Jenny is three years older than me. We have the same blond hair, intense blue eyes and wide mouth.

"How are the family?" I ask.

"Richard has taken Jake and Matt to the park on their bikes to get rid of some of their excess energy before bed. They miss you. We all miss you."

"And I miss you all." Jake is twelve and Matt is ten. We have spent countless weekends together flying kites, playing chess and other board games, cycling and swimming and there is a gap in my life that makes me feel suddenly lonely.

"Any news from Mum?" I ask quickly.

"She's still on the beach in Thailand with Roger. I spoke to her last week and she sent her love to you."

"I suppose she's worried about me?" I joke.

"No but I am." Her voice takes on a bossy and petulant tone. "Kat phoned me again. I don't know why you just don't speak to her Ellie. She's still in love with you, can't you see that?"

"She isn't. She just doesn't like to lose. She's a control freak. Can you not see that Jenny? She's used to getting what she wants and I've always given in to her."

"I feel sorry for her."

"Don't. That's what she wants. She's a saleswoman, one of the best in the UK, it's a trick. She knows just how to play you like she does everyone else, including me. She'll flash those big green eyes, flick her auburn hair over her shoulder and hold a tissue to her nose. I've seen it all before. She betrayed me."

"She says it wasn't like that. She says you have misunderstood everything."

"I worked for months on that project. It's a lesson learned. Never sleep with your boss."

"She was more to you than that, Ellie, don't exaggerate. You were together two years."

"It was two years too long."

"She forgave you sleeping with Angela Sheen."

"It was one night - besides she had been having an affair for three months but it's not about that. It's about my dream job going to an idiot…"

"You stormed out and look where it's got you. How long do you intend sulking over there?"

"I'm not sulking. I have a job."

"It's crap compared to what you were doing over here."

"I like it."

"Rubbish."

"My month's trial is almost up and if Simon asks me to stay on. I think I might."

"What about that guy who's been giving you a hard time?"

"John? Simon's sending him on a sales course so hopefully he'll learn some manners."

"Well, you're not always the most—"

"I know, I know, likeable, loveable, smartest, easy-going, the list is endless." I wave the tea towel at the screen.

"Kat says, if you won't come home, she's moving out of your apartment."

"That's fine. I'll rent it out. I'm still paying the mortgage and I assume Kat's paying the bills."

"Ellie? What do you want?"

I'm looking out of the lounge window, across the Lough. "I don't know," I say, "I wish I did."

"Why don't you come home?"

"Because I don't know where I belong any more," I answer truthfully.

"You should have gone to see Dad and Tia Luisa in Malaga. It would have been a lot more fun and much, much warmer."

* * *

I'm sitting at my desk on Monday morning daydreaming about Friday night with Maria in the Bistro and I'm lost in the memory, smiling, recalling our conversation, the stories and anecdotes.

"We went on holiday to Greece last summer," Maria had said passionately. "I loved it. There's something about the islands on a quiet summer's evening that is so wonderful and peaceful."

I think of her and Michael swimming in the sea; both good-looking, smiling and laughing with Lily between them.

John's raised voice floats in from Maria's office and interrupts my reverie. His tone is aggressive and accusatory. "Thanks for your support last week," he says.

I miss the next piece of the conversation so I save the work on my computer and walk over to stand at the door listening intently.

"What is wrong with you?" Maria says, "You've done nothing but criticise Ellie since she started working here. You pushed her too far and now she's retaliated. We're supposed to be a team John. We're all working together for this company — for Simon. But Ellie is not from here and she needs our support and deserves our help. She certainly doesn't need you knocking her back down when she's trying to get more business for the company. That new deal she has signed has saved us. You have no idea how bad things were because you bury your head when it comes to finances…"

I peer through the crack in the door but I only see a glimpse of his shirt hanging out.

"Just like Siobhan?" he replies.

"What's Siobhan got to do with it?"

"Well, last week you had a go at me because I asked Siobhan out to dinner, and now this week I have to be nice to Ellie. I haven't come to work to please you, Maria. I come here to do a job and I don't need you breathing down my neck everyday telling me what to do and what—"

"I'm only saying that Simon—"

"Simon? He's not here. He's away in Germany or Greater Manchester or Ghana or somewhere else in the world trying to set up pathetic deals for buying cheap hardware." He waves a stubby finger in the air and his voice rises, "And while he's away, it is me that's in charge here and if I want to be nice, or nasty or rude, then I will."

There's a movement and I step back.

"Oh John, come on. We've worked together for a long time, we're friends."

"If only she—" One of them closes the door. I can't hear any more so I return to my work. Ten minutes later John stomps downstairs. He doesn't stop by my office to say hello and at lunchtime Maria walks in with a smile on her face.

"There's good news and there's bad news," she says.

"Okay. I'll have the good news first."

"John asked me if you had a boyfriend, and I said no and

that you left him behind in London."

I feel my body tense.

She smiles and continues, "So, he thinks you are a very spirited and sexy woman and, he's now decided that when he gets back from his sales course, he's going to ask you out. He thinks he can tame your wild side and provide a shoulder for you to cry on." Her laughter is warm and throaty as she speaks. "I did ask him if he would go on the back of your motorbike but he said, 'You're bloody joking. Those things are a death trap.' So I told him, that I think you are a match made in heaven." She smiles with sarcastic satisfaction.

"Okay," I sigh dramatically. "So what's the bad news."

"He's serious. He's giving up smoking for you."

Chapter Five

I'm daydreaming, drinking coffee in the deli and staring out at the afternoon traffic on the Lisburn road when I see Michael walk past. His stride is purposeful. His hair is blown back by the wind, off his face, revealing a determined jaw-line.

I don't think he has noticed me but then he does a double-take and his gait falters. He stops, tilts his head to one side and grins.

I smile warily. My mouth falls open when he turns around and walks into the coffee shop and slides into the seat opposite me.

"How's the girl with the red leather jacket?" He makes it should like a dragon tattoo and I shift uncomfortably trying to keep my face pleasant. "And how's life in the fast lane at Bizweb?"

I shrug. "Okay."

"Is John treating you well? Has he asked you out yet? He will either bully you or be your best friend. There is no middle ground with John. He's an all or nothing type of guy and that's probably why he's such an enigma."

"Maria understands him."

"Ah, Maria is an expert at dealing with difficult people. Look at me." He laughs. "I'm not the easiest man to live with but she knows how to handle me. We get on well. I can be difficult to please, even selfish and grumpy but she handles all that. She takes everything in her stride. Nothing phases her. She's a good mother and Lily adores her."

"Lily is very special."

"Yes, I wish I could take credit for my lovely daughter but it's Maria who has all the influence and charm with her. Sometimes they're so close I feel left out and so I behave badly like I'm the ogre in the family. I need lots of attention." He turns down the corners of his mouth like a clown. "But I am lucky. I couldn't live without them. You're not married? You don't have children?"

I shake my head.

"You should. A woman isn't really complete until she's had children, is she?"

I stare at him.

"I mean, that's the role of the female; mother-earth, mother-nature, giving birth. It comes naturally for all you women, doesn't it? Not like with us men. I would hate to get pregnant and have a baby." He pats his flat stomach. "I'm more of a Tarzan, myself." He bangs his chest and makes a playful jungle cry. "But I do like trying to make babies that's more my style. I like to have fun." He is being crassly macho but his joking takes the sting from his words and I marvel at his complete lack of sensitivity and clumsy attempt to flirt with me. He maintains eyes contact.

"I love your smile Ellie. It's beautiful. And I enjoy your company." He stares at me and there is no denying that he is a handsome man, square jawed with penetrating eyes and soft skin. "There's a certain mystery about you. You have this air of confidence. You drive a fast Harley which makes me think that there is something edgy and dangerous about you. You're a girl who likes to take risks and live life to the full. I bet that's how you lure all the men into your honey-trap."

When he smiles I wonder how many women he has practised his boyish grin on. He tilts his head as if waiting for an answer.

"I'm not that exciting," I reply, sipping my coffee, using my cup as a shield between us. "In fact, I'm really quite dull."

He laughs aloud, and again, I am taken aback by the easy charm of his reply. "You could never be dull, Ellie Bravo. You wouldn't know how. You are very exciting—"

"I thought you were working away this week — in Galway or somewhere," I say to change the subject.

"I'm flattered you take an interest in me—"

"I don't."

He leans his elbows on the table and stares intently into my eyes and I feel the heated scrutiny of his gaze. I shift uncomfortably before turning my attention to the traffic outside.

"Can't you feel it Ellie?" he whispers. "You must be able to."

"What?" My coffee is finished and I am looking for a way to leave but I suspect he is heading to the office and I don't want to walk with him.

"You must feel the chemistry between us," his voice is a soft rumble. "You felt it the last time we met when you sat on your bike outside the office in your leathers—"

"No - I actually didn't." I stand up.

He blinks but his smile doesn't waver. "You're the sort of girl who likes to be chased, aren't you? I've met women like you before and I must warn you - I am a very patient man."

"You're also a married man, Michael. Isn't Maria waiting for you in the office?"

He reaches for my hand. "I want you Ellie and I always get what I want."

I gaze down at him and prize my fingers from his grip. "You are married to my friend and colleague and you are completely out of order. I am not interested in you. Besides, you are not my type."

"Well, it was worth a try, wasn't it?" He grins.

"Don't waste your energy," I say and I leave the deli, walking quickly, hoping that he won't catch me up in the street.

Once I get to my desk I immerse myself in emails and phone calls. After a few minutes I hear his footsteps and his loud laughter in Maria's office. Ten minutes later Maria's door slams and she puts her head into my office.

"Michael has surprised me," she says smiling. "So, I'm leaving early."

I see him over her shoulder. He winks and he waves to me as if we are best friends. His other arm is around his wife's waist.

"Hi Ellie," he calls out. "Don't work too hard. It will make you very dull indeed."

* * *

"So, when are you taking me out on the Harley?" Lily asks.

"When you're eighteen," I reply.

She groans and leans dramatically across my desk. "Come on, Ellie."

I'm tired, I've been in meetings off-site all day and now I'm skimming the internet. It's Friday afternoon and I've been wondering how I will spend the weekend. I'm thinking I may take off on the Harley and ride around Ireland for a few nights just to quell the loneliness that is seeping into my life. I haven't been sleeping well and I think a change of scene will do me good.

I look up when Maria appears in the doorway. "Simon is buying white lab coats for the techies. He thinks it will be more professional like a uniform, and by the way, this proposal you've done for the Independent Travel Group seems pretty realistic but it does mean they will want a twenty-four service seven days a week, including bank holidays."

"They will have to provide that service if they want to be the core supplier for the corporate market that they are going after."

"Simon's insisting we take on someone with more experience to oversee this project so John's hired a new techie. He's due to start next week. His name is Mark Bowman and according to his references he's a whiz kid and a university graduate from Glasgow. Simon also wants John to get an app specialist."

"Great. Things are hotting up and John is getting more staff." I smile.

"We can afford it with these new contracts. You're certainly making a difference around here."

"I need help too," wails Lily.

Maria ignores her daughter's bored yawn and she leaves the room.

"But what do you think, Ellie?" Lily's voice is persistent and whiny. "Do you think I should ask Charlie?"

"Ask Charlie what?" Maria walks back in and tosses a folder onto my desk. "You're going to your ballet class now, so stop bothering Ellie."

Lily has kicked off her shoes. Her school blouse is creased

and her blue tie hangs loose. She pushes her glasses up onto her nose. "I still don't know what to get Charlie for her birthday," she sighs dramatically.

"We'll find something." Maria perches on the arm of the chair and places her hand around Lily's shoulder. They seem to mould into each other like two felines taking comfort from the body of the other's embrace in a loose hug.

When I look up Maria is staring at me. "You look tired, Ellie. Are you working too much?"

"No chance."

"What are you doing this weekend?"

"Haven't decided." I begin to stack papers and tidy my desk. I feel suddenly close to tears and I'm annoyed that they're tears of self-pity.

I want to say, I'm lonely.

"Do I have to go to ballet tonight?" Lily moans. Her eyes shine from behind her glasses. "We could go to the cinema instead, the three of us."

"You have a ballet class, young lady. So, stop your antics," Maria replies.

"What are you doing, Ellie? Do you want to come and watch me?" Lily says.

"No, she doesn't. I'm sure Ellie has better things to do — something far more exciting."

"Do you?" asks Lily.

I think of Auntie Annie's empty house. Tonight is her bridge night. I swallow hard. "Of course."

"You could join one of those singles clubs." Maria stands up and pulls the unwilling Lily from the chair.

"What? And mess up my chance with the lovely John?" I blink back tears.

"Ugh! John! No way!" Lily puts a finger to her mouth as if to vomit and I laugh.

"Mum, Ellie needs to be with someone really lovely, don't you think?"

Maria stares at me and I am rooted, unblinking and trapped in the headlights of her smile. If there's any chemistry then it is between Maria and me, not Michael and me, but my heart sinks. I cannot bear to be without her and I hate this feeling of infatuation.

* * *

The following week Maria and I are sitting in the park finishing our sandwiches. It turns cold when the sun disappears periodically behind scuttling clouds. Five schoolboys pass us, carrying a football, jostling each other, laughing and teasing.

"I told you Michael is working on the cycle path between Dublin and Galway? It's like he spends more time there, than he does here. He says he doesn't want to go but…" Maria lifts her face toward the sun languishing in the warmth. Her neck is raised and tilted like a beautiful sunflower. She wears small diamond stud earrings. "Marriage is a strange thing," she adds quietly.

I'm not sure if it is statement or a question, so I wait and listen.

"I think it's only in fairytales that people live happily ever after," she adds.

I have an overwhelming urge to speak. I want to tell her that I agree, and all about Kat and my unfulfilled love life, and my awful loneliness.

Behind us a black bird sings its merry tune from an ornamental cherry tree. I should feel happy and relaxed in the sun with Maria at my side but today I'm melancholy and tired. I should have gone away at the weekend but I didn't. Instead I worked at home on some more projects, refining and honing the details of the Independent Travel Group (ITG) project for the new techie from Glasgow, Mark Bowman.

A bumble bee buzzes past. It settles on the arm of the green bench where the empty sandwich package balances precariously.

"My sister Jenny is very happy," I say, closing my eyes relishing the warmth of the sun on my cheeks. "Richard is lovely. Matt is twelve and Jake is ten. They are the perfect family. They seem to complement each other. I think they have the perfect balance. I still assume all marriages should be pretty much like that apart from my own parent's marriage of course but, I guess, I'm still old-fashioned and I believe in a happy ending."

Maria turns and I feel her smile on my face. "Do you?"

When I open my eyes she has turned away. I watch the bumble bee fly away before I continue, "When I was a child I took it for granted my parents were happy. I never heard them argue. It was only when Grandma moved in with us that I realised they weren't happy. One summer during the school holidays Dad went back to Spain and he never came home. Mum said afterwards that relationships are like that. As you go through life you have different needs and expectations and one person can't fulfil them all. What you want at twenty is different to what you want at thirty or forty. Now I'm beginning to understand what she means." I stretch my legs, cross my ankles and wrap the remains of our picnic in a plastic bag.

"Does that mean we should have a different partner every ten years?" Maria asks.

"Probably, or renew your marriage periodically."

"As in a contract?"

"Yes, like a gas bill - every three months."

She laughs. "Your mother's attitude is ideal but very hedonistic. My mother is the complete opposite. She married my father for life and even though there were bad times, she wouldn't have left him."

"Wouldn't or couldn't?"

"Umm. Couldn't more likely. Divorce was unheard of and certainly for a Catholic woman in the heart of the Troubles. Even now it's still frowned upon. It's still not really accepted."

"Just as well things have changed in most other places. There's no point in being stuck in a rotten marriage and everyone being miserable."

"She would be mortified if Michael and I split up. It would ruin her life in our community."

"Best to stay with him then, just for your mother's sake," I say quickly.

"I would stay with him for Lily's sake."

I stand and stretch. "Good. Well, I believe in fairytales and happy endings so come on, it's time for the two Princesses to go back to the castle dungeons, check on the minions and face John the Old Ogre."

* * *

Later that week Maria pops her head around the door of my office. "Any chance of a lift to Mum's? Michael's in Galway and I lent my car to Pat as she was going for an interview this afternoon and she's not back, so I'm stuck."

"No problem. It's a perfect afternoon for a ride on the Harley." I'm only too delighted to have something to do after work and somewhere to go and with Maria, it is an even happier idea.

Lily normally goes to her Grandmother's house on the Antrim Road after school apart from on Friday afternoons when Maria collects her and brings her to the office before her ballet class. The thought of a leisurely drive fills me with delight and I am unable to concentrate until we are on the Harley.

I weave the bike in and out of the traffic and open her up on the motorway. I turn up onto Cave Hill and glance at the sun shimmering on the blue water below. We are on the north side of the Lough and, on the south side, Holywood stretches along the shoreline and into the distance. It's a beautiful view and one that I want to savour.

At a red light, Maria taps my shoulder and yells over the wind. "You've taken the wrong road."

"I want to see the view from the castle," I shout back.

"You're crazy." She laughs.

"Don't tell me you're in a hurry."

"Never."

Belfast Castle is an elegant turreted sandstone structure originally built by the Normans and situated in the Cave Hill Country Park. It's surrounded by ageing woodlands, hazelwood, and is rich in birdlife and wild plants. Grey squirrels dart from trees to shrubs, daffodils bloom and the grass has been freshly mowed. I smell the optimism of spring.

I park the Harley near a low stone wall and we pull off our helmets and gaze at the view spread below us. The fast flowing tide is flanked by green hills and clusters of grey houses. Church spires of all denominations glisten in the sunlight. Warehouses and roads in the industrial area near the port look like a toy-town set, and the iconic landmarks of the Titanic Museum and yellow cranes of the Harland and Wolff shipyard are easily identifiable. A ferry trails out to sea leaving a white V-shaped wash in its wake and overhead a plane rumbles and circles across the city through fast-moving fluffy clouds.

We lean on the wall and I inhale deeply and close my eyes enjoying the air against my skin and sunlight on my face. It is calm and peaceful. A perfect spring day.

"From over here you can almost see your Auntie's house in Holywood."

I have told her where I live but I dare not open my eyes. Little does she know how often I look across the Lough and think of her in Jordanstown.

Maria leans against me like a light wind. Her perfume envelopes me in an invisible mist and I'm aware of the soft contours of her body.

I inhale slowly smelling her apple shampoo and when I sneak a glance there are small crow's feet at the corner of her velvet brown eyes.

My arm is covered in goosebumps and I wonder if she can feel my emotions and the closeness of our bodies. I swallow then cough. "Look at that tree over there. Isn't it wonderful? Is it a horse chestnut?" My voice is tense and my tone nervous.

"It is unusual," Maria agrees quietly. She doesn't move and seems lost in her own thoughts, relaxed and comfortable beside me, I reach for my helmet and fiddle nervously with the strap.

We stand quietly without speaking and after a few minutes and with mutual understanding, we know it is time to leave. She holds my gaze for a fraction of a second longer than is normal and I turn quickly away.

"Come on," I whisper.

And, as we ride down the estate road toward her mother's house, I make a silent vow never to let myself be in such close proximity with Maria again. She's a happily married women.

Maria's mother lives in an imposing Victorian building in a long leafy road and as we pull up to the kerb Lily is watching from the bay-fronted window. When she sees us she opens the front door and comes hurtling down the gated pathway.

"My turn," she shouts, and hitching her school skirt between her legs she pushes between us and straddles the bike wedging herself firmly between me and her laughing mother.

Lily thumps me on the back. "Come on Ellie, let's escape. Quick! Let's go the three of us."

Maria climbs off the Harley and her laughing eyes meet mine as she stands on the pavement and removes her helmet. I cannot speak. The intimacy of us together at Belfast Castle on Cave Hill remains with me and my skin continues to tingle. Over her shoulder I'm distracted by a small plump woman pushing a straggly fringe from brown flinty eyes. She strides purposefully down the pathway with a sense of urgency toward us.

"I want to see who Maria got a lift with," she says, by way of greeting. Her eyes bore into mine and she doesn't bother to smile. Her accent is strong and my helmet makes it harder to hear, so I remove it. My short hair flies loose in the wind and I wipe a bead of perspiration from my neck and give her the benefit of my charming smile.

"Mum, this is Ellie Bravo. Ellie, my mother Brenda, as if you couldn't guess."

I hold out my hand. "Pleased to meet you." (It's only a white lie.)

"Maria's been happier recently," Brenda says, "I thought she might have a fancy man at work. I had to come and see for myself when I saw you on this thing."

"Chance would be a fine thing," Maria laughs and pulls a reluctant Lily from the bike.

"There's always John," I say, gunning the bike and replacing my helmet. "He's a fine thing and a great catch."

"Who? Who's John?" Brenda shouts over the engine, a patchwork frown creases her forehead and she glares at Maria.

"He's yuk!" Lily allows herself to be pulled off the bike and squeals when Maria tickles her.

"You'd better tell me about him." Brenda is staring hard at Maria.

When I smile Brenda turns and scowls back at me.

Maria raises her eyes to the heavens and mimes, *thanks for that.*

"De nada." I smile and say, "It's the Spanish in me. We're an inquisitive bunch."

* * *

It's Friday afternoon. It's a bank holiday weekend and I am sitting in Simon's office. Like the techies downstairs, he is wearing his new white lab coat. I don't have one. Both Maria and I said we would save the company money, we didn't want to wear one.

"Business has certainly improved since you've been here,

Ellie. We got the OUT Magazine contract and now the ITG contract. They are both big deals and that's in the space of a month."

He rubs his palms together and I feel a surge of elation.

"Perhaps you'd think about staying on permanently?"

"That's a big decision to make," I say. "I'll stay another month but I will have to go back to England. I have my flat in London and my home is over there." I don't tell him that I have no friends and no social life here and that I feel very alone.

"Promise me you'll think about staying longer, Ellie. Now that we have closed the deal on the ITG project things can only get better. We're on a roller-coaster and I know it's a long way away but if things are this good by Christmas I'd like to offer you a more secure future in the company, financially speaking of course, shares or directorship. Something that would make it worth your while to stay."

"Christmas? That seems months away."

"I know but I have to incentivise you to stay here." He smiles.

"That sounds interesting Simon, thank you, but what about John and Maria? How would they feel? They've obviously been here much longer than me and if you were to offer me something more—"

"Don't worry. I'll sort it. Maria will be pleased to have you here and I'll speak to John nearer the time. It is just something for you to think about and something to work towards. I don't want you to feel you are not appreciated. You have made a difference to the company and you need to be financially rewarded. I know I cannot match the salary you were earning in London but I hope that the long term prospects of staying here will be an enticement for you."

"So long as the business is out there, we can compete and

hopefully win more accounts."

"The sales course John is on this week might be the making of him. You know that I'm often out of the office, and um and um, well to be honest, it makes sense for you to take over in my absence. You're a natural born leader."

I have been concerned at the amount Simon travels and his long absences from the office but I say nothing. I still remember Auntie Annie telling me that they want children and the difficulties that must bring to their marriage. No wonder he looks strained and tired.

"I haven't decided on my future, Simon. It is all up in the air but I feel happy that you have been upfront enough to entice me into staying. Thank you. Just give me a while to think about it?" I ask.

It was more than Kat had done at Proctor and Gower in London. She had wanted me to leave. She had wanted me out. She had pushed me to go. She had ruined everything.

Fifteen minutes later I am sitting at my desk mulling over our conversation when Lily's face appears at the door.

"Nice haircut," I say.

It has been cut into a neat brown bob and it makes her look very serious.

"It's horrible." She scowls and flicks her fringe roughly. "I would love short blond hair like yours that sticks up and out at all angles," she says wistfully. She is wearing her school uniform. One sock is gathered around her ankle, her blouse is open at the neck, and her tie pulled off centre.

"You look like St Trinian meets Harry Potter." I laugh. I look forward to her weekly visit and our Friday chats.

She wiggles onto the chair opposite me. Her feet don't touch the ground and she swings them energetically thumping them against my desk.

"Mum's on the phone. Dad's in Dublin and he's going to be there all bank holiday weekend," she groans. "There's nothing exciting happening and I'm bored. Will you take me for a ride on the Harley?"

"Not unless you want me to fall out with your mother."

"No, I don't want that. You're the only one who makes her laugh."

"I'm sure that's not true," I reply but my stomach flutters. I can't help but wonder what relationship Michael and Maria have together.

"Mum's always happy with you. She's always laughing. She tells me you sometimes have lunch together in the park and you went out for dinner. Dad never takes us out. We never do anything or go anywhere apart from Grandma's."

I rearrange pens and paper, and put the calculator, ruler and stapler in a neat line before flicking imaginary dust from my keyboard. I don't know what to say.

"Have you asked her then?" Maria appears in the doorway. She wears a printed floral dress with short sleeves and she looks radiant. She stares expectantly at Lily who shakes her head.

"Go on then, ask her quickly, or we'll be late for your ballet classes."

"Ask me what?" I say.

"Have you seen the new Disney film?"

"If you mean the very latest one that's on at the cinema, then no."

"Would you like to see it with us?" There's something in Lily's manner that holds her back. Is it shyness? Is it the fear of being turned down — lack confidence?

"I'd have to consult my busy diary," I reply teasingly.

"Tomorrow night?" Lily looks hopeful.

"Great. That's precisely the evening I had nothing planned," I reply quickly and she giggles.

"It's only that Michael's in Dublin." Maria explains and she nods at Lily as if wanting to please her. "And it is the bank holiday weekend so we should do something special."

"*Without* Grandma!" adds Lily.

"Well, that sounds like a plan, but only on one condition," I say.

Lily's eyes shine warily from behind her glasses and she blinks quickly. "That I take you both for dinner. We can try one of those restaurants nearby, there's the Indian or the Chinese?"

A smile spreads across Lily's face and her feet bang rhythmically against my desk in perfect time with my own rapidly beating heart.

"Charlie said the Indian is great. She goes there all the time. Oh wow, Ellie, this is going to be a great night out."

Chapter Six

The cinema is my true love. The magic of the big screen, the colours, sounds and the vitality of other people's lives absorb me like no other. I step into the screen and disappear into another world, into other people's problems, emotions and excitement. It makes me forget my lonely life.

Lily sits between us stuffing handfuls of popcorn greedily into her mouth. She is thoroughly engrossed with the film. Over her head, in the flickering lights, my eyes occasionally meet Maria's and we smile.

I try to ignore the tingling in my skin and have serious a conversation in my head.

Stop playing with fire. Never get involved with a straight woman. It only leads to heartbreak.

After the film Lily pulls us in the direction of the Indian restaurant.

"Charlie's Dad brought her here with his girlfriend and Charlie said it was one of the best meals ever."

"It must be good then," I reply, and Lily nods seriously.

On the restaurant wall are pictures of long sandy beaches in the Indian Ocean, drooping coconut palms overhanging a turquoise sea and thatched huts hidden in bountiful tropical gardens.

I imagine the sun on my skin and Maria in the sea, her hair wet, her eyes laughing. She is tanned and—

"What are you thinking Ellie?" She leans toward me. "You have a very naughty smile on your face."

I blush, laugh too loudly and gaze quickly down at the menu. "I was just wondering how hot the curry would be."

"I don't think so. You were staring at those lovely beaches. You were miles away."

I smile wondering, for a brief second, if she has direct access to my mind.

"So what'll we eat?" I ask Lily.

"Dad would have steak wouldn't he, Mum? He doesn't like Indian, does he?" Lily pushes her glasses up her nose.

"Probably." Maria is studying the long list on the menu. Her face is filled with concentration and she doesn't look up.

"He's coming home tomorrow now, isn't he?" Lily persists. "We'll have the rest of the bank holiday together."

"Yes we will. What will we order?" Maria replies as the waiter appears at her side and all we order from the menu.

While we wait we talk about the film and programmes on television.

Lily exclaims delightedly when steaming dishes are placed on the table; chicken in creamy Korma sauce, lamb with onions, garlic and peppers, hot sizzling beef, and mounds of pilau rice.

"We'll never eat all this," Maria says, breaking garlic nan bread and passing it around.

"Oh yes, we will," Lily and I reply in unison.

We idle away the meal, chatting and teasing each other. We watch as people pass by the window on their way to the cinema to to restaurants or to the bowling alley. There are groups of animated girls in miniskirts wearing heavy makeup and young lads with hair, like the girls, equally tinted and groomed.

"Years ago when I was a student…" Maria says over coffee, and Lily raises her eyes mockingly toward the ceiling. "We would go into the pub and no sooner did you have a drink on the table there was a bomb scare, so we were all kicked out to stand in the road. In the winter it was freezing cold so we stopped going out and got used to socialising at home."

"So how come you don't have people over for dinner now?" Lily asks.

Maria pauses before replying. "We're too busy."

"You mean Dad's too tired or he's at the golf club with Connor." Lily shoves her elbow against my arm nearly sending my coffee flying. "Mum's a great cook, can Ellie come over for dinner one night?"

Rather than returning Maria's gaze, I seize the moment to order the bill. My heart is racing and I'm wishing that Maria didn't have this effect on me.

Outside the restaurant we look over the rail to the ground floor where a queue is forming to bounce on a giant trampoline. We watch as bodies fly and twirl in the air, happy to gaze down on their energetic performances.

"Can I have a go?" Lily asks.

"You would be ill after eating that food," Maria replies.

Lily shrugs and wanders off for a closer look.

I lean against the rail watching those around me. I look at the clothes, tattoos and makeup, and listen to Maria's comments about fashion. Then very gently she takes my arm and pulls me closer.

My heart skips and then beats quickly in rapid succession. I smell her warm Indian breath. She tucks her arm through mine, leans against me and points to the floor below us.

"Look," she whispers

Stuart is talking to an attractive girl. He smiles and when the girl lifts her face for a kiss, Maria says, "That's Siobhan. Isn't she stunning? It's no wonder he asked her out. Good for him. It's about time there was some love and romance in the office, don't you think?"

Our faces are inches apart. I can't speak. My mouth is dry. I am aware of the goose pimples that are spreading down my arm and across my chest and the tingling sensation rising in the tips of my fingers.

"Dykes!" A group of tough-looking young boys walk past us.

One has his head shaved and his muscled biceps are covered in blue ink and a Union Jack flag.

Another wears a T-shirt that says: *I'm not Mr Right but I'll hump you until he arrives*. "Lesbos!" he says.

Maria's cheeks flush red. She pulls her arm from mine and runs away and down the moving staircase. But before I follow her I turn on the tattooed yobs.

"Dick-heads," I hiss.

* * *

Tonight Auntie Annie's best friends - the Greys - are hosting a farewell dinner for her. I remember them from the St. Patrick's lunch and I am pleased that I thought of an excuse not to go with her. She leaves for Canada tomorrow and she will be gone for six weeks.

If I was lonely before it will be worse without her.

So instead, as it is a beautiful warm evening I ride the Harley up the coast road to Ballycastle where I eat an ice cream and walk around the fishing boats in the harbour. I motor along to the Giant's Causeway then tear back on the motorway as fast as I dare, opening the throttle, taking unnecessary chances. I need the release of speed but not speeding points.

It is almost nine when I unlock the front door and my mobile begins ringing.

"Guess who has been here for the past two hours?" Jenny says by way of greeting. Her tone says, don't mess with me and she speaks quickly and insistently. "Ellie, you've got to speak to Kat. One way or the other you have to sort it."

I tuck the phone under my ear and find an open bottle of Rioja in the kitchen. I pull the cork and pour a large glass.

"Why should I phone her? She was the one that wrecked my career?"

"She's really sorry. She's upset about everything. She said she moved in with Marcella for a few days because of what happened at work. Things aren't great between them and so she's back in your apartment and she wants you to come home."

"That's convenient." I gulp quickly and the wine spreads comfortingly through my body. "She wants me to go back to London as if nothing has happened?"

"Don't play the saint. I know your track record too."

"Mine wasn't serious. It was a fling, one night, and it certainly didn't affect our work."

"That's not the point."

I stand at the window and gaze across the Lough listening to Jenny pleading Kat's case. "She misses you. She said she still loves you."

"She ruined my chance at the one career I wanted and I was

good at. I worked hard on that project and she gave my job to a moron. She knew what it meant to me."

"She never expected you to run off to Belfast. None of us did."

"I couldn't bear to be in London. You know that. I was angry. Besides, I spent a few weeks staying with you and I've been here in Belfast for over a month, so she's had time to get over herself."

"You're in a job that pays you less than half of what you earned over here. You're living with Auntie Annie when you have a lovely apartment near the river in London. You've left all your friends and family behind, and on top of all that, you don't even sound happy.

"Well, I am happy." I stare out of the window across the Lough. "I'm making new friends and I'm settling in. Simon has asked me to stay on and there's a chance of him offering me shares in the company at the end of the year if we do well."

"Is that really what you want? Do you want to spend the rest of your life in Northern Ireland, so far from us?" I imagine her blue inquisitive eyes challenging me.

"No, I—"

"Ellie, have you met someone?"

I let the silence hang in the air.

"Ellie?"

"She's just a friend." I ruffle my hair conscious of the perspiration on my neck.

"Oh, no. Who is she?"

"Her name is Maria, and she's a happily married woman with a lovely daughter. There's nothing in it. We're friends. We work together and she's straight."

"Does she know you're gay?"

"It's not important."

"Oh Ellie, don't get involved with married women, especially one you work with. You're very vulnerable at the moment. Don't rush into another relationship."

"I'm not rushing into anything. A trip to the cinema and dinner with her and her eight year-old daughter hardly constitutes a budding romance or is even classed as being involved with—"

"Don't fall for someone who's not in a position to return your affections. What you had with Kat was very special."

"If it was that special, Kat wouldn't have been having an affair with Marcella for eight months and she certainly wouldn't have given my promotion to an incompetent arse, would she?"

"She really does regret it. The two of you were invincible before and there's no reason why you can't be again."

"If we were so invincible then why did we split up?"

"These things happen but they can be repaired."

"This can't." But there is no sense in arguing with Jenny so I change the subject. "I'm taking Auntie Annie to the airport tomorrow. She's flying to New York then up to Toronto."

"You're going to be very lonely without her."

"I'm lonely now," I whisper.

* * *

It is bank holiday Monday and I drive Auntie Annie to the airport. My emotions are mixed. I'm caught up in her excitement yet selfishly I know the house will be empty without her. She will be seeing her son Michael and her brother — my Uncle David — and family. I smile and reassure her that I will be fine on my own and that I will make more friends and go out more.

"You're only thirty-three," she says, "I was married with a son at your age. Go out and have some fun."

"I will, I promise."

"Treat my house as your own. Entertain, have dinner parties and enjoy yourself."

"I will."

"Invite friends over from London to stay."

"I will."

"Find a boyfriend!"

I kiss her goodbye, push her through passport control and hide my tears.

"Live dangerously." She laughs.

* * *

Simon is determined to buy and sell hardware to the public. I've told him it's a crazy idea but he won't listen so I spend the rest of the week reviewing suitable locations for secure warehouses or a retail outlet and I speak on the telephone to a new client. Her name is Mickey Bleu. She's from Haiti and she's a restaurant owner and chef. We run through the spec of the technology service she is looking for and I tell her I will send her some details and suggest a meeting. It is almost five o'clock when I have time to look in on Maria. I've hardly been in the office this week and I haven't spoken to her all day. She looks up from mounds of invoices and smiles with tired eyes.

She has a cold.

"I must have caught it last Monday but I've hardly seen you this week. I haven't even had the time to tell you, we went to the zoo on bank holiday Monday."

She laughs at my reaction and holds up the palm of her hand.

"I know. Don't say it. Michael hasn't realised that Lily has grown up. He was trying to get us all to behave like we did five years ago being silly and pulling faces at the monkeys but you know how Lily likes to be quite a grown-up now." Maria shakes her head. Silver pendent feather earrings flutter from her lobes. "I refused to join in. I couldn't wait to get out of the place, I felt so ill. What did you do for the bank holiday?"

"I dropped Auntie Annie to the airport, took the Harley up the coast, and walked down at the sea in Holywood. It's beautiful along there."

She rests her face on her hand thoughtfully. "You can look across the Lough to us in Jordanstown."

That's exactly what I had done but I say nothing, instead I turn and look out of the window.

"Ellie? Is there something wrong?"

I stand beside the window. She has not mentioned the incident with the tough guys calling us names last Saturday in the Odyssey but her reaction at the time said it all. She had been embarrassed and humiliated.

"Am I that transparent?"

"Do you want to talk? I always unburden myself to you and tell you my problems. So, speak to me, please." Maria waits and concern floods into her eyes.

"My ex went to see my sister." I look down at the busy road before turning back to Maria. I want to tell her the truth but I don't know if I can. What would she say? What would Simon say and the rest of the guys in the techie lab? I would be a social outcast again. It was bad enough in London after Kat had told all our colleagues but here would be infinitely worse. These people don't know me. They have probably never met a gay woman before and they would automatically feel uncomfortable or worse — threatened?

I cannot speak. Even though I want to — so I remain silent and staring like a child caught in the act if something bad.

"Let me guess. He wants you back," she says softly. "I wouldn't blame him."

Now is the perfect moment to tell the truth.

I can be honest.

I take a deep breath. But what if it complicates my relationship with Maria? What if Simon finds out that I am gay. I may lose my job. Even though there is sexual equality and no discrimination I don't believe that it is embraced so widely and accepted in daily life. There might be another excuse to get rid of me.

I speak slowly, "He wishes I had never left…" My voice trails away. It's easier to lie and to pretend that Kat is a man.

"And, what do you think?"

"Sometimes I'm so lonely I think it would be easier to go back to London," I answer truthfully.

"Are you still interested in him? Do you think it could work out?" Maria's questions come quickly and I study the ends of my maroon-painted nails before I reply.

"No. My relationship is over. I'm not very forgiving and I don't know if going back to London is the answer."

"I know you haven't said much about him but affairs are affairs. It would be great if we could all have affairs and go back to our partners and expect to carry on as if nothing happened. We would all do it, including me."

"You wouldn't have an affair."

"Sometimes I think a fling would be lovely. A naughty

escapade would be wonderful."

"Maria!" I reprimand her but I smile. "What about the guilt factor?"

"Ah yes, guilt. We Catholics are very good at guilt but I could train myself in that department but only if he was exceptionally good-looking, and the sex would have to be pretty special too," she jokes and I am pleased with the diversion.

"Brad Pitt?"

"George Clooney."

"Not John the Ogre then?"

"Definitely not. He's back in the office on Monday. I wonder how his sales seminar went and I do hope he's given up smoking for you." She smiles at me and I cannot tear my gaze away from her transparent gaze and deep brown eyes. She makes me laugh and that's always a bonus.

* * *

On Saturday morning I'm restless. It is early, there is a crescendo of birds singing and when I fire up the Harley the road is deserted. Five minutes from my house I'm in the country riding over the hills, winding down country roads until I don't want to know where I am.

I don't want the road to be familiar.

I want to explore randomly.

Hedgerows are thick with white hawthorn, bluebells on the forest floor are swaying in the breeze like dancing girls, pungent white flowering garlic flutter in clusters by the roadside, and baby blue forget-me-nots cuddle together like best friends. In the distance sun shines on a shimmering blue sea and fields of colourful Picasso-yellow rape seed bend and ripple in the breeze.

When I stop on top of a hill to admire the view I feel vibrating in my chest. I reach into my pocket for my mobile.

"Hello?"

My day is radically changed. With zest and excitement I turn the Harley toward home filled with anticipation of the day ahead.

An hour later I meet Maria, Lily and her best friend Charlie in town outside the City Hall.

"I hope you didn't mind me calling you at such short notice but I couldn't face this alone," Maria says.

"I was thinking of coming into town anyway,' I lie.

Lily hugs me and Maria introduces me to Charlie. She is the complete opposite to Lily. She is overweight, has pixie ears and a hooked nose. I warm to her immediately.

"It's my birthday tomorrow," Charlie announces. "I'll be nine and I love shopping."

"It's my birthday in August, I'll be thirty-four and I hate shopping," I reply.

"I didn't realise I was a year older than you. I thought I was much younger," Maria teases me.

"God bless your imagination."

"You really don't like shopping?" Lily screws her nose up at me.

"No. Unless it's on the internet and I get it delivered like I did this jacket." I tug the lapel of my red Harley jacket.

"I want a leather jacket," Lily announces.

"You won't want to wear leather in the summer, it's too hot," Maria says. "Besides it's not your birthday today."

"I need shoes," Charlie announces. "High heels for my

holiday."

I meet Maria's gaze above their heads. Her brown eyes are warm and sparkling.

"And Maria - what do you want?" I ask.

"Is it too early for lunch and a large glass of white wine?"

"Never."

It's a warm day with a cold wind. We dodge the showers, dashing in and out of the shops. I'm happy to wait with Maria while the girls are in the fitting room, trying on tops and skirts, giggling and posing. We pop into a few shoe shops then wander around accessory shops avoiding the pricey designer stores in the main shopping mall.

I drag them into the high street bookshop and we amble between the shelves discussing novels, writers, and the merits of bestsellers. The girls have read Roald Dahl, Enid Blyton and Doctor Who so I buy them both the adventure loving books by Ali Sparks, *The Shapeshifters Set*.

Finally Maria and I share a mutual look of understanding and breathe a sigh of relief.

"It must be time for lunch now," she says.

"We've earned it." I grin.

The restaurant is warm so I throw my jacket over the back of the chair. Underneath I wear a short-sleeved checked blouse and I rub my hair feeling cooler but leaving it messy and tousled.

We are eating lunch, burgers for the girls and salt and chilli squid for me and Maria, and I have a mouthful of food when Charlie suddenly lunges across the table and tugs open the neck of my shirt.

"Wow! Look at that!"

She must have been peeking inside my blouse because she

spots the tattoo on my chest and across the top of my shoulder.

"*Not all who wander are lost,*" she reads.

Three pairs of eyes turn on me and I blush.

Lily is upset she has not seen it first. "Ellie!" she screams, and almost rips the material to get a closer look at my shoulder so I hold the palm of my hand at my chest clutching the buttons. "You never told me you had another one. Let me look. I want to see it. Mum, when can I get a tattoo?"

"When you're eighteen." Maria is physically restraining Lily from climbing into my blouse.

I spend the next half an hour eating lunch and trying to distract them, attempting to deflect the attention from my body art and to talk about other things. Eventually when we leave the restaurant the girls walk on ahead and I feel Maria's eyes staring at the inky stars under my ear lobe.

"What have you done to my daughter?" she asks, "she thinks you're wonderful."

I blush. I'm still reeling from their unwanted attention and I say nothing.

"As a matter of interest, do you have any more tattoos, I should know about?" she whispers and then laughs aloud at my obvious embarrassment.

* * *

It is late on Monday evening and I am clearing up the files on my desk when I hear footsteps on the stairs.

"Simon?" I call out but there is no reply.

I'm weary and the thought of going home to Auntie Annie's empty house doesn't inspire me. I grab my bag and I turn out the light when I am confronted by a shadow at the top of the stairs. I gasp holding my hand to my mouth.

"John?" I focus on the darkness and reach for the light-switch and a face comes into view. "Michael? What do you want? What are you doing here?"

His breath is sweet and he pushes me backward very gently against the wall. His lips brush mine and I push him angrily away, reassured that the lights are still on downstairs in the techie lab and some of the guys are working.

"What are you doing, Michael?" I raise my voice. "Michael?"

He lets me go and says, "I've come to get Maria's jacket from her office. She left it behind. She's waiting down in the car."

I take a step but he blocks my path.

"Don't pretend you don't want me." His palm brushes my breast.

I slap his hand away. "Get off."

"You are quite irresistible, do you know that? Are you on your way home?"

"Get out of my way."

He laughs and backs off.

I run.

* * *

A couple of days later I am in my office preparing papers for the weekly managers' meeting. I have made notes about the progress of the ITG and OUT magazine contracts and I am also working on figures to prove that investing in apps and gaming software will be more profitable than Simon's ridiculous idea of selling hardware through a retail outlet.

"Are you busy?" John appears in my office. He flicks open his white lab coats, flops down onto the chair opposite my desk and watches me.

"Hey John, how are you? How was the course?" I hope my upbeat tone covers my serious dislike for the toad.

His eyes twinkle mischievously and he licks his lips. His hands are wedged in the front pockets of his tight trousers and there's a roll of fat hanging over his waistband.

"You did me a good turn. It was a good sales course and very revealing."

"Great. Have you come back with new ideas on how to increase sales?"

"The course really opened my eyes." He stands and walks restlessly to the window as if suppressing excitement where he stands like a coiled viper.

"Dublin's a lovely city. I must get down there again," I say, wishing he would get out so that I could finish preparing my notes.

"Who was in Dublin?" he asks.

"Wasn't your conference in the South?"

"No. I went over to London."

"Oh? OK, well, I've prepared a time schedule for the ITG project." I lift papers in my hand.

"Happy Days!" He winks. "See you in the boardroom."

Half an hour later we are all sitting around the table. Simon is working through the items on the agenda.

"Mark Bowman the new computer graduate starts work today to oversee the ITG account," John confirms. "Liam is co-ordinating with Sally Richman from the OUT magazines. He has the skill and talent to oversee the tailor-made package for them and he will liaise back to Stuart who will provide the techie experience of programming and hosting." As he speaks he maintains eye contact with me. He has a sly secret smile lingering on his lips. Perhaps he thinks he's sexy. I hope Maria wasn't serious when she said he is going to ask me out.

We finish by discussing targets, new contracts and other future projects and when the meeting closes we all stand and I gather my papers. I need to return a call to Mickey Bleu, the restaurant owner, about our meeting.

"You enjoyed the sales course?" Simon pats John's shoulder.

I move toward the door.

John raises his voice. "That sales woman you recommended, Simon, was fantastic."

There is something in his tone that makes me pause.

"Had Proctor & Gower started the sales seminars when you left them, Ellie?" Simon asks.

I pause.

"Katherine Small. Does that name ring a bell?" John insists.

"Kat?" I whisper.

"She remembers you…" He smiles.

"They had a cancellation and I thought it would be a good opportunity for John," Simon says.

Maria throws an inquisitive glance at me.

"I must make a phone call." I push past them.

"Has Ellie told you Maria?" John is balancing on the balls of his feet, rocking backwards and forwards.

"Told me what?" There is a frown between her inquisitive brown eyes.

I pause at the door and to turn look from one to the other. I shake my head at John. It's a deja-vu feeling. London is happening all over again.

His tongue flicks over his lips. "She's Ellie's ex!"

"What are you talking about?" Maria says.

I run. In my office I toss my notes onto the desk, grab my

jacket and helmet. I jump down the stairs two at a time and pause on the last step with my hand on the rail. I'm trapped as John's voice floats down wafting after me like a bad smell and I am caught in the simplicity of truth.

"The sales director at Proctor and Gower - Katherine Small - is Ellie's ex-lover. Didn't you know that our marketing manager is a red hot Lesbian?"

Chapter Seven

The following morning I make fresh coffee and the croissants are still warm from Maud's cafe. I hear Maria's footsteps on the stairs and I wait for her holding open the kitchen door but she ignores me and walks past so I follow her into her office.

"I'm sorry. I should have told you," I say. "I know it wasn't fair that you found out that way."

She removes the jacket of her light brown suit and without glancing at me walks into the kitchen. I follow in the wake of her familiar and invisible *Chanel* perfume, conscious of the muffled sounds downstairs of the techie team arriving to work. Siobhan and Stuart are talking, Liam barks a quick laugh and John coughs.

I close the kitchen door behind us.

"Maria, please don't be angry with me."

"It's nothing to do with me. It's not my problem." Her voice is strong and firm.

"Don't block me out. I thought we were friends."

"Friends? That's funny, so did I." She slams the fridge door. "But I wouldn't treat my friends like this."

"I couldn't tell you," I whisper.

"Why? You know everything about me. I tell you about Lily and about Michael, and my problems—"

"It's not the same."

"No, you're right! It's not the same. It's fine for you to lie."

"No — it's not—" I push hair from my face. "Not everyone understands."

"Is that the best you can do?" Her angry eyes challenge me.

"Do you have any idea what it's like to have to hide your feelings every day and to pretend you're someone you're not?"

"Don't look for sympathy. It's been your choice." She slams the kitchen door on her way out and I follow her, keeping my voice hushed.

"I understand what I did was wrong. There is no excuse for my lies when I pretended that Kat was a man but it was the easiest thing for me to do. I didn't know you well enough to tell you the truth. I didn't know how you would react. I've never told anyone. Not even Auntie Annie." I sigh and lean across her desk. "Maria, I'm truly sorry. I value your friendship and I really want to talk to you about this."

She looks at me over the mug in her hands, *The World's Best Mum,* her generous lips are set firm so I sit opposite her.

"I didn't want to tell anyone, especially in Belfast. At first, when I arrived here, I was too upset. Then to explain to a happily married heterosexual woman with a loving daughter that my lifestyle isn't as conventional as theirs, well, it just got harder and harder..." I push up my hair, my neck is damp.

"If you can't speak to your friends then who can you trust?"

"I know. It's just that..." I massage my temples.

"I deserve the truth. Not some made up stories."

"I know, I know, but everyone pretends they accept the gay lifestyle until it comes to their own family or someone they know. Even though Civil Partnerships exist there's prejudice still out there. We still live in a very homophobic society. Gay people are judged and defined by their sexuality not by their love. There's a stigma attached to being gay. Look at John, for example, look at his reaction. It's malicious, so please don't tell me he understands—"

"It's not John I'm thinking about and it's not about you being gay either," she pauses then lowers her voice. "It's the fact you didn't tell me. You didn't trust me—"

"But I—"

"How do I know who you are? How does anyone know who you are — when you lie?"

"It's difficult to discuss my feelings—"

"Well, Kat obviously doesn't feel the same way. She told John, a complete stranger, on a sales seminar."

"Kat is different to me. When I met her, we spent our first Christmas together, she got drunk and told my family on Boxing Day over dinner. Believe me, I didn't get a choice. MY sister, Jenny — and Richard — have been brilliant about it and even the boys know but my mother thinks it's like a dose of flu and I'll get better and be over it soon."

"Bird flu?" she says quietly, and her glare turns into a weak smile.

"I know I have hurt you, Maria—"

"You've really pissed me off."

"I couldn't tell you because I was frightened—"

The phone rings.

I lean forward, across the desk an put my hand on hers. "Leave it," I plead.

Our eyes lock and when it rings again Maria picks it up.

* * *

Several days later I'm in Simon's car and we are driving back from meeting a client in Fermanagh.

Simon's grey eyes are firmly on the road. "I'm going away with Louise. I'm taking her to America for a week. I've had a word with John and he won't say anything to anyone, you know, about Katherine Small and your um…"

"He just wanted to get even with me. He's a vile man." I'm still angry with him. I haven't seen Maria since our chat after the meeting when he dropped the bombshell and I'm still unsure how she will be with me.

"John is the way he is," Simon responds calmly. "It's unfortunate he knows about your personal situation but you're going to have to deal with it."

"How could Kat confide in John, of all people?" I wonder aloud.

"It's not a big deal, Ellie. Just do your work, be professional and don't take any rubbish from him," Simon insists. "No-one else has to know. I'll support you, but you must to speak to Maria. She's your friend. She hasn't said anything to me and she's refused to speak to John and I think she's very upset. She considered you a friend."

"I don't think she wants to speak to me either," I mumble. "She's been avoiding me."

"Try to speak to her again. Perhaps this afternoon at the celebration you will have the opportunity."

I had forgotten about the company drinks party today, and at five o'clock, I venture downstairs and into the techie lab.

Simon has bought a few crates of beer and a few bottles of wine and we're toasting, at his insistence, the new contracts we have recently signed.

It will ease his conscience, I think, while he swans off to

America for a week.

Stuart is laughing with Siobhan and Maria, while the boys stand in clusters drinking beer from bottles. They all look like scientists in white lab coats. It's only Maria and I who don't wear them. Liam, John, and the new guy Mark Bowman are discussing the latest computer game, and Steve, Adam, Jeff and Mike have boy-band hairstyles with thick long fringes so I've nicknamed them Boys Aloud. They wave me over and pour me a glass of warm white wine.

It's only Ray, the quiet one who stands to one side not participating and not speaking.

Then Simon clears his throat and we fall silent and he makes a fine speech about the company, its growth, its potential and of course the hard working team which gets an enthusiastic cheer, whistles and catcalls.

"And, we will be celebrating with the company's sixth anniversary party on the twenty-first of June," he announces. "It seems that dinner in Bert's Jazz restaurant is the most popular choice for our celebration this year."

This creates a spontaneous burst of applause and a few more piercing whistles.

My smile is fake. I'm thinking I'll be back to London by then. Perhaps I'll leave this weekend. I definitely won't be here for the party in June.

After Simon's speech, John take Maria's elbow and he leads her toward his office. Their heads are bent in animated discussion and her face darkens into scowl. She glances in my direction and I turn quickly away.

Stuart stands with his arm casually draped over Siobhan's shoulder and I think of the time we saw them together and how Maria linked my arm in hers and leaned affectionately against me before the yobs walked past and called us names and she fled.

When I look back at Maria she is staring at me.

Liam tops up my wine but I feel nausea. My stomach is like an empty pit. I glance at my watch and place my untouched glass on the desk. I need to get out. and I have almost reached the door when I feel Maria's fingers tugging on my arm.

"Where did you go on Friday evening," she whispers, "after work - after our chat that morning?" Self-consciously she releases my arm and flattens her long hair with the palm of her hand.

"I went for a ride on the Harley. Why?"

"I waited for you. I went to your Aunt's house. I wanted to speak to you." She glances over her shoulder. "I left Lily at Mum's but you weren't home."

"You came to my home?" I say, remembering how I sat staring at the sea for hours. Thinking. Worrying.

"I wanted to speak to you but then Michael came back and I couldn't get away again over the weekend."

"It was late when I got home. It was almost nine," I say.

"I waited as long as I could." Her pupils are large and she looks tired. Her long lashes blink quickly and she glances over to where John is talking with Simon. "He's trying to cause trouble," she says.

"Maria, I—"

She holds up the palm of her hand. "But I won't let him. I told him not to mention it again. Not to me or to anyone else. I told him I will tell Simon he was moonlighting last year when Simon was away. He worked for an engineering company for a few weeks and he knows that was wrong."

I cannot suppress a small giggle. "My goodness, Maria.

That's blackmail. I'd never have thought you had it in you. I'm very impressed."

"You may be very surprised Ellie Bravo," she replies, "at what I have inside me."

* * *

I'm weary and when I return home and there is a car parked in Auntie Annie's driveway. It's a red Audi and Michael is leaning against the bonnet.

"What are you doing here?" I say, ripping off my helmet.

"Bitch!" He's filled with restrained anger.

"What is your problem, Michael? What do you want?"

"You've been taking the piss out of me. You've led me on. John told me." He grabs my wrist.

"Michael, I haven't— Get off—" I pull free.

"You know you want it," he sneers. "What is it with you? You've flirted with me and now it turns out you're a feckin' dyke—"

"I haven't flirted with you—"

"John said he knew from the beginning that you hated men."

My neighbour, a man with ginger curly hair arrives home, parks his car and he waves. His two sons, teenage boys, have the same colouring, fair skin and a scattering of heavy freckles.

"How's Annie?" he calls.

"Great. She's having a wonderful time."

I watch them as they disappear into their house using the time to control myself.

"Is it Maria?" he asks.

I turn my head sharply.

"Ah? So it's my wife, is it? I see that look in your eyes. You're frightened she will find out about us. You swing both ways, don't you?" He smiles.

I shake my head. "I think you had better go."

"Aren't you going to invite me in? You'll enjoy it. I promise—"

"Michael—"

He clicks his fingers, taps his head and laughs then his tone turns harsh. "Of course, how could I have been so stupid? I know what it is. You're with someone else. Who is it? A woman? You're a cock-teasing bitch."

I fumble for my front door key, calculating how quickly I can reach my neighbour's house in a fast sprint.

"Go away, get out of my driveway and don't come back, Michael, or I will tell Maria that you have been following me and—" He pins my arms behind my back and pushes me against to door. I struggle but he is stronger and his grip is tight. His face is pushed against mine and there is spittle on his lips.

"Mention this to Maria and you will regret it. I know some very nasty people and if you think you are going to affect my life and my marriage then think again. I can be a very, very bad person. Don't mess with me." He pushes me sideways and steps back. I stumble and wipe his saliva from my cheek with a shaking hand. I watch him get in his car and reverse out of my drive.

✳ ✳ ✳

Several days later Maria and I are eating lunch in Cafe Maud's beside the office. I have been deliberating if I should say anything about Michael. I am not scared of his threat, I'm only frightened that his behaviour will isolate Maria from me and affect our friendship.

I have a ciabatta half way to my mouth when she says, "I'm having terrible trouble with Lily."

She is wearing a lavender blouse that has drained all colour from her cheeks leaving her face drawn and exhausted. There are dark circles around the hollow of her eyes.

"What's wrong with her?"

Maria gazes out of the window, her sandwich lays untouched and her coffee is growing cold.

"Michael wants us to move to Dublin. He says that some property is cheaper now down there and we could afford to move. He says it would save him commuting but Lily is having none of it. She is stomping around the house saying she isn't going and she'd prefer to live here — with Grandma."

We stare at each other.

"That is bad," I agree. I put the half eaten ciabatta on the plate. My appetite has disappeared. "Why does he want to go to Dublin so suddenly? How do you feel about moving?"

She shakes her head. "I'm confused. It's all so sudden. His behaviour is becoming quite irrational."

I contemplate telling her but I can't. I remember my fear at Michael's anger. I want to take her in my arms and hold her close.

"I've had a weekend of it," she says. "Arguing and discussions. Michael is insisting. He's adamant. He got really angry. Lily is resisting and I'm in the middle." She places her thumb to her lips and nips at the nail with her teeth.

"Do you want to move?" I ask and hold my breath.

"No!" She slams her fist on the table and her eyes bore into mine. "Of course I don't. This is my home. This is where my family are and Lily is happy at school."

I breathe again.

"My mother isn't helping," she continues. "When I tried to discuss it with her she insists I must go with Michael. It's my duty as his wife—"

"What about your job and your life here?"

"She doesn't seem to think that counts."

"Why am I not surprised?" I can't hide my sarcasm but she doesn't seem to notice.

"It's awful." Maria places her face in her hands.

I pull a tissue from my bag and pass it to her.

"Michael's been so bad-tempered and angry recently, so that doesn't help."

"With you?"

"And with Lily." She dabs her eyes. "He's not at home that often but when he is, he's always finding fault with her, or with me, or the house or something. I assume it's the stress of commuting between here and Dublin and over to Galway."

"Lots of people commute. They don't have to turn into an asshole." I can't help myself.

"Pat is on Michael's side. My sister's always had a soft spot for Michael, and now Connor and Kate have got involved. They say it's me being difficult and that I must get around Lily. I have to tell Lily that we're moving and not take any of her tantrums."

"So, the whole family has an opinion on what you should do."

"He brought it up again over Sunday lunch with the family. I think he does it on purpose. He knows they all adore him and he can do nothing wrong. They don't know how hard it is to live with him once that icy charm wears off."

"It's not easy Maria. Don't worry, everything will work out in the end." I make my voice light and encouraging. "Concentrate on one step at a time. Tackle the small hills and don't think of the mountain. Explore all angles and you'll do the right thing. Speak to your Mum and explain to her that you need her support and then speak to Lily."

She picks up her cold coffee and smiles with tired eyes. "You're right. Thanks for listening, Ellie. I'm pleased we're friends again. It means a lot to me. I don't know what I'd do without you."

I want to say that I don't know what I would do without her. The thought of them moving to Dublin fills me with weary sadness.

* * *

I have not seen Maria since lunchtime on Wednesday in Cafe Mauds. I've been in meetings off-site with Mark Bowman and Boris McCabe the Director of ITG. He's a formidable man who wears designer suits and a large gold signet ring.

I've also squeezed in a few meetings with companies looking for apps and I've secured a meeting for Simon to view a suitable retail outlet near to our office when he's back from America next week.

I stop for an hour in the late afternoon sunshine to look at the sea and stare mournfully across the Lough. It's Friday and I haven't gone back to London for the bank holiday weekend because Jenny and Richard have taken the boys to Malaga to see Dad, so I go home to Auntie Annie's house, restless and bored and my mood is volatile.

I pour a strong gin and tonic add plenty of sliced lemon and ice, and I drink greedily.

Tony Braxton, *I'm a Woman*, sings to me from the radio and my mobile phone rings.

"It's me," Maria says, "Where are you?"

"At home."

"Can I come over?"

Thirty minutes later I answer the door.

"Where's Lily?"

"Watching *Dirty Dancing* with Grandma, for the fifteenth time."

She wears blue jeans, flat moccasins and a low cut, beige T-shirt. She accepts a glass of red wine and exclaims with delight over the house; the fitted kitchen, large terrace doors that overlook a neat garden and I follow her through to the lounge and she gasps. "This is amazing." She walks past two comfortable beige sofas, a large television, an unlit fireplace and stands at the floor to ceiling window and gazes across the Lough. I watch her figure and her slow movements and then I return to the kitchen where I begin washing salad and rinsing tomatoes.

"I hope you haven't eaten. There's pasta, salad and garlic bread," I call out.

"It's a beautiful house." She stands in the doorway watching me.

"Auntie Annie modernised it. She's like me in that sense, she hates old houses and antiques."

We speak about houses, families and heirlooms. The conversation flows and we talk freely as I set the table beside the window overlooking the garden.

"It's too cool in the evening to eat outside," I explain.

"This is a lovely treat. I didn't expect dinner."

"The unexpected can often be a welcome surprise," I reply.

She watches me silently as I place a salad bowl and then steaming aluminium-wrapped garlic bread on the table.

"Why did you assume I was happily married?"

I don't turn from the hob.

"Aren't you?"

She doesn't reply so I change the subject.

"I'm pleased you're here. It's nice to eat with someone. I miss Auntie Annie and I miss not cooking every night; not having dinner parties, or barbecues." I place the macaroni on the table. "I always cooked for Kat. She was lousy in the kitchen. This is Dad's favourite too."

"Does he know you're gay?"

"Yes."

"Does it bother him?"

I look out of the window. "I suppose it did. I'm sure he would like me to marry and have children and to be happy."

"Is marriage and children the recipe for happiness?"

"I don't know. You tell me."

We eat slowly.

She's quiet and thoughtful so I speak about Spain, my father and my parent's divorce and then I end up telling her how I met Kat.

"Were you faithful?" she asks.

"I was — she wasn't. Then I had a casual fling with a client, one night, and she turned nasty and vindictive."

"Did you have many relationships before her?"

I think the wine has emboldened Maria and I smile.

"I had a girlfriend at University in Madrid. It is easier in Spain to meet gay people. There are gay bars in London but it's very hard to meet the woman of your dreams that way."

"Why?"

"Well, it's like going to the pub. How many people meet their partners in a bar? It's much nicer if you meet someone through work or you are introduced through mutual friends. That way you get to know someone first, don't you think so?"

She doesn't look at me when she replies, "I met Michael when I was very young. We were still at school."

"Have you been faithful?"

"Of course."

"Have you never been attracted to another man since you've been with Michael?"

"Not really, no."

"Never?" My voice holds a note of surprise. "You've never met anyone you were attracted to in all these years?"

"I envy you," she says but she doesn't look at me. She breaks off a lump of garlic bread and places it in her mouth. "I envy the fact that you are so free. You can do what you like. You have no ties and you only have yourself to please."

She misses my point. Deliberately?

"I'm not single from choice," I say icily, "I'm a sharer and I like to give. I would be much happier in a relationship."

* * *

By Sunday afternoon the morning sunshine has been replaced by dark thundering clouds and a sea mist and heavy rain is lashing against the lounge window. It obliterates my view of the church spire across the Lough, dashing my hope of riding the Harley down winding roads with wild irresponsible speed.

The fire is roaring and the Sunday papers are strewn across the floor. I pace restlessly as I have paced since Maria left on

Friday night. Our conversation has been replayed over and over inside my head, tumbling and mixing so quickly that I do not remember the truth of our conversation now, only the shape of her jaw, the laughter in her voice, her brown speckled eyes, and the way she self-consciously touched her hair, tilted her head and gazed at me.

Had she been flirting?

The storm rages outside and I stand spread-eagled pressing the palms of my hands against the floor to ceiling window. I am hot, cold, energised and exhausted, leaning in supplication of the powerful electrical surge that seems to ripple through my body as cracking thunder splits the billowing black sky and driving wind rattles the pane. My forehead rests against the cold glass until the storm subsides and the clouds break apart then I pull away from my trance-like state and begin pacing the room like a caged tiger — backwards and forwards.

The doorbell rings.

I move with stealth, slow, deliberate, paces. My body is taut and lithe.

Maria stands on the step. Her hair wet from the rain. "Can I come in?"

I stand aside. She walks past me and into the lounge. She stands at the window, taking my place, gazing outside.

"Are you okay?" I ask.

Her voice is muffled. "Looking across the Lough is like looking at life from a different perspective. I've just been standing on the other side, looking over here. From here everything is so easy and uncomplicated." She sighs. "I could be selfish and independent. Yet when I'm on the other side, looking over here I'm confused and claustrophobic."

I pass her a hand towel and stand beside her at the window.

"I had to get out." She rubs her hair. A tang of *Channel* from her wrists reaches my nose and I inhale deeply. Her voice is soft and thoughtful. "Looking across the Lough, you never know what people's lives are like on the other side. How different we all are. All the things we hide. The feelings we try not to have. The yearnings we suppress."

Her warm breath leaves a cloudy mist on the window where I stood a few minutes ago, stretched against the glass.

"Where do we draw the line between what we want and our responsibilities? Is my life over because I can't stand up and say I want something more exciting? Am I a bad mother because I crave excitement and passion or even lust? Is that really so shameful?"

"You are not a bad mother—"

"But a bad wife? I wouldn't say all this if I was a happily married Catholic woman, would I?" Her eyes burn into mine. The towel hangs limply at her side.

"You can't help your feelings, Maria. You can't help who you are," I answer softly.

Her eyes are like dark velvet. The tang of her perfume invades my senses enveloping me in its misty embrace. There is a small tic near her left eye and when her head moves toward me it tilts gently like a sunflower turning toward the heated rays of the sun.

When our lips meet I'm surprised by the softness of her full mouth and her probing tongue that explores tentatively and gently; my lips, my tongue, my teeth.

Eventually we pull apart.

My breath is rapid. My chest is shaking and the skin on my arms is covered in goosebumps. I lay the palm of my hand against her cheek and she smiles and kisses my fingers. I release the ribbon holding her damp hair and I let it fall to the floor beside the damp towel.

She pulls me closer and, very tenderly, she trails her nail across my skin to the inky star tattoo under my ear, looking at me with infinite scrutiny. Our foreheads are pressed together, our noses touching and our smiles turn into bubbly giggles.

"Make love to me, Ellie," she whispers between gentle kisses. "I want you. I need to kiss you and touch every part of you.

"Are you sure this is what you want?"

"I've never been as sure of anything in my whole life. Besides, I want to check you out and make sure you don't have any more body art that you haven't told me about."

Chapter Eight

After the bliss of Sunday afternoon and making love with Maria my life has plunged downhill faster than an Alpine skier. It has gone from bad to worse, or as my father would say; from Guatamala to Guatapeor.

Simon is back from America and we've been dealing with the logistics and strategies for all the existing and new contracts and services that we are now providing to our clients.

At four o'clock we are sitting with a new client Mickey Bleu, a restaurant owner and chef extraordinaire, in the boardroom. She is a black Haitian with wide red lips, a flat nose and eyes the size of horse chestnuts. She wears a flamboyant low cut bright red, yellow and green dress with a matching turban, a voice as deep as the ocean and a cleavage as impressive as the Grand Canyon.

She is beautiful.

It's as if the boardroom walls are breathing.

This woman radiates energy and I'm clearly not the only one in the room attracted by her magnetic charm. John is unblinking. He is enthralled with her. His mouth hangs open and he stares hypnotically at her heaving breasts that expand and constrict as she speaks.

"We recently moved from Haiti. I am opening a new

restaurant in town beside the Ulster Hall. It's in a trendy and popular street and I think I could do well.

"The food will be simple and filled with spices from my Caribbean homeland -it will be fiery and fierce like its people." She raises her chest as she speaks. "We are resilient. We know about hardship. We know about pain and loss and suffering. Three and a half million people were affected by the earthquake and my country was devastated. Over two hundred thousand died. Four thousand schools were destroyed and at one stage over one and a half million people were living in camps. If the storms and flooding weren't bad enough there was an outbreak of Cholera in October 2010..." She shakes her head. "Emmanuel's family all died apart from one nephew and I lost my sister and her four children. We worked hard. We saved as many lives as possible. We fed as many as we could. And we begged for more food parcels. So many families were devastated. Children were orphaned..." her voice trails off and she wipes her damp eyes. "Covid hasn't helped," she continues.

It is almost five o'clock. I had wanted to see Maria before she goes home but I can't move I'm so saddened by Mickey's story.

Simon strokes his cheek and his pale grey eyes become remote. And I think that to diffuse the emotion of the situation he calls Maria into the boardroom. Just the sight of her entering the room causes my throat to constrict and when she sits down she tilts her head and smiles at Mickey. She doesn't look at me but I'm filled with the memory of kissing her swan like neck and trailing my fingers across her breasts.I think of the small mole she has on the top of her thigh, the scar from Lily's Caesarean birth and her soft voice explaining why they never had more children.

Suddenly Maria looks up and focuses on me and when I blush there's a small smile playing around her charcoal eyes.

After Mickey Bleu has gone, I have one final meeting with Mark Bowman to review the ITG project. He is a slim Glaswegian with a mop of thick hair brushed across his forehead that he continually smooths down with the palm of his hand. He is efficient and we work well together but it is late when we are finished and I am exhausted and frustrated.

It is my second night working late and I've been unable to talk properly with Maria.

In the quiet solitude of my office, I imagine Maria at home with Lily, eating dinner, watching television and going to bed. She has told me the daily routines of her life. She has also told me of her fears, joys and loves.

My back is aching. It feels it is breaking so I yawn and stretch. I don't want to leave a message so I dial her mobile.

"Hi," she says.

"Are you alone?"

"No."

"Are you okay?"

She doesn't reply.

"I'm thinking of you."

"Thanks for phoning." She hangs up but not before I hear the smile in her voice.

I'm satisfied yet empty. Downstairs I call out goodnight to Mark and Stuart who are working late and I thank them for their help.

In the street the air is cool on my face. Curry from the Indian takeaway on the corner lingers in the air making my stomach retch. I can't face food. My stomach is knotted. My lips dry. Jenny's words form in my head.

Don't get involved with anyone. Don't get involved with a married woman. You're too vulnerable.

Was Maria a conquest?

How will I see her again — alone?

What will happen?

I need her. I think I am in love. What have I done?

* * *

"I park my Harley in the same place everyday. In the side street, near the front door of Bizweb Solutions," I repeat slowly for what seems to be the tenth time to a child. I'm exasperated and angry.

The policewoman in her green uniform doesn't bother taking notes. She just circles my Harley regarding the damage. She has dark circles around her eyes, thick eyebrows and a long face. It makes me think that she has seen far worse things during her career and is pleased to be called out for something more mundane.

"Nice bike! And you said it was perfect when you left it this morning."

"Yes."

"What time was that?"

"About seven thirty."

Her colleague is fat. He has greasy hair and wears a yellow high-vis jacket over his uniform. His radio punches into life with a static voice and a series of codes. He turns to off and continues to gaze at the Harley.

"This does happen, unfortunately. There's a lot of vandalism, joy-riders, that sort of thing, and sometimes after they've had their fun we find the burnt-out cars dumped on waste ground. So you're very lucky it's not worse."

"What sort of person would want to trash my bike?"

He shrugs. "We normally have a good idea who they are but it's trying to prove it, so the chances of catching anyone are—"

"They've slashed the leather seat with a knife and sprayed graffiti over the chrome. This is not normal. Who would do such a thing?" I am trying my best to keep my voice level and calm.

"Someone with a grudge?" The policewoman raises her solid eyebrows. "Have you any enemies?"

"I've only been in Belfast a few months. I hardly know anyone."

"Have you upset anyone?"

"No. What about CCTV?"

"We could check but don't hold out too much hope," the policeman says.

"If we caught them, they would still get away with it. It happens all the time. The courts are lenient. There are worse crimes up here." She sounds like she's already defeated.

"It's ridiculous," I say, running my hand through my hair. "What sort of society do we live in?"

"It's probably just a couple of lads—"

I am thinking of Michael or John — or both.

* * *

It's late on Friday afternoon. I've finished my final phone call so I lean back and stretch my arms above my head releasing tight muscles from a gym workout this morning.

Last night when I called Maria, Michael was there and she

hung up quickly but not before I heard her name on his lips and it still haunts me.

There's no ballet class today and so no Lily. I'm not sure if I am relieved or anxious that I haven't seen her since I made love to her mother five days ago. Would Lily sense something between us?

The thought of not seeing Maria over the weekend fills me with dread. I need to speak with her — about us. Was I just a fling? A one-night stand or a cheap experiment to satisfy her need for excitement? I take long determined strides to her office but it's empty. Her desk is clear. There's a noise in the kitchen and I spin around and spy her through the glass in the door. Her back is to me. She stands against the sink. Her blouse has come loose and her long hair is unruly and hanging from a bulldog clip.

When I push open the door she turns and a smile spreads across her lips. "Did you drop the Harley at the garage?"

"Yes."

"It's just kids. Third generation of the unemployed with no respect. Can they fix it?"

"It will take a few weeks."

"That's the main thing then. Don't lose any sleep over it. Did you have lunch? I know what you're like when you're working. You forget to eat," she says.

"I'm not hungry." I walk slowly toward her, my eyes don't leave her face and her smile broadens into a naughty grin.

We stand inches apart and I feel her warm breath on my cheek. Her familiar scent begins ruffling and stirring my sense and when her lips part I'm drawn to her like to the core of a magnet, unable to resist her touch and willing smile.

I don't mean to kiss her but I am propelled by some

unknown and magical force. She leans toward me. Very softly and very slowly our lips meet. At first our kiss is tentative and she responds with a seductive gasp and a sigh of pleasure. She murmurs my name and presses her hips against me reaching her arms behind my neck pulling me closer. Her lips become more passionate, her response more urgent and her breasts push against me.

"I want you so badly, Ellie."

"I've missed you," I whisper.

She brushes her lips over my neck and unhooks the top button of my blouse trailing undulating kisses across my skin, under my ear and across my inky stars. She kisses the top of my chest and the words *Not all who wander are lost,* then she raises her head to my mouth. She groans huskily when our tongues meet and I am lost in the depths of her kisses.

BANG!

Outside, in the corridor, a door thuds. Quick footsteps echo and a voice calls out.

Instinctively we break apart.

I pull my blouse together, grab a magazine from the table and flick it open. My hands are shaking. My heart is thumping rhythmically and loudly like tribal bongo drums and I force myself to turn a page slowly. I master my breathing and appear to be nonchalant, swallowing the lump in my throat.

John throws open the door. He stands in his white lab coat with his hands in his pockets. His small cobra eyes flick from me then to Maria, who faces the sink and doesn't turn around.

"I've been phoning your office," he says to me.

"Oh? Is it important?"

"It's Kat." He is rocking on his heels smiling. "Katherine Small."

Maria runs the tap.

"Please put the call through to my office. I'll take it in there." I close the magazine decisively and try to push him, in front of me, from the kitchen.

"She's not on the phone," he says, standing his ground and looking defiant, and I'm filled with relief and my body sags.

"She's downstairs in reception," he adds.

* * *

Kat holds out her arms but I still feel the warmth of Maria's lips on mine and the electric passion that surged through me in the kitchen and I turn my cheek from her kiss. A flicker of uncertainty crosses her green eyes. Her mouth is a red pencil line and she tosses her long auburn hair with irritation.

I grab her elbow and steer her from the reception speaking quietly, "Come on, there's a wine bar up the road."

I don't want her to see where I work or meet any of my colleagues and a few minutes later we are sitting in the window of the bar with a bottle of Shiraz on the table between us.

My pain, resentment and anger are directed at Kat but more strongly and hurling together inside my stomach is the tenderness and passion that I feel for Maria.

We drink. Kat talks. I listen. Kat is still speaking thirty minutes later. "I know that you'll probably need time to forgive me but I'll wait. I can be very patient. I want you back."

I glance out of the window. The rush of the afternoon traffic has calmed. Shops are closing: the hairdressers, the Estate Agent, Cafe Maud and the art gallery are all shuttered up and secured for the night.

"You look tired." Kat reaches across the table and her fingers grip my hand. Her palm seems foreign in mine and her touch cold and unfamiliar. She brings my fingertips to her mouth. I am in a trance-like state thinking only of Maria. My lips still feel her warmth and a small groan escapes my lips. With sudden lucidity I snatch back my fingers and glare at Kat who seems like a stranger to me.

She speaks but I am behind a veil like a sheet of thin muslin and I struggle to understand her words. The wine fuddles my mind and I turn my attention to the darkness of the street.

Friday night.

The weekend stretches ahead of me like an artist's blank canvas.

The wine bottle is empty.

Maria would be at home by now. She would be with Lily. What are they doing?

Kat buys another bottle of wine and returns with a ceramic dish filled with green olives, salted nuts and dried fruit. The wine is reassuring and it hits the back my throat, sliding down quickly. She talks about our friends in London, our work we once shared and the marketing and sales seminars we worked on.

"Peter hasn't worked out as we expected, in fact he's terrible and so your job is still open. I want you to come back." She sits motionless like a sculptured porcelain feline. Her auburn hair hangs loose around her shoulders and her almond-shaped green eyes flash as she speaks. "Come back, Ellie please. We all miss you—"

"He was a dick. I told you before but you didn't listen." I gulp wine. It's easier to drink than to think so I take another reassuring swig.

All around us are men in business suits and young giggling girls with optimistic smiles full of weekend promises. The stress of the working week is dissipated by each glass of alcohol: a smile replacing a frown.

"I couldn't believe John was working with you." Kat nibbles an olive. "It was fate or I would never have found you. Jenny wouldn't tell me where you had gone."

"Thanks for telling him I was gay."

"I didn't."

"You did." I pause with my wine glass at my lips.

"Well, we'd had a few drinks after the seminar and I was missing you." She smiles. "I couldn't believe it when he told me that one of our ex-employees had moved to Belfast and when he told me your name. I couldn't pretend I didn't know you…"

Outside rain is falling in long striped sheets against the window distorting my vision. Dirty puddles lay at the side of the road, cars splash the water high and an old lady takes refuge in a bus shelter.

Where is Maria? What is she doing?

My head begins to throb as Kat's voice continues above the voices at the tables around us. "I only stayed with Marcella for a few weeks. You were so bad tempered and you took the work 'thing' so badly. I told you I was coming back once you calmed down. You know we belong together."

"I don't want to be here," I say and I look at my watch and I realise I have left my handbag and mobile phone in the office. I run out of the bar and through the rain to the office. But the door is locked. It's closed for the weekend.

I am swearing loudly when Kat appears beside me.

"They normally work late and I have no telephone. No

phone numbers…." my voice trails off. I pat my pockets and find the key to Auntie Annie's house in my jacket.

"We'll get a taxi. Everything will be all right. I'm here now. I'll look after you." Kat puts her arm around me and whispers, "I love you. I only want to be with you."

Her face is tinged with yellow light from the streetlamp. The words are right but the accent and voice is all wrong.

I want Maria.

At Auntie Annie's house I drink two cups of strong black coffee, eat a thick cheese sandwich and take a hot shower.

It is midnight when I stand looking at the flickering lights across the Lough and I imagine Maria curled up asleep, her eyelashes flickering, living a dream, and the regular breathing of her chest.

I rest my head against the cold pane and sigh. Was she asleep with Michael? Cuddled together in bed? Making love?

Was it only today - yesterday that I kissed her in the office?

"I've left it too late, haven't I?" Kat's voice cuts into my thoughts. I watch her reflection through the window. She sits behind me curled on the sofa, her eyes are large and green.

"Yes." I don't turn around but continue to stare across the Lough.

"You loved me once." She unfolds her body, stretches and walks slowly to stand beside me. She pushes hair from my face and strokes the outline of my cheek. "You're still very beautiful Ellie…"

I stare at her for a while then turn away. "Sleep in the spare room Kat and I'll see you in the morning."

In the quiet of the house I watch a car's headlight flicker across the bedroom ceiling. I imagine Maria beside me and I turn to press my nose to the white cotton pillow, imagining where she lay, trying to find a trace of her perfume on the sheets but a dull ache of foreboding seeps into my soul.

Lily is the most important person to her. She will protect Lily and keep her in a safe and happy environment. Maria couldn't live life as a closet lesbian as I did. We would never have a normal life with her family. Her mother Brenda would be impossible.

As a dank dawn struggles to begin a new day. I listen to the rain lashing at the window. I watch the sun as it strives for survival in a pale liquid sky, fighting ominous cumulus clouds and I know how it feels to fight the inevitable.

An hour later I am dressed.

Kat is booked on the first flight to Heathrow and I am determined she won't miss it.

* * *

On Monday Maria doesn't come to work, nor on Tuesday and so far she hasn't appeared today. She is not taking my calls either. I resort to another text, telling her that I am worried. If she doesn't call me I will go to her house. I don't care about Michael.

After lunch she finally answers the phone.

"Are you okay?" I ask.

"I've a stomach bug."

"Tell me the truth." I know she's lying.

"I've been sick." She is definitely lying.

"Are you upset with me?"

"What do you think?"

"I have to see you Maria."

"How was Kat?"

"She was full of apologies. She wanted me to go back to London; back to my old job and start over again."

"And?"

"It's not going to happen."

"Why?"

"Because," I pause, "Because I don't love her."

"I have to go Ellie."

"Wait! You have been off work and you haven't answered my calls. Is everything okay? What about Michael? I miss you, Maria. I've been worried about you."

"But not too worried or concerned enough to phone me over the weekend."

"I left my bag in the office. I had no mobile. No phone numbers. I couldn't remember your mobile and I don't know your address—"

"You were busy with Kat—"

"It wasn't like that—"

"No? You were kissing me passionately and as soon as John said Kat was downstairs, you ran. You couldn't get down the stairs fast enough."

"I did that to protect you. To protect us. I didn't want him to catch us — to see us together."

"You never even spoke to me, Ellie. You never said goodbye."

"Maria, I'm sorry, I—"

"You don't know how awful I've felt. I spent the weekend hoping you would phone me. Hoping you would contact me. I was waiting for you. I even slept on the sofa. I needed you. I spent the weekend fighting with Michael. He's been so awful. I can't stand him near me. In the end I even went down to the sea at Jordanstown - just to look across the Lough - to see if I could see you in Holywood. I wanted to see you desperately.

I can't live like this Ellie. It's killing me." She is sobbing.

"But why didn't you come to Auntie Annie's house?"

"Because I knew she was there with you."

"She wasn't with me! All my telephone numbers are on my mobile. I couldn't phone you until Monday morning. I was lucky I had the house keys in my pocket."

"How convenient." She stops crying. Now she is angry. "At least you had somewhere to go with Kat. Somewhere you could make love to her. Somewhere you could be alone with her. Somewhere that you could rekindle that lost love—"

"Maria—"

"I saw you," she shouts, "I saw you sitting in the window of the wine bar. She was holding your hand. I saw her stroking and kissing your fingers and you didn't stop her. I stood across the road watching you and you didn't even see me. You still love her—"

"No. I took her to the airport first thing on Saturday morning. Nothing happened—"

But Maria doesn't hear me. She's already ended the call.

* * *

I have a meeting in town and it is mid-morning before I'm back in the office. I am weary and bad-tempered. Maria's office is empty but her jacket hangs on the back of her chair so I'm heartened that she's in the building.

Muffled voices in the boardroom propel me to open the door. She is sitting at the table with Simon and John but she averts her gaze.

"Great. You're back," Simon says. "Sit down. Maria's been doing a quick budget for us on the additions to the ITG project that we discussed yesterday." He passes me photocopies of figures. "I'm beginning to realise that selling hardware is not a financially sound option. The shop would be too costly and you're right about being competitive in our pricing. So you'll be please to know that retail is not for us. We'll have to rethink our strategy."

I sit down. I don't tell him that it was his strategy, not mine.

"Maria, do you want to talk us though all of this?" asks Simon.

Her undulating accent fills the room and soft vowels roll from her tongue as she explains the figures. She's wearing a cream cotton blouse and my eyes rest on the freckled skin on her chest. She is concentrating on the paperwork and when she does look up there are dark circles under her eyes. Her face is pale and drawn.

John and Simon ask a few questions but I can barely breathe.

Are they moving to Dublin? Has Michael decided to move? Is she going with him? Was I just an adventure for her?

"Ellie? You've not said a word. Does this all sound okay, to you?" Simon stares at me.

I drag my eyes from Maria, cough and clear my throat. "Fine."

She will not look at me and continues to be fascinated in the figures or with John or Simon. She looks everywhere but not at me.

When the meeting ends Simon leaves the room quickly already speaking into his phone.

I linger behind wishing John would leave but to my despair he puts his hands in his pockets and rocks on the balls of his feet.

"I bet it was good to see Kat again, was it?" he asks.

I freeze.

Maria looks at me.

"It looked as if she was on a mission on Friday." He smiles heartily. "She couldn't wait to see you. You must have been in a hurry yourself too. I had to turn your office light off. You even left your bag behind."

I think about him telling Michael I was gay. When did he do that? Why did he? I want to thump him but instead I reply slowly and quietly, "It's none of your business John but Kat left on the first flight on Saturday morning. Now, let me tell you something. I may have to work with you but I don't have to like you. And if you ever, ever, mention my private life again you will regret it." His smile fades. "This is the only warning you're going to get because if you make any reference to Kat or I hear you speaking about or discussing my private life, I will haul your arse into court for sexual harassment quicker than you can say Happy Days. I will make your life hell and no employer will want to touch you after I've finished with you. So stay out of my life."

"I don't want to upset—"

"Shut up John, or I'll see you in court and sue your fat arse and take you for everything you have." I leave the room not bothering to glance at Maria.

It is almost four o'clock when I have calmed down. I've spent the past hour pacing my office; my caged tiger walk, backwards and forwards, leaning my head on the glass as if it's a bar on a prison cell. I'm wishing I had behaved differently, more moderately and with more control and I take a deep breath and venture into Maria's office. I lean against the door frame with my arms folded.

"Maria?" I say.

Her hair flops across her eyes and she pushes it aside. We look at each other unsmiling.

"How are you?" I ask quietly.

"Fine." She shuffles papers.

I take a step forward. "How are you really?"

"Fine, really!" She studies the figures.

She can't still be concentrating on them.

I put my palms on her desk and lean forward, and she has to sit back to look up at me. I see into the depths of her pained eyes. A flicker of sadness crosses her face and her pupils are extraordinarily large and beautiful.

"Let me ask you something. Do you understand my pain and hurt knowing that you sleep with your husband every night? But I say nothing to you about that. I don't ask what happens between you and Michael, even though it kills me to know that you have a husband and that you share a bed. But I will tell you this. I had nothing with Kat. She wanted to and yes she took my hand in the bar but I pulled away. I was thinking of you. I can't stop thinking about you. I'm not interested in her. It was over before I came to Belfast but she just wouldn't accept it." I take a deep breath, stand straight and I fold my arms. "So now that I have explained that, tell me, are you moving to Dublin?"

"No, Michael has decided he's going to do an internal transfer so he can spend more time at home with us here in the north."

"That's great then." My voice is heavy with sarcasm.

"It will be much better," she says positively. "It means we can spend more time together as a family, and Lily is really happy now she doesn't have to move."

"And us?"

Her eyes are dark. "There is no us. I have to concentrate on my marriage."

Her words are like a sharp spear ripping open my gut.

Chapter Nine

What does a woman do when she's unhappy? She goes shopping. I only shop on the Internet and boy, when I shop - do I shop?

It's a classic Mercedes. Beige soft top. It's the car of my dreams.

I can't really afford it but as Kat has moved out of my apartment in London and I have it rented out from next week, money is not one of my immediate problems.

I send photos of the car jenny loves it and I ask Richard for his advice. He knows about things like this. Matt and Jake tell that they want to come and stay and they want to drive my new car. I promise them that if they come over I'll let them wash it for me.

I send a picture of the car to my father. He phones me back immediately and tells me about my Tia Luisa - his sister, and my other Spanish aunts and uncles and my countless cousins. Then he tells me that there is someone special he wants me to meet.

"A woman?"

"Sí cariño!" He laughs. "Her name is Marta and you will love her. She is funny, kind and charming."

"At last," I say, "You've been living like a monk for the past ten years."

"Hardly a monk, but she is *muy especial.*"

"I'm pleased for you," I say truthfully.

He doesn't ask about Kat. He doesn't ask if I am happy and he doesn't ask if I have anyone *muy especial.*

On Sunday I drive the Mercedes up to the north Antrim coast. I stop in Ballycastle and walk up to Torr Head where the views over to the Mull of Kintyre are spectacular. The sky is clear, wall to wall pure unadulterated blue, bigger than an ocean. The air is fresh and the sun is warm on my cheeks.

I try not to think about Maria. I try not to imagine her beside me in the passenger seat, or holding my hand as we walk over the cliffs, or as I sit on the harbour wall gazing at the fishing boats, and I realise that I'm speaking to her. I'm holding imaginary conversations with her in my head. I see her brown eyes sparkle and the way she tilts her head at me when she is teasing.

I am not sure if thinking about her makes me feel warm and happy or sad and depressed. But her words echo continually in my head.

There is no us.

On my way home I stop in Mickey Bleu's restaurant. It's early evening and I'm surprised to see her serving behind the counter. She is dressed in a blue and gold long dress, and matching turban and she waves her hands in the air in greeting like a jazz singer. Her smile is wide as she places steaming coffee on the bar in front of me. "It's going very well, Ellie. I can't believe how lucky I am. We've been really busy."

We chat as she serves customers. Disjointed conversations as she moves between the bar and the tables, helping the waiters, removing dirty plates and replenishing drinks. I watch her deft and precise movements and I tell her about my new car. We talk about the restaurant, business and life in the north.

Then she says, "I like to keep my hand in serving customers as well as cooking. I don't want to become an unknown face." Her voice is baritone. "I like to know my regulars but I also like to get home and spend some time with the girls before they go to bed. I'm almost finished here. Do you fancy driving me home as it will save Emmanuel turning out to get me?"

She loves my new car. I turn the music up full volume and drive her to a modest house in a pretty and shaded tree-lined street. She insists I go inside to meet her husband and Cassandra six and Flore who is five.

Emmanuel is serious with a grey goatee beard. His hand-shake is firm and his eyes teasing. His dark skin glistens against his pristine ironed shirt and he smiles at his wife and daughters with happy indulgence.

The two girls have their father's slimmer frame yet their mother's wide features and happy chuckle. Tentatively, they shake my hand then run into the garden shrieking with laughter. The house smells of garlic, cooked tomatoes, onions and fresh herbs.

"It's my Jambalaya Crock Pot," Mickey says, watching me wrinkle my nose in delight. "Simon and Louise love it."

"Simon and Louise? You'll be telling me next that John has been over for dinner."

"Not yet," she replies. "I'm not quite ready for him. He's a strange one."

I smile.

"Emmanuel, honey?" she continues, "Make this gorgeous girl one of your special tropical fruit juices. She's staying for dinner and if you are very good she might take you out for a drive in her dream machine."

Over dinner I feel the tension easing from my shoulders and I relax and revel in the atmosphere of their home. They are laid back and their teasing laughter is contagious. Their energy is enviable and their company easy. We eat, laugh and talk, but it doesn't matter what I do, where I go or who I'm with. I can't stop thinking about Maria and the impossibility of our situation, her marriage to Michael and life as a lesbian. But as the evening wears on, I realise I'm simply in love. Maria has seeped into my pores and under my skin and when I'm alone and in my car driving home, a silly and a familiar song enters my head from *The Sound of Music*.

"How do you solve a problem like Maria?" I sing louder and louder, more frantically and furiously and tears stream down my cheeks.

* * *

On Wednesday evening I've watered pots of colourful geraniums, hosed the patio and tidied the house, plumping up cushions in the lounge and I fall exhausted onto the sofa. My stomach churns at the thought of food and I feel sick. But I open a bottle of wine which an hour later lies almost empty on the table beside me where I am stretched out on the sofa like a star fish.

My attempts to keep occupied have failed miserably. My thoughts return again and again to Maria and I am angry and upset that she has declined any offer of lunch or coffee. Our conversations in the office have been polite but minimal. She's not even my friend. She's blocking me out of her life.

How could she blank me so easily?

I lay staring at the ceiling remembering our love-making. She was completely at ease with me. Our bodies fit together perfectly. It felt so right — for both of us. It was special. She told me that she had never felt so much emotion, passion or tenderness in her entire life. She loves me. Where has that love gone?

"She doesn't love me," I say aloud and my voice turns into a pathetic wail. "She just doesn't want me."

Doesn't she know the pain that she is putting me though? How could she treat me this way when she said she loves me? She is ruthless and cold and hard. She cares nothing for me. She is selfish.

I close my eyes and imagine the few times we were in the office this week; in the boardroom, in the reception with Siobhan and Stuart, and this afternoon in the techie lab just before she went home.

Each time she wouldn't meet my gaze and she looked quickly away. Now that Michael is back in Belfast she is playing happy families and the thought of them together makes my stomach turn. I never told her about Michael or that I suspect it was him who damaged my Harley. Perhaps I should?

"Nah. Let them get on with it. I'm not going to ruin their marriage. They deserve each other," I mumble. "Maria belongs with me, I know she does. It just feels so right when we are together. She can't love Michael like she loves me. We laugh and have fun and Lily loves me too."

I fumble for the remote control and eventually find the volume to the television. I tune into a music channel and turn it full blast.

I sing a slurred duet with Shania Twain, *"Man! I feel like a woman...*" And I tip the remaining wine from the bottle into my glass, cursing softly when it spills onto my blouse. I brush it with clumsy fingers but the stain spreads like blood.

My mobile rings. It sounds muffled and far away. It slipped between the cushions. I make a lunge for it but my fingers are slow and it falls from my gasp. I can't find it but I try again and then I smile and hold it like a trophy in the air before squinting at the caller's ID.

It's Maria's mobile.

I gasp and swing my legs to the floor. I try to sit up. "Hello?"

There are muffled noises. Someone is whispering. I frown, hiccup, and struggle to keep my balance.

"Hello? Who is this?"

"I don't care..." It is Lily's petulant voice but she isn't speaking to me. "Let me speak to Ellie."

I hiccup again. "I'm getting bored with this game. I'm going to hang up."

More muffled noises.

"Ellie?... Ellie... Hi, it's me, Lily."

"Is everything okay?" I slur.

"I was just talking to Mum. Can you come to my school concert on Friday? I'm singing in it."

"You're singing?" I giggle, thinking of Lily's bespectacled serious face. I feel a warm glow that she wants to see me but then my mind races. What about Michael? Will he be there?

"Ellie, can you come?"

"What does your Mum say?"

"Hold on. She wants to speak to you."

"I'm sure she doesn't," I mumble and smother another hiccup.

There are more muffles then Maria's voice sounds clear and

crisp. "Michael has had to go to Dublin so he can't go to Lily's school concert," Maria pauses, "so, Lily wants you to come."

"Is that okay with you?" I try to sound sober.

"I don't get a choice. She doesn't want anyone else in the family, just you. Not even her grandma, her uncles, aunts or her cousins." Maria sounds very annoyed and I'm pleased she is angry.

"Okay, I'll go."

"I know how busy you are Ellie, and Lily will understand if you can't make it and so will I—"

"No, I won't," Lily shouts in the background.

"I'm not busy. I couldn't let her down. We're friends," I say pointedly. "Give me the details and I'll be there." I fumble for pen and paper before she changes her mind or thinks of another excuse why I shouldn't go.

After the phone call I lay on the sofa with my arms above my head staring happily at the ceiling talking to myself. "Well, this is a turn up for the books. The doting father is back in Dublin and Maria is irked because Lily wants to be with meeeeee." I laugh aloud and swing my legs to the floor. "Score one point for Team Ellie Bravo! Maria, if you want to play games then I will play them too. If you want to cold-shoulder me at work and hide your feelings then that's fine with me. And, if you want excitement which I am beginning to suspect you do then I will give you all the excitement you need but on my terms. I'm not going to let this opportunity, at Lily's concert go to waste. Let the game begin. Team Bravo is about to fight back." I raise my arms enthusiastically and when I try to stand I fall off the sofa and land face-down on the floor.

* * *

The school corridors are packed with children in matching navy blazers, blue skirts or trousers and striped white ties. They all look identical. Clones. Then there are groups of proud parents who smile encouragingly. They greet each other air kissing and shaking hands and I feel like the new girl on her first day: shy and out of place.

"Ellie!" Lily waves and I push through the throng of people trying not to lose my balance and my cool.

She reaches up to grab my neck and kisses my cheek enthusiastically. I'm surprised and return her affection with a squeeze.

"Your hair's grown," I say, tugging her fringe.

Her skinny arm is still around my neck and she pulls me to her and whispers, "I've used straighteners. I want hair like yours. It's funny. It sticks out like a baby duck's."

I laugh. "You look great, Lily. Hi Charlie, you look smart in your blazer."

Charlie has put on weight. Her collar is stretched under her thick neck and her cheeks are flushed and rosy. "Have you got any new tattoos?" she asks.

"Not recently."

Maria stands with her back to the wall. Her dark hair is recently trimmed and tied with a black ribbon. She wears a yellow and beige summer dress which is cut low and reveals a tempting cleavage. Only her brown eyes betray deep anxiety. She looks everywhere, and at everyone, except at me.

Charlie nods at a group of kids moving into the hall. "Come on Lily, we'd better go and get ready. They are going in."

"Yey, Rhianna and Beyonce, sock it to them." I high-five them both.

"Sing loudly I want to be able to hear you," Maria calls

encouragingly, as they disappear into a sea of blue uniforms.

When they are gone I turn to Maria. "What is it about a school that makes you feel like you were only just out of uniform yourself?"

Maria casts a wry smile.

A peroxide blond woman clinging to an older man's arm stop in front of us. She chews gum like a cow in a field chews grass and looks utterly bored. The man's grey hair is wild and unkempt and he stands gazing at my breasts.

"Is this your sister, Maria?" he asks, raising his eyes to look at me.

Maria flinches. "No. A colleague from work." She says to me. "This is Charlie's father and his… friend."

"Dawn," she says, "and in another few weeks we'll be married, won't we, hun?" Her mouth is open and I watch her masticate slowly.

Maria mutters something about getting a seat in the hall and pulls on my arm and we don't bother to say goodbye.

"Relax," I say when we are out of ear-shot. "What did you think I was going to say to him? That we are lovers?"

Her eyes flash me a warning and I can't help laugh aloud but she refuses to meet my gaze or to smile. Her face remains stony as we sit on hard, plastic chairs and when I cross my legs I accidentally tap Maria's toe and she glares at me.

"There's more room on a charter flight," I grin.

"You didn't have to come."

"Well, at least Lily still enjoys my company."

Maria's lips are set in a tight line. She looks down at her hands. She is wearing her wedding ring. Her chest rises in a deep breath.

"You used to enjoy my company too," I whisper, "or have

you forgotten?"

"We don't need to speak about—" She breaks off as the head-teacher appears on stage. He clears his throat and after a few words the concert begins and we sit through a medley of pop and folk songs.

I spot Lily singing with her head tilted back and her mouth moving erratically. I glance at Maria and I have a smile on my lips and our eyes meet. I don't look away. I can't. Her brown eyes are so dark with emotion that I am momentarily shaken. My love for her stirs my senses and I yearn to reach out and touch her.

"Ellie, don't," she whispers.

"What?"

"Please don't look at me like that." Her eyes fill with tears.

My heart begins beating erratically. She knows how I feel and I know she feels the same. She sits close to me, our shoulders almost touching, yet she is so far away from me; mentally and emotionally. We are a life apart.

I sit for the next hour wondering what our lives may have been like had we met before she knew Michael but then she wouldn't have had Lily and I cannot imagine her without her daughter. I play with the idea that in an ideal world, I may have been Maria's partner and Lily belongs to both of us. I think what I would be like as a parent and I know I would do a better job than my own selfish mother and my absent father. I have a greater sense of responsibility. A wave of sadness overtakes me at the unfairness of our situation. I love this woman sitting beside me and when I look at her in profile I know the contours of her face, the smell of her skin and the passion that lies beneath her. I understand her. She is my world.

When the concert is over we stand in silence by the front entrance watching parents and children leave the school, waiting for Lily. She comes sauntering along pulling at her fringe, flicking it from her eyes and adjusting the collar on her blazer.

"Here comes our Music Award nominee," I say.

"Could you hear me above everyone else?"

"Was that beautiful voice yours?" Maria replies.

"Charlie sang a wrong note and came in too late for the high bit at the end. Mrs Burrell was really angry but she knows Charlie's parents are here with their new partners. Charlie's mother thinks she's having a baby." Lily sticks out her tongue dramatically. "And no-one likes her boyfriend."

"I can understand that." The words out of my mouth before I think.

"Do you know him?" Lily looks up at me, her eyes are round in surprise.

"No, but my mother had a good few boyfriends that I didn't like. I don't even like the one she has now."

"Really?" Lily is enthralled and grabs my hand. "What's he like?"

I wish I hadn't spoken.

"Come on, let's go home." Maria ushers us toward the car park. "I'm sure Ellie doesn't want to talk about this."

How well she knows me.

"Are you coming home with us?" Lily pulls me toward their car.

Maria looks at me. I imagine their house. His house. His garden. His books. His music. His furniture. His life. His daughter. His wife.

"Maybe another night." I disentangle my arm, wave and

blow a kiss to Lily. I don't look at Maria. I can't.

***

It's six in the morning when I go to the gym. I smile at a few early risers, call out to the receptionist, wave at the cleaners and make small talk with the gym instructor. I recognise a stocky weight-lifter with tattoos, a slim girl with black glasses who smiles at me and a plump man at the water dispenser. I run hard on the treadmill for thirty minutes until my body is perspiring heavily and my legs ache. Afterwards I shower quickly, listen to the banter of the other girls in the changing room, and smile again at the slim girl with black glasses.

In the office Simon's office door is ajar so I tap and walk in.

"You're in early," I call brightly but he looks terrible. His face is ashen and he hasn't shaved. His hair is unbrushed and when he stands up his shirt and chinos are wrinkled.

"Did you sleep the night in here?" I ask.

"I didn't sleep much." His bloodshot eyes stare back at me. It looks like he's been crying and his face is puffy and nose swollen.

"What's happened Simon? Look, the techies will be here soon. Go to the bathroom., smarten yourself up and I'll organise breakfast then we will chat," I order him.

Ten minutes later he's washed but still has dark stubble on his cheeks. His grey eyes light up gratefully when I place a steaming mug of coffee on his desk and bacon bagels from the deli next door.

"Eat," I command taking a seat opposite his desk. "Then we will talk."

He chews slowly and methodically, scrutinising each mouthful and following it with slurps of dark, thick, rich coffee.

I wait patiently until he finishes his second bagel and I toss my rubbish into the bin under his desk. "So? What's happening? What's wrong? Is it the business? Financial problems?"

He shakes his head. "No, it's nothing to do with the company."

I'm relieved yet my heart sinks. That means it's probably something more personal and I know my advice always borders on the erratic with suggestions like; pack and run, fly and hide or close your eyes and block your ears.

"It's Louise," he mumbles.

"Oh?" I smile broadly, feigning more confidence than I feel. "Well, that's lucky for you. Because I do have some experience in the ladies department. Fate has been kind to me in that way, so I may be able to help. Tell me."

He grins and rubs the stubble on his chin. "She wants children."

I nod and put on my — I understand and I am encouraging you to talk — face. "Most women do," I reply. "It's often called a maternal instinct."

"But we can't. That's the problem. We've been to London, Germany and to America but none of the treatments or the IVF has worked. She's miscarried four times and I…" He runs his fingers through his hair and pauses. "Well, now she wants to adopt."

"That's lovely," I pause. "Isn't it?"

He brushes his nose with the back of his wrist. "I'm not cut out for adoption, Ellie. I don't want to raise someone else's child, a child that isn't mine, someone else's kid."

"Is that a macho thing?"

His eyebrows knit together. "What do you mean?"

"Is it a man-thing that the child has to be yours, you know, from your sperm? Do you want your child to be your mirror image, with your eyes or your temperament or character? Is that what being a father is all about to you? Why do people want children? What's the point of having children?"

"To have a family."

"Exactly — a family."

"What do you mean?"

"Families come in all shapes and size, Simon. Nowadays there can be two male dads or two mums living together. Sometimes the child originates from sources unknown or even inserted with a turkey baster but it doesn't matter. If two people love each other then there are many ways to have a family. It's all about sharing, loving, giving and more importantly it's about enriching your life, having fun and caring for others."

"But what if — what if — I don't like the child? Or what if, in a few years' time, they're awful? What if they are a horrible child?"

"Ha. Well, you've no guarantee that you will like your own son or daughter, Simon. Life is full of surprises. Some kids have been dealt a rotten hand before they even come into the world but if someone kind or someone with a beautiful heart can give them a better start in life or help change that adopted child's destiny for the better then doesn't that make life just that little bit brighter and happier — for everyone?" I add quietly.

He looks over my shoulder and when I turn around Louise is standing behind me. She looks tired, worried and frightened.

My heart goes out to them both. But only they can resolve

this problem. I stand up and pick up the dirty mugs. "Morning Louise. I'm just about to make coffee. Have you had breakfast? Would you like a bacon bagel?"

* * *

The office is an emotional nightmare. Simon is either shut in his office or he walks around in a daze. And, as if aware of his problems, John passes me phone calls from clients with the words, 'I don't think it's important but can you just speak to…' Leaving me to deal with the day to day running of the office.

Maria doesn't look great either. She scurries into her office to avoid me and when we do speak it is with polite caution. We don't have coffee and we don't eat lunch together, and when we pass each other on the stairs Maria is tense and silent and I feel her strength of will and the torture in her dark eyes.

The game I had wanted to play, to tease her and to flirt with her into submission, is too painful to play — for both of us.

I know I have lost her. I have lost the woman I fell in love with. I don't know where she has gone but wherever it is I can't follow her dark path. I want to be her friend. I want to help her and provide a shoulder for her to cry on but my feelings would become entangled. I want to hold her and kiss away her pain but she doesn't want that. She doesn't want or need me either. Time will tell if we have a future as friends but only once our feelings for each other have dissipated forever.

My deep sadness lies in the fact that I have revealed more of myself to Maria than to anyone in my entire life. She understands me without me having to explain, she accepts me and there is a chemistry between us that I have only ever read about in book or seen on television, and probably more importantly she makes me laugh. She makes me feel good. But now I have withdrawn into my solitary self. Never will I share myself so readily or so easily again. I need and deserve more. I want to be valued and not treated as if I am of no importance, and her rejection makes me feel both ashamed and humiliated.

* * *

OUT Magazines should be a relatively simple task but the contract seems to be getting complicated. They're asking for more specs priced for and when Maria points this out to John he decides that I should help soothe things over and help Liam. So I am in the Tekkie lab and the meeting is laborious and time-consuming. Liam's client Sally Richman from OUT Magazines has speckled grey hair and thick-rimmed glasses. Her nails are as manicured as her shoes are glossed and polished. Her voice is slow and her manner tedious and I feel myself becoming tetchy. I know that my thoughts and my indignation relate to Maria and I resent time spent with this client that Liam should be dealing with.

Sally is insistent so I concede a few changes but I am frustrated. I need to speak to Maria. I have this compulsive urge to see her and I can't get out of the meeting fast enough. I want to speak to her before she goes home.

I rush up the stairs, two at a time, hoping for a few minutes of private conversation. She is pulling on her summer jacket as I walk into her office. Her computer is turned off and she frowns when I appear at the door.

"I haven't had chance to speak to you—"

"What about?"

"About things. I need to speak to you—" I break off mid-sentence. I can see she doesn't want this conversation and I'm torn between saying what's on my mind and making a fool of myself or retreating into myself and hiding my feelings.

She gathers her handbag and another shopping bag in her arms. She's ready to leave and I feel like a pathetic schoolgirl, over anxious, over excited and eager to please.

"Everything has changed between us. I miss our lunches and our chats. I miss the friendship we had."

She gazes at me. The frown lines on her forehead are a small patchwork of fine lines. She speaks slowly and softly, "I don't know what you want me to say. This isn't easy for me either."

I perch against her desk hoping to keep her in the office for a few seconds longer. "Does it have to be like this? It's killing me."

"How else can it be? You seem to think that you're the only one hurting in all of this. That is is only your feelings that count."

"It's your decision to block me out."

"I have to — they are my family."

"And I don't count?"

"I didn't say that."

"Well, I'm obviously not important to you—"

"You don't understand, Ellie I can't live without them."

"And what about me? I thought you loved me?"

"I do — I just can't live like this. My head is a mess. I'm confused."

"Let me help?" I take a step forward.

"You can't." She glances at her watch. "I must go. I have to collect Lily—"

"I miss seeing Lily too."

"You came to her concert last Friday." It's a stern reprimand and I am rebuked. "You can't do this to me, Ellie."

"That's fine." I stand up and move away. "I won't bother you any further. I see your feelings have changed. Is it because Michael is in Belfast and you are back playing happy families?" I can't hide the bitterness of my words. They spill out and I'm ashamed but I can't stop. "Was I just an experiment for you? A one-night stand? A bit of excitement in your boring marriage?"

She holds up the palm of her hand and her mouth opens but I can't stop. All the pent up feelings, emotions and thoughts that have been my companion night and day for the past weeks spill out between us.

"I understand perfectly that your life is with Lily and Michael. I knew it all along. I knew you were married. I knew the score but—" This time I hold up my index finger. "I think I deserve a little more kindness, a little more thought and a little more decency. We could still be friends or perhaps you can't look at yourself in the mirror knowing that you have been unfaithful to your husband and you enjoyed it more than any other experience and that is why you are taking it out on me." I move away, toward the door.

"Ellie."

"You accused me of not being a good friend when I didn't tell you I was gay and look at how you are treating me now. You avoid me at every opportunity. You eat a sandwich on your own, shut in your office, and you scurry out after work hoping to avoid me. Well, it won't happen again Maria. I promise you. I will not mention this ever again but nor will I beg for your friendship. We shared something very special. Something very tender and passionate. It was a love that I had never felt before. It was important to me, and I'm not going to ruin the memory of it by embarrassing you, or me, ever again."

I don't wait for her to answer. Instead I take the stairs two at a time back down to the techie lab. My heart is pounding and the memory of Maria's surprised O-shaped mouth, and the image of her face stays with me for the rest of the evening and I know it is something I will remember for the rest of my life.

Chapter Ten

June. It is the evening of the company's sixth anniversary. When Simon announced it at the drinks party I thought I would have returned to London by now. But with him struggling emotionally at work and with a truce between me and Maria, I've managed to survive the past few weeks by working hard.

It's the official company celebration that I would cheerfully boycott it, given the opportunity. The thought of an evening with a group of techie guys, the soulless John, the reclusive Maria, as well as the emotionally wounded Simon and Louise, all leave me uninspired and weary.

When I arrive at the jazz restaurant in the prestigious hotel, drinks are flowing at the long table where the team are sitting. The guys greet me with wolf–whistles and although I laugh, my mood is heavy. I slide into a vacant seat at the end of the table beside Simon and opposite Louise. They both appear tense and strained although they sit with fixed smiles, and Simon behaves like a politician on a flagging election trail.

Maria sits at the far end of the table between Liam and Stuart. She doesn't look at me but her false smile is tense around her dark eyes. I know she can feel my eyes on her but she deliberately ignores me.

Anger rises in me. I've revealed myself to this woman and made love to her as I have to no-one else and she cannot even look at me. Pathetically humiliated, I'm torn between going wild and getting very drunk or succumbing to my inner self and ignoring the frivolity at the table. My mood sways like a smuggler's lantern on a Cornish beach luring a gold-laden ship to its doomed fate on a rocky shore.

The increasing decibels of laugher at the table only serves to fuel my discontent and, as the jazz band swings, I decide I'm not in the humour to be frivolous or fun. I'm isolated like an island or like the tide that ebbs and flows as I drift in and out of conversations and laughter. I'm swimming for survival. Floating on the flotsam of hollow conversation that glides past me as I push my food around the plate pretending I'm enjoying each morsel.

The music gets louder and the banter more raucous until Steve, Adam Jeff and Mike (Boys Aloud) and Ray (the quiet one) drift toward the bar. John and Maria sit with their heads together in conversation. Stuart and Siobhan are swaying on the dance floor, and Louise and Liam are attempting some sort of complicated jive movement. He is twisting and twirling her and I'm surprised at his easy style.

"Liam must have had dance classes." Simon leans into my ear and shouts. "Louise went to classes when we first met. She said it would be a hobby for us in our old age. This place is a bit loud but it's what they all wanted. Last year it was black tie and too formal. I think they're enjoying themselves tonight though."

I smile and sip non-alcoholic beer. I'm not relaxed enough to drink alcohol. I follow his gaze and we watch John and Maria move onto the dance floor.

I try not to notice the way she moves her hips, her arms and her sensual body. She is laughing and her smile is encouraging and teasing. I feel sick. I want her to look at me like that. I turn away. I wish it was me holding her in my arms.

"Come on, Ellie. Let's show them how it's done." Simon grabs my hand with resigned determination and I know that if I refuse, I would look churlish and miserable.

I manage to keep to Simon's rhythm. He is skilful and playful and I find myself laughing and relaxing. It's been a long time since I danced with such a good partner. I'm breathless by the time we finish three dances and I head for the bar to stand with Boys Aloud. But as I draw close Mark pulls me onto the floor. Then Stuart wants to dance with me and finally I manage a sip a non-alcoholic beer before Liam won't take no for an answer. He's a sophisticated dancer and he poses with his film star looks at every opportunity. I'm not sure if it's for my benefit or for the watching diners but he's funny and he makes me laugh. We dance well together and I sway in his arms, pull apart, twirl and jive according to his subtle hand and body movements.

Half an hour later, I'm drinking soda water and lime at the bar when Louise appears at my elbow and pulls me to one side.

"Thanks for speaking to Simon," she raises her voice above the music.

"I didn't."

"I know you did." Her tired smile is genuine and her eyes are sad. "After he spent the night in the office. I do appreciate it."

"I didn't say much Louise, but if it helped…"

She's drinking vodka and orange very, very, quickly. "He

won't listen and I don't know how to get through to him. I don't know what else to do. I want a child. I need a family. We all do, Ellie don't we? But he is so stubborn."

"Yes, I know he is. It's like the time he wanted to buy retail premises and sell hardware instead of expanding apps and games."

"What?" she shouts.

"I said," I speak louder accentuating each word. "He'll come around in the end."

After more drinks and several dances Simon kisses me on the cheeks. "Louise and I are going home and the boys will relax after we've gone. I've put some money behind the bar for a running tab so it should be a good night. Thanks for everything, Ellie."

I kiss his cheek and hug Louise who leans against his shoulder in weary exhaustion. When I scan the room I can't see Maria. I've kept her in the periphery of my vision all night and I'm disconcerted. Perhaps she's left without saying goodbye.

The techie guys are drinking shots, Car Crashes: Baileys and Guinness straight down. I make an excuse and go to the Ladies and I'm standing at the mirror, washing my hands, when the door opens. In the glass above the basin Maria is standing in the doorway staring at me. My heart pumps faster and my hands begin to shake and I curse myself for the weakness that runs through me.

She nods for me to follow her and I don't hesitate. We pass through the reception in the hotel lobby and outside where we pause on the step. Her eyes are dark and there is a challenging half-smile on her lips. I sense a quiver of excitement from her and I smile.

"Taxi?" she says.

"I've got the car. Let's run." Rain pelts down on us, flowing into the gutter and we totter and giggle on our high heels, dodging puddles, down narrow cobbled streets and around the corner to where my car is parked. We are still laughing when I pull open the passenger door. I run around to the driver's side and slide into my seat. Rain falls from our hair down our cheeks, and our warm breath mists the window. I flick on the air, switch on the ignition and pull the car onto the deserted road.

"Wow, this is wicked. Lily will love this car." There is something about her tone that makes me realise I have my Maria back again.

"It was retail therapy because you ignored me," I reply.

"Money well spent." She places her hand on my thigh.

"I think so." I want to reply that she looks beautiful, sitting beside me, instead I ask. "Where to?"

She blinks and gazes steadily ahead watching the window wipers frantically clear the rain. The traffic lights change to red. I stop the car. Reflected light from the yellow street-lamp weaves a patchwork pattern across her pale face.

"Maria? What do you want?" My heart is thumping so loudly I imagine she can hear it. My voice is throaty with desire and I guess she can sense it and I feel suddenly vulnerable.

Very slowly, she takes my hand from the steering wheel and places my fingers against her damp cheek. She kisses my palm and then my wrist before pulling my face toward hers and she places her lips on mine. Her kiss is deep and filled with longing. "I need you," she whispers. "I want you Ellie."

* * *

Later, it's as if we've never been apart. Our bodies recognise each other in the candlelight and our skin moulds into one as we caress and explore each other with our hands, our tongues and our lips. She fills me with desire. There is chemistry between us, as we move, explore and discover new ways of sharing our love. We speak quietly, encouragingly, tenderly and lovingly. She is giving, passionate and sensitive, and she holds me close whispering my name and talking of her love for me.

"Ellie, you are my love, my life. I adore you."

"We fit like a jigsaw puzzle," I say, looking down at the entwined-tangle of our arms and legs. My arm is around her and she is snuggled against my shoulder.

"You're beautiful," she replies huskily, stroking my stomach with her finger. "I've never experienced anything like this before, Ellie, you're amazing."

She fills me with a passion and longing that I've never known before. I run my fingers through her hair and caress her cheek tracing the outline of her mouth and looking deeply into her dark eyes.

It is as if she knows we are on borrowed time. She wants more and more of me, and I feel her need. Our bodies are sensitive and receptive to the gentlest of movements. And when our feelings explode I'm close to tears. I hear a sob escape her lips and I hold her tighter to my chest lost in the closeness of our bodies, our minds and our hearts.

I hold her in my arms tracing wide circles across her shoulder with my finger and listen to the softness of her voice.

I inhale the natural scent of her dusky body and I'm wondering what it would be like to sleep and then to wake with this woman for the rest of my life when she says, "Ellie, this can't continue. You know that don't you?" She squeezes closer against my body and kisses the hollow of my neck and throws her leg over my hip. She reminds me of a kitten and I am caught in the embrace of her front paws while her back ones kick me gently away. "I don't want you to get hurt."

"Do you think you will hurt me?" I return her kiss.

"I've hurt you already. It's not intentional but I have responsibilities. I have two people in my life who I must put first. They are my life — my family."

I'm stroking her back in wide arcs with the tips of my nails in increasing and decreasing circles. There's lemon scent from her hair and the taste of her on my lips. She lifts her head from the crook of my shoulder and we kiss deeply.

"What do you want?" I ask, not wanting an answer, not wanting this conversation.

"I want what I can't have. I want you, Ellie." Her hand caresses my stomach and then she stretches her head and kisses me under my left earlobe where my star tattoos are etched in ink and trails kisses along the inky words, *All Who Wander Are Not Lost*. A shiver runs down my spine and I feel a sense of doom, fear and foreboding.

"I can't do it Ellie. I can't live here in Belfast with you, even if I wasn't with Michael. My family wouldn't approve of you. My mother and even my brothers and sister would hate me. They would block me out of their lives. I would be a social outcast. I couldn't do that to Lily. And then imagine the taunts Lily would have to endure at school. Children can be cruel and ruthless - especially up here. You heard what those yobs called us that night we went for dinner in the Indian restaurant. There's no tolerance here for gays."

"But they have an annual gay parade," I argue.

"Yes, and they also have a marching season in July and all sorts of other parades — but it doesn't matter — I'm speaking about the average person in the street. They don't understand. But, I promise you, I wouldn't mind any of that, Ellie." She rises up on her elbow and her brown soft eyes stare into mine. "If it wasn't for Lily and the secure family environment that she needs, I would be with you. I would spend my life with you. It would be my dream. My heart belongs to you but I have to be with them. I cannot live without my family and I couldn't put Lily though all that trauma. It would be torture for her at school if anyone found out. It wouldn't be fair."

"You're making excuses."

"No, I'm not Ellie."

I sense Maria's determination and her resilience, so I say, "I've missed you Maria. You've been avoiding me." I stroke her cheek and pull her toward me."I need you in my life. I need your friendship."

We kiss and when we break apart she replies, "These past few weeks have been torture. I've been so miserable. I can't stop thinking about you Ellie, but it isn't fair. I can't give you what you want. I can't give you any more. You're a warm and loving person and you deserve more in your life." She rests her cheek on my shoulder and I feel the dampness of her tears on my skin.

I feel weak. Like the sap has been sucked from my body. A sense of desolation washes over me leaving me helpless and forlorn. "Would you like me to leave Belfast?"

"No, Ellie, please don't leave. I couldn't bear it if I couldn't see you again."

I brush away Maria's tears and when she raises her head I kiss her lips. I feel the rhythm of her figure as her love envelopes me and she pulls me closer into her embrace. Her passion swells and her body moves against me. She kisses my neck with tender and loving kisses and our desire grows again and I'm totally absorbed in my love for her.

I pull her body to me, feeling the strength of her arms and the softness of her skin as she presses her body to fit the contours of mine. Never have I felt so totally in love and that someone is so perfect for me. Maria is everything to me. I've known this since I saw her getting out of the car on my first day at work.

"You are *The One*, you know that don't you?" I say.

"Yes, and you know that you are *The One* for me too. I knew it the first time I saw you that morning sitting on your Harley outside the office."

* * *

Dawn is breaking and we shower together. We lather each other's bodies, whispering, teasing, laughing and kissing. Afterwards we dry our ourselves and dress. I make tea and toast and we stand in the kitchen watching the sky turn crimson as the daybreaks. As I close the front door of the house behind me, birds are chatting like excited children and we whisper as if we are eloping and stealing away into a new future as we climb into my car.

When I drive, we hold hands like teenagers. Clinging to each other valuing the precious minutes together. The motorway leads us over the River Lagan, past the Victoria Centre's illuminated blue dome, and the car park of the Odyssey lies as vacant and forlorn as my hollow heart.

Across the Lough, I glance back to the lights of Holywood. An underlying sadness clings to us both suffocating our spirits and our laughter and a melancholy air descends between us. Maria receded into herself. Her emotional shutter is being pulled down as she takes her hand from mine.

There are no answers. There are no solutions. There is no remedy.

She stares ahead unblinking, directing me through the winding streets to her home on a large estate. There are big houses with double garages and gardens filled with trampolines and bicycles. They are family homes occupied by a husband, wife, two point two children and probably a family pet. It is suburbia.

"Which house is yours?"

She points to a double-fronted house with bay windows and a navy front door. I drive past and park at the end of the street. I don't want to let her go. My insides are screaming my heart is crushed.

Behind the windows families are sleeping. Curtains and blinds are drawn and a baby's hungry squealing reaches us where we sit silently in the car.

"Patricia's babysitting Lily," she says. "As a thank you for me lending her my car."

I regard her sleeping house and imagine Lily curled on her side, her hands clasped as if in prayer, surrounded by soft toys and teddy bears, snoring softly.

"When is Michael back?" I ask staring at his house.

"Tomorrow, although they transferred him to Belfast, they still need him in Dublin to sort things out. He's been going back and forth quite a lot again," she says vaguely.

I try not to think of him arriving home and I try not to think of how Maria is when she's with him.

"You don't love me enough." My voice cuts through the stillness. A serrated knife edge deftly slicing my dream.

"Please don't say that, Ellie. I do love you. It's the circumstances. It's hard. It's lonely and it's difficult for me too."

"But it's your decision," I argue. "At least you have a reason and a purpose. It's your daughter and your family that you want to put first. I'm too far down the line to compete with them. I will never be first in your life. That's why I say, you don't love me enough."

"It's not about that."

"Then what's it about?"

"I don't want to upset or hurt you."

"So, what do you want?"

"You know, Ellie, we keep going over this. The circumstances are awful. What should I do? Tell me what you want me to do," she says, urgently.

I say nothing. If I have to tell her then it wouldn't come from her heart. She should know what she has to do to save our relationship. She should know instinctively that if I am *The One* and she loves me and she wants me in her life, she should know what to do. But she doesn't.

"I'd better go." She reaches for the door handle.

I know she's holding back her tears. I feel her anguish mixed with my pain and it tears the core of my soul. I'm helpless in the path of her chosen destiny.

"Wait Maria," I whisper urgently. She pauses with my hand on her arm. "We could run off. We could take Lily with us and live abroad where no one knows us. We could start a new life. We would be happy together."

She hesitates with the door ajar and a cool breeze gusts inside and my body gives an involuntary quiver.

"It's a lovely thought," she says. "But it's just that. It's a dream, Ellie. Just a dream." She gives me a wry smile and steps out of the car and into the stillness of the stirring street.

* * *

We go live with the ITG software on Sunday when the travel agents offices are closed. And for the following three days I'm with Mark Bowman and Stuart working until gone midnight. We're in the office at six o'clock each morning; sorting problems, providing back-up and running system software updates.

On Wednesday we meet with Boris McCabe, Director of ITG, who has brought two assistants with him to our office. They're experimenting with the reporting system and have detected a few glitches that we are correcting on the live-site.

Boris's eyes are set close together and when he speaks he has a nervous habit of dipping his head forward like a hungry sparrow pecking a worm and I have to control myself not to imitate him when I reply to his quick fire questions.

Stuart and Mark are rewriting and editing the software, and I explain the reporting processes, feigning interest while secretly daydreaming about Maria.

I re-run conversations in my head. I argue, reason, cajole and tie myself in knots coming to the conclusion that she doesn't really love me. She's acting out a fantasy or a romantic dream of forbidden love to provide some excitement in her mundane life. She's insincere and fickle in her emotions;

switching from me to Michael when it suits her or when she wants sex or when she needs excitement. I fluctuate between anger, humiliation and despair. I remember her touch, her declarations of love and her passion and I'm devastated to realise I will never make love like that again. There can never be another - *The One* - it just isn't possible.

They must have been hollow words with no meaning or substance but why did she say it, if she didn't mean it? Our conversations haunt me. My memories unsettle me and I want to cry as equally as I want to reach out and punch the wall.

I imagine her in her office beside where I sit in the board-room, on the other side of the wall, and I cannot stop thinking about our love-making last Friday. My body reacts to the memory and I cross my legs and tug on my bottom lip remembering her languorously slow kisses and the probing of her tongue.

Siobhan brings us copious amounts of coffee, tea, biscuits and sandwiches but I cannot eat. I've hardly eaten since Friday. My attention wanders and sometimes I find myself at the window, staring down into the street, hoping to catch a glimpse of Maria.

I remember my first morning at work when Michael almost knocked me off my Harley and I saw her for the very first time. I remember how Lily's arms caught her in a hug and how Michael drove the car quickly into the traffic. There had been an instant connection between us and since then, our emotional reaction has been enhanced and heightened as if surrounded by a special and magical aura that binds us together and unites us perfectly.

She is *The One*. But why? When she clearly has no regard for my feelings.

"Tea?" Siobhan appears with a tray of tea and hands me a note in Maria's handwriting. I scan it quickly and make my excuses.

Maria is waiting for me in her office. It's the first time we are alone since she stepped out of my car and back into her life on Saturday morning — it seems an age ago and I want to wrap her in my arms and kiss her lips but her dark eyes regard me warily.

"Hi Ellie, I just wanted to know how everything is going with the ITG project. Simon is so strange at the moment. He's hardly ever here. I feel so isolated and John's not even around to ask..." She turns away putting the table between us, ignoring the desire in my eyes and the excitement etched on my face. "It's lonely in here sometimes."

I retract my hand and I don't sit down. Instead, I lean forward resting my elbows on the back of the office chair as I recount the trials of the past five days; of our new software programme, the late nights we've worked and the actions we are performing to correct systems, the data input and source codes.

I speak for maybe five or ten minutes and her eyes don't leave my face. "It's hard without Simon being involved, Maria, so I am just making decisions on what I think is best. John is in town, he's gone to sort out a problem with Mickey Bleu's website."

"Thank you," she says, when I eventually take a breath.

"No problem. Anything else?"

She shakes her head. Her eyes are sad. Is she acting?

I know she can read my mind just as I can read hers. We feel the same sense of futility at our situation and the same sense of loss. I need her with an intensity and passion I've never experienced before and it is so excruciatingly painful that it brings tears to my eyes but I will not cross the boundary. I will not do anything to jeopardise our friendship. Not this time. Not ever. I must remain in control. I need Maria in my life — even as a friend. I must banish and forget my feelings, so I breathe deeply trying not to imagine her lips on mine or her mouth exploring and awakening my body. I must be strong. I must think of her with Lily and with Michael. They are her priority. She loves them more than she loves me.

"You look exhausted, Ellie. I bet you haven't eaten today." Her voice is soft and I dare not speak. I shake my head willing my tears not to bubble in my eyes. "It's not good for you. You must eat," she insists.

My throat has closed over. Tears are pricking the back of my eyes like tiny darts and I'm ashamed at my weakness and my overpowering feeling of love. I'm pathetic and stupid.

"Maybe we could have lunch one day?" she says.

"Please, I'd love that." My voice shakes and I cough.

Liam calls my name from the boardroom and Boris's bird-pecking voice floats in and I raise my eyes to the ceiling in mock exasperation and Maria giggles.

I smile. "Let's get this system up and running and then I'm all yours - oops, figuratively speaking, of course." I tease her and my gaze lingers on hers just long enough for me to see that her gleaming brown eyes are also filled with tears and I know it is an image I will carry with me for the rest of the day.

* * *

By the end of the week, the Harley has been repaired and I ride it to the office. It now has a new leather seat and the chrome has been expertly polished and restored. It's good to ride the bike again. I need fresh air. I need to feel free. I need to feel alive. But I am exhausted. It's been a stressful week dealing with one problem then another. Even though Simon has returned and sits in on the meetings, he's vague and distant. His mind is clearly focused on another agenda and I'm still left to solve difficult issues, deal with clients and make decisions.

By six-thirty I am exhausted. My body is weary and my head aches. Maria left the office a few hours ago and I didn't even get chance to say Hi to Lily, as I was tied up in discussions with Boris McCabe. Now the meetings are over and it's the weekend. I grab my leather jacket, flick the lights switch and close the door.

Last Friday was the company party and it seems an age ago. Another place, another life. I need a drink. I glance into the techie lab and I am surprised to see Siobhan still in the office. She stands twisting lime green strands of her hair extensions around her fingers. I open the door, step inside and she throws me a worried look.

"It ridiculous. We take every precaution…" John's voice trails off.

"What about the firewall?" Simon's face is grey.

"We're checking it," Liam says. "We're going through everything."

"It's impossible!" Stuart thumps the desk angrily.

"What's happened?" I take a step forward into the room.

Simon shakes his head. He doesn't speak. He appears lost and more distant and vacant than in this afternoon's meetings.

"We have a virus attacking our system." John thrusts his hands into his pocket. "And we can't seem to stop it." He's standing behind Mark Bowman who is frantically tapping keys and swearing softly at the computer.

"How?" I move further into the lab.

"If I knew that, it wouldn't have happened would it?" John explodes. "It's not only infiltrated our system but it's latched onto the new ITG data system. It's infecting all their computer files and it's wiping out all their source codes, tracking lines, accounts and information."

Mark's Glaswegian accent cuts across the room. "That includes all their bookings with tour operators, airlines and ferry companies," he explains, glancing up at me. He moves to another computer beside Ray as he speaks. "It's erased all records of their accounts and monies taken from clients and suppliers in the past year."

"It chaos. It's a bloody nightmare." Simon scrapes the stubble on his cheeks, stands up and crosses his arms.

The phone is ringing and Siobhan returns to the reception.

I remain rooted to the spot watching the boys tapping keys on the computers, considering the consequences.

"This could close the company. This could be the end for us all," Roy, the quiet one says.

"How did it happen?" I ask.

John flicks his white jacket behind his elbows and thrusts his hands deeper into his pockets. "Hackers get into the White House. They download medical records. Even the Ministry of Defence has problems keeping their software safe—"

"But why?"

"Some hackers want to be famous," Mark replies. "But I'm with Ellie on this one. Why us? Why would anyone want to do this?" He swears loudly striding between Liam and Ray who are all at their computers, punching keys rapidly.

"We have to limit the damage," Stuart says. "I think we can contain it." His fingers fly across the keyboard but he doesn't look up.

"If these guys can't sort it. No-one can," Liam says nodding at Mark and Stuart.

"That's it. We've paused it. I think, for the time being." Mark looks up from the screen and leans back in his chair. His face taught with weariness. "At least I've isolated it. We have contained it so it won't destroy any more data. These things happen all the time. We just have to be more careful. I just can't work out how it was done." The phone at his elbow rings and he answers it and speaks quietly.

Simon sits staring at the wall. He's lost somewhere in the middle-distance of his mind or in the recess of his consciousness and he doesn't speak.

"Someone will have to handle Boris," Marks says, hanging up the phone. "He's on his way over here and he's not happy. It will take me a while to assess the damage but we will need to stall him, until we find a solution."

They all turn to look at me.

I toss my jacket and helmet to one side. "Okay, I'm your woman. We need to show him that we're confident about our systems and our software. You'd better bring me up to date as to what I can say."

Mark claps me on the back. Simon smiles and it's the first time his anxious eyes lighten gratefully. Steve, Adam Jeff and Mike (Boys Aloud) also look relieved.

"I'll help too, if you need me," says Liam.

When Boris arrives in less than thirty minutes we take him to the boardroom and Simon and I spend the next few hours in damage limitation. I make promises, provide reassurances and rebuild the confidence in our company. Mark has already told me that he can make a quick fix and that he had the foresight to back up the raw data and he can reinstall it overnight.

"It will mean that the twenty-four hour service the ITG want to provide for clients will be unavailable," I explain to Boris. " I would prefer to be upfront and honest, and offer any of the agents our phones or our staff to help out in the next few days."

Boris plays his hand carefully like a card shark in the casino. He's a shrewd businessman and I've worked with many like him before. "So this will be deducted from our final invoice?" he says.

There is no-one as formidable as Kat. I am well-trained and well-accustomed to dealing with his type of business mentality and these type of sales negotiations, and we discuss the situation for over an hour until Boris is satisfied that everything is under control and we reach a financial agreement that's fair to all sides.

Mark is a star. Stuart sits with him as they reinstall the old system and I wait with them long after the others have gone home. I'm in it for the long haul with the lads - they're my team and I will support them.

I buy us fish and chips and during the night I make endless tea and provide cans of soft drinks. They work throughout the night diligently and methodically and it's the beginning of a very, very long and arduous weekend and somewhere in the back of my subconscious I'm thinking that last Friday night, I was in bed with Maria. I wonder what she's doing now. And I try to block the image that forms in my mind of her in bed making love with Michael.

I imagine her lips on mine. Does she kiss him like she did

me? Does she have the passion for him that she has with me? Is she as adventurous and as exciting in bed with him as she has been with me? Is she pretending when she says she has never felt intense love before — because if that is the case — then how can she stay away from me?

** * **

On Monday morning I drag myself out of bed at five and no sooner am I in the office than I'm caught in a frantic whirlwind of activity. I'm on the telephone speaking to travel agents, receiving and recording the damage, checking with the boys in the techie lab for constant progress reports and work out the weekly strategy.

We decide personal contact with each travel agent is the best form of defence. So I leave the office with Liam to visit an annoyed and unhappy travel agent who has been forced to shut down their systems over the weekend.

In their agency, Liam listens and makes notes but unfortunately his film star good looks are not enough to help us out of this mess as we trudge from one office to the next and from one disgruntled client to another.

Boris calls me on my mobile each hour to tell me another agent wants to pull out of the contracts, so I take their details and call them. I make an appointment to visit and reassure them, explaining that it is only a temporary glitch and that we can repair our software and their system.

During the day, Mark replaces and reinstalls the old software while Stuart retraces all new bookings and tracks invoices, payments and reservations. "We cannot let one travel agent cancel or they all will want to pull out and the deal will fall apart. Not only will we lose money but our reputation will be jodida - as my father would say," I explain to Liam. "We cannot let that happen. Our company reputation is at risk. We could lose everything."

He nods. His handsome face is grim and set with determination.

Back in the office, Simon floats between us all breathing over shoulders and looking for updates and progress reports. John works with Mark and Stuart, and by Monday evening when we assemble together we are calling the worm Dominator like he is our oldest and closest enemy.

"The damage has been huge but it would have been worse had we not advised the travel agents to shut down the system and revert to their original software," Mark informs us.

"The three biggest travel agents have taken the brunt of the damage but it has affected all the agents linked to the system in the north of Ireland. Over one hundred travel agencies in total." Stuart confirms. His eyes are rimmed-red and I realise how little sleep we've all had.

"I'll concentrate on goodwill visits to the agents this week," I reply. "I'll do some PR and organise a positive message." My head is tired and muddled and I'm not sure how I will tackle this yet. I need a good night's sleep. I also need Maria. I miss her.

"The problem is far from over. We must track Dominator back to its origins and find out who did this." Mark's Glaswegian drawl is more pronounced with his tiredness. There are purple circles under his eyes.

"Let's leave it for the time being," John replies, "We're all exhausted."

Liam yawns loudly and stretches his well-muscled arms

behind his head. "It's important that we've stopped Dominator. Let's concentrate on getting back up and running."

"We have to show the agents we can manage the software and host their bookings. It's our reputation that's at stake," Stuart argues.

Simon stands up and rubs his chin. "We'll meet up tomorrow. Let's all get a good night's sleep before making any decisions. Thank you all for everything."

After days of tactful negotiation, persuasion and reassurances my head throbs and my back aches. I want to climb into a hot bath, enjoy a glass of wine, eat home made food and sleep for a hundred years. Ideally, I would also like to listen to some soul music and hold Maria in my arms. I imagine her face on the night of the company party when she danced with John. She was happy and alive and vibrant and I would love her to dance like that with me but I must keep within the realms of reality — we are friends — nothing more. At home and after two glasses of wine my resolve disappears and it is ten o'clock when I call her at home. I need to speak to her. I need to hear her voice. I've decided that if Michael is there, I have a legitimate excuse to tell her about Dominator and the progress we've made.

When she picks up the phone her voice is hoarse. It's almost a whisper.

"I spoke to Simon just now," she says by way of greeting. "He told me what happened and that Mark managed to stop Dominator. He says you've been busy with damage control and building up positive PR for the company."

I'm surprised she has spoken to Simon. It's late and I thought she would have waited until the morning — or more importantly — call me first.

"Mark wants to find out how it happened." I sip red wine and lean back on the sofa. "I just hope that it wasn't done deliberately. It's been crazy and the agents haven't been happy," I pause. "I'm sorry, Maria, I didn't get chance to phone you or to call into your office but it's been crazy."

"I know. I understand." Her voice is flat.

"Has something happened?" I frown and sit up.

"I'm taking Lily on holiday tomorrow."

"What?"

"We're going to Lanzarote."

"What? Why? What's wrong?"

"I've told Simon. It's for the best." Maria inhales deeply. Her voice is shaking and I hear her struggling for control.

"Is there is something wrong? Are you crying? Maria—"

"Michael has left—"

"He's gone to Dublin again?"

"He's gone for good! He's been having an affair."

"What?"

"Look, Ellie, I don't want to discuss it on the phone. Lily is in a terrible state. I have to go."

"Wait. Maria. Don't do this to me. This is a shock. It must be awful for you. Did you know? Did you suspect? How long ago did his affair start?" I stand and walk to the window to gaze across the Lough and I think of him flirting with me and the damage done to my Harley.

"It doesn't matter."

"Tell me."

"Over a year ago," she whispers. "He met her before we went to Greece on our family holiday last summer."

"Oh God, Maria, I'm so sorry. I never... Can I see you? Can I come over?" My heart is breaking for them. My head is on fire with questions. I want to strangle Michael for hurting them.

"No, I need to be with Lily. She's very upset."

"I can imagine. The poor thing. Would you have left without telling me?"

"No, of course not—"

"I must see you—"

"I can't—" Maria begins sobbing. "We can't—"

"Let me take you to the airport."

"You're exhausted Ellie. You've hardly slept."

"I don't care. Please Maria. I have to see you. I'm your friend. Please let me help you. Please," I beg.

"Okay, but it's an early flight."

Even though I can barely keep my eyes open I say, "I don't care. I need to see you."

"Okay. Pick us up at five in the morning."

* * *

Despite a relaxing bath, wine and a home cooked pasta, I can't sleep. My eyes feel as though they're filled with tiny grains of grit. My body aches and my heart is filled with pain. I lay in bed thinking about Maria and Lily and I'm reminded of my parents' separation when I was nine years old and the confusion, hurt, fear and the sense of loss. Nothing will ever be the same for either of them.

Over the past week, I've been trying to come to terms with the fact that Maria would be my friend and only my friend. I've worked hard to suppress my feelings, believing that they would eventually dissipate or disappear. I even held onto a small glimmer of hope that I would, one day, become part of their family circle and Michael and I may have become friends and I would have met her mother and siblings. I cannot believe he has been having an affair. How could he do that to her? So why did he flirt with me?

I decide, I must have been delusional or very tired. I will never be a family friend. Whatever happens — the crux of the matter is — is that I am gay. Even as a friend I cannot mix in their social circles. It would be a constant reminder to Maria that she has dallied — with the other side — and that she had feelings for another woman. She could not lead a double life. She would never cope with that. She could not pretend. She could not lie in the face of her family. It would be easier to block me out of her life and pretend that I didn't exist or, if I did, it would be as a work colleague only.

I rally my tired body from my bed and drag myself under the shower. It's already light outside as I drive into the sleepy estate and I'm reminded of this route when I dropped Maria home, on the night of the company party, barely two weeks ago.

This time I park in the drive and the front door opens immediately as if someone has been waiting.

Maria barely looks at me. Instead she fusses around a sleepy Lily who wordlessly stretches out her arms. I give her skinny body a big hug and she embraces me tightly. With her arms still around my neck I stroke her hair, kiss her forehead and settle her into the small space in the back seat. I realise how young and vulnerable she is and I'm overwhelmed with a sense of protection. I have a fierce desire to look after them both and I'm angry with Michael.

Maria locks the front door and pulls a suitcase to the car. I want to reach out and hold her. This is my last chance to feel her in my arms but she's in a closed cocoon in her own mind. She wears an invisible armour-plated suit protecting the shattered emotions inside her heart. Her invisible shutters are down and there's no way I can penetrate her soul. Her dark eyes are puffy and swollen. There are fine lines between her brow and around her mouth that I haven't noticed before. Her half-smile is tense and her shoulders are hunched in sad defeat. When our hands brush together she instinctively pulls away from me.

On the way to the airport, I glance at Lily through the rear mirror. She's listening to music through headphones and gazing listlessly out of the window. Maria turns in her seat and gives her a brave and reassuring smile then stares straight ahead.

It's not until we join the motorway that she begins to speak, disjointedly and distractedly and I wait as each sparse sentence falls from her lips and she tells me how her life has fallen apart.

"I checked our joint bank account. He'd taken her to a posh hotel in Cork for the weekend. He admitted it to me on Saturday. He only came home to pack a bag. It's some girl from his office in Dublin and she's younger than me. He insisted on telling Lily. He obviously isn't going to change his mind."

'He used your joint bank account?"

She nods and the silence stretches between us until she says, "I haven't told the family. I couldn't face it. Mum will be beside herself and Pat will be angry. I just booked the first tickets available. I have to get away. I have to leave. It will give us time to digest it all. It will make me stronger to face everyone when I get back. I know it isn't a good time at work but—"

"It doesn't matter. Look, I'm sorry Maria. It's a shock for

you both." I glance in the mirror. Lily's eyes are closed. She is locked in her own world.

"I'm so angry," she whispers. "It's easy for him just to get up and go and start a new life without any thought or consideration for anyone else. Poor Lily is distraught. She is very upset and has hardly spoken."

At the international airport I park the car and inside we check in the baggage.

"Coffee?" I ask.

"No, we'll just go through."

"I need the bathroom," Lily says.

We wait for her as holidaymakers bustle around us with tired good-humour getting ready for their flight with eager anticipation.

Maria's hands clasp their passports and flight tickets and she stares at the floor.

"There's no point in you hanging around, Ellie. You look exhausted. All those problems and hours you've spent in the office. I'm sorry I'm not here to help…. Besides, I can't talk now. We can't, I can't—" Her eyes fill with tears.

Very gently I pull her close to me and she slumps effortlessly against my shoulder. I trace the outline of her shoulder blades and inhale the scent from her hair.

She speaks quickly, her voice is partly muffled against my summer jacket. "I can't believe that he was with her last summer when Lily and I were in Greece. We went on ahead with Connor, Kate and the children and when he arrived, he wasn't happy. He said he had problems at work. He only spent a few days with us before he flew home early. I've been so stupid, Ellie. He couldn't wait to get back to Ireland. She lives in Dublin. That's why he's been spending so much time there.

It's been nothing to do with his work; roads or bicycle paths or going to Galway. He told me everything. He's been asking for more work down there so that he can be with her. It's been going on for over a year."

I rub her back in wide soft circles between her tense shoulders, pleased I never told her about my encounters with him.

"I'm worried about Lily and what this will do to her," she adds.

"She's strong. She's like her mother." I smile although I want to cry. "Be strong Maria," I whisper into her hair, her lips are inches away from me and her face is so close to mine that I can read her pain etched with fine red lines in her tired eyes.

Lily walks toward us and we move apart.

"I'll pick you up next week," I say.

I bend down and revel in Lily's skinny arms around my neck. She holds me so tightly and it reminds me of my first day at work when she grabbed her mother for a hug from the car window before Michael drove recklessly into the traffic.

"I wish you were coming with us. I'll miss you," Lily says, pushing her glasses onto her nose. "I love you, Ellie."

"And I love you too, Lily. Perhaps next time. Now, don't forget my postcard and use plenty of sun cream," I say as brightly as I can but I feel sick.

They're leaving me and my heart feels hollow and empty. I feel useless. I cannot control my destiny or theirs. I can't do anything positive for them, instead I must let life happen and wave them goodbye.

Maria leans forward and kisses my cheek. It's like the soft tip of a butterfly's wing tickling my skin. Her familiar perfume is intoxicating and my heart constricts. And, it's at that exact moment when she drops the bombshell.

"We're going for three weeks."

Chapter Eleven

With Maria and Lily gone, I feel that a part of me is missing. But worse than that, I feel helpless. Three weeks will be a lifetime. It seems that the day will never come when they return. What will I do? How will I survive without them, without Maria?

I can't do anything to support them, to comfort them or to mend their broken lives. I can only wait. Time will be their guardian as much as it's now my enemy and I resign myself to the fact that I have a very long wait ahead of me.

In the office I try and get my head around the damage limitation situation. I decide the best method is to tackle the problem head-on so, as a gesture of goodwill, I suggest we invite all the travel agents for lunch in an expensive hotel the following day.

"It will cost us money but we must look after our clients. They must know we care and value them," I tell Simon. "We can provide reassurance and remind them of our professionalism."

Boris likes the idea and when Liam and I arrive at the hotel he is already there, smiling enthusiastically and greeting travel agents as if he's the bridegroom on his wedding day with a glass of wine in his hand and a smile on his flushed cheeks.

Liam, with his Johnny Depp cheekbones, is charm personified. He wears a casual beige jacket, mustard-coloured shirt and brown jeans. His hair is trendily tousled and the young girls nudge and stare at him.

Unlike me, he radiates confidence and oozes sexuality but like me he wears *Paco Rabanne*. He's equally charming to the men deferring to their questions, listening to their comments and he answers them with an air of authority which, quite frankly, impresses me. Today he could probably match Kat for professional charm and people skills. He's a showman; smooth and genuine, and I'm left watching him with awe. My energy is ebbing. Maria has taken my heart and my soul. Now it lies somewhere off the coast of Africa in the Atlantic Ocean - in the Canary Islands.

Before we sit down for lunch, I begin a presentation explaining the importance of the new software and why they came to us. I reiterate our aims and objectives. It's always a good ploy to remind them of what and why they're spending their money. Then I ease into the functionality of the software and the future role of travel agents. The benefits of using the system which is another reminder of their money well spent before explaining about Dominator and the type of worm that infiltrated the system. Liam takes over and minimises its effect. He ends the presentation by reassuring them that everything is under control. The new system will be back up and running tomorrow. Finally, he reminds them of our professionalism, dedication, efficiency and dependability. They clap enthusiastically and we give a mock bow. We're all friends again and they love us.

Over lunch we pour wine, deflect the conversation and charm them. There are one or two grousers as always and

I'm delighted that Boris is on our side. He's telling everyone how hard we've worked and how brilliant we are. His agency manager is a brunette with a low cut blouse, and she is practically on Liam's knee and Liam is clearly loving being the star turn. By the time lunch is over he, is everyone's hero including mine.

"Forget Pirates of the Caribbean — you're the pirate of computing," I say in the taxi back to the office. I yawn loudly relieved it's all over and wondering when I will sleep again. "Well done Liam and thank you." We high-five and grin at each other.

In the office I have phone calls to make and emails to answer. I try not to think of Maria as I run up the steps and I glance at her office door wondering when I will see her again.

Three weeks is an eternity.

When I finally take a break it is almost the end of the working day and I sit wondering what Lily and Maria are doing. I'm gazing thoughtfully out of the window when Mark walks into my office and flops down into the seat opposite me.

"We've got all the new data on a secure site and we've readjusted the programmes to allow bookings, financial transactions and historical client data to be recovered and protected. The accounts have been balanced with the transactions registered on the old system and so far the results are good."

"Great! Well done and thank you." I speak sincerely but I have a feeling he wants to say more.

He wears his white lab coat over jeans and when he leans across my desk there is a furrow between his deep set eyes. "I think it was deliberate."

"What?"

"Dominator. It was done on purpose. I'm convinced of it." His Glaswegian accent is strong and it takes me a minute to register the significance of his words.

"Why?"

He shrugs. "People do it for a variety of reasons, more often it's for fame or notoriety. The idea is to create the biggest, cleverest worm. They like upsetting things. They like to prove they're better than any system and they take great delight in destroying and creating havoc. It's every hacker's dream to let loose the perfect worm and Dominator did just that. Think about it." He ticks his fingers as he speaks. "One, the pleasure of seeing the company in disarray. Two, to drive the price of a company down if the company is for sale. Three, to cause havoc so it reaches the newspapers. Four, to get known in the IT world—" He looks at me with raised eyebrows and smiles. "Or five, sometimes they do it just because they're prats."

"But we have managed to contain it," I argue. "There will be no fame here."

"Unless it was a trial run for something worse."

"Would anyone really do this deliberately?" I find it hard keeping the incredulity from my voice.

"Yes."

"So, if it's a hacker? How do we find them? They could be anywhere."

"We may find them, we may not, but I think it could be an inside job. I want permission to see if I can pick up the trail and find out who it is."

"An inside job?" I look out of the window and think carefully before I speak. "Why have you come to me for permission?"

"Well, Ellie, you're the only one who..." He ticks off his

fingers and smiles. "A - couldn't design a worm. B - would have no interest in it and, C - would not benefit from it. Plus, D - I trust you."

"Who else do you trust?"

"No-one."

"And you think, it could be anyone in the company?"

"Is it for sale?"

I stare at him. My mind is whirling and I think of Simon's schemes and erratic thought processes and off-beat ideas, and I shake my head. Eventually I say, "Okay. Do it. Keep it quiet and when, or if, you find out that it is anyone in the company bring the information back to me."

"Thanks, Ellie."

"I just hope that you are wrong, Mark."

"I'm not. Trust me."

After he leaves my office his words continue to reverberate in my head. His Glaswegian accent persists in occupying my thoughts on my drive home and, over a meagre omelette for dinner, at night when my head lies on the pillow his words return to haunt me.

Is the company for sale? If so, who would benefit? John? Simon? Maria?

I toss and I turn, bashing the pillow into shape around my neck as if it is a punchbag in the gym. I take no consolation in the fact that it prevents me from dwelling on Maria and wondering where she is and what she is thinking. Does she miss me?

* * *

The following morning I'm drinking coffee when I hear a

noise from the office next door. I jump up and spill hot liquid over my arm. Cursing aloud I investigate only to find Siobhan sitting at Maria's desk.

"Hi," she says cheerfully. Her hair is cut short and dyed white. "Isn't it strange without Maria here? The office seems empty without her. She did tell me where everything was before she went on holiday but I can't find a thing."

It isn't strange without Maria. It's depressing. "Can you find what you are looking for? Can I help?"

"Thanks Ellie. I need to find an invoice for the OUT Magazine group."

We spend the next twenty minutes searching through files and invoices together. A recurring question is forming in my mind burning my curiosity and eventually I say, "So, Maria had time to tell you she was going away and show you where things are in the office, that was lucky."

"Yes, on Tuesday. You and Stuart and everyone were bogged down with Dominator so she said not to say anything. I was here when she booked the flight tickets. I felt so sorry for her. She wasn't happy."

"No?"

"I have a feeling she's got problems at home. You know, with her husband."

"Why do you say that?"

"She looked like her whole world had caved in. Besides you don't just up and off like that from one day to the next for three weeks — do you?" Siobhan picks up the file she was looking through. "I'll take these down to the reception to work on when I'm quiet. It will mean that Maria won't have so much to come back to."

"That's very kind of you, Siobhan. She'll appreciate that."

"It was John's idea. He's always looked out for her. She's just another one of his crushes." At the door she pauses and frowns. "Ellie? Can I speak to you about something?"

Surprised, I nod.

"You see, I've been offered a modelling contract in London. It's a step on the ladder to being an actor which is my dream…"

"That's fantastic Siobhan, modelling what?"

"Different things. The agency called but they said there would be some acting work too. I wasn't going to take it but now this has happened. You know, with Maria and her problems then Simon and Louise, you know about that…" she whispers, "You know they're getting a divorce."

"What?"

"I know it's a shock but—"

What does this have to do with your modelling career?"

"Think about it, Stuart and I are very young. I'm twenty-two and he's only a year older. It's too young, isn't it?"

"For what?"

"To settle down. Don't you see? If I don't follow my dream to be an actor and go to London then I might regret it and I could end up resenting him. Then if we were to have children — that's why Simon and Louise are separating — because they can't have any. I might resent him for the missed opportunity. I don't ever want a divorce. My family would be dead against it. And anyway, acting is all I've ever wanted to do." She takes a deep breath and shakes her white head at me. "You've got the right idea, Ellie. You're a rolling stone. You'll gather no moss. That's the way to be. Independent."

"Well, I don't—"

"I love Stuart but this could be my big break. My lucky chance. My one golden opportunity to do the one thing I've ever dreamed of doing. I want to be an actress. I don't want to work in here until I'm thirty or end up in an unhappy marriage."

"Right."

"So what do you think?"

"Is it a reputable agency?"

She undulates the words as if I'm stupid. "Yes. Of course."

"Well, it seems a good opportunity then, if—"

"Great. That's what I think. Make sure you say that to Stuart won't you? Thanks Ellie, I'll need all the support I can get when I tell him." She taps up the folders in her hands. "Got to go. Work to do. The techies will be wondering where I've got to."

But as she goes she leaves in her wake the idea of Simon and Louise getting a divorce that washes and waves over me.

* * *

I'm at home staring out of the window sipping a gin and tonic, thinking. It's my new and dangerous past-time. I make up conversations and I imagine situations and events. I puzzle the divorced lives of Simon and Louise. The sale of the company. Dominator and the destruction it could have caused had it not been for Mark and the possibility that this was just a taster for what may come next. I think of John and the techie boys and then everyone's motives for wanting to cause havoc. But it's Maria who pushes everyone from my mind. She's with me day and night and, in my darkest moments. Sometimes I press my lips against the back of my hand and pretend they are her lips on my skin. I remember her delight, her shining eyes when she discovered our pleasures.

"I've never spoken so candidly and openly about lovemaking before," she'd said.

"Why ever not?" I'd replied.

"It's just something we never really talked about. We never discussed what turned us on — we always just assumed."

"How strange. You would discuss everything in detail with your partner if you were buying a new sofa, so speaking about lovemaking should be just as important and just as honest."

She had gone into shrieks of laughter at that point and I smile at the memory of her radiant face and her naked body lying on the sheet beside me, and her saying. "Come here and let's buy a sofa."

They've been gone a week now but it seems as though she's been gone forever. Two more weeks to go. I'm only one third of the way through their holiday. It's endless. So much has happened since she left. So many thought processes and possibilities. I'm exhausted.

I imagine her with Lily in the sunshine, on the beach and in the sea. But Lanzarote seems a million miles away. They might as well have gone to Australia.

I pour another drink and turn up the volume to Yasmin Levy's *Olvidate de mi*, which is suitably melancholic and depressing. I'm singing aloud and tears swim in my eyes when my mobile rings.

Maria's voice is distant, as if she is at the end of a long tunnel, so I shout like an old deaf woman.

"Maria? Is that you?" I sound stupid, so I take a deep breath and calm myself. "How's everything?"

We chat for a few minutes about the weather, the hotel and I tell her about work and the office but I don't mention Mark is looking for the hacker.

She sounds happier than on the journey to the airport a week ago and she's friendly. "Lily wants to say hello," she says, and I hear the smile in her voice as she passes the phone to her daughter.

"Ellie? You should have come with us. I miss you," Lily shouts.

"Hey! Are you having a good time? Is the water warm?"

"We were on the beach today. I've met some friends…" She launches into a detailed account of her new friends until eventually Maria grabs the phone and Lily reluctantly says goodbye. I blow her a kiss and hear Maria sending her into the shower.

"We're going down for dinner in half an hour," she explains.

"How are you coping?"

"Okay," she pauses. "Lily's in the bathroom now so I can talk more. We're doing okay. It's great that Lily has met some children of her own age to play with, she seems to be coping—"

"What about you?"

"This will give me time to think. I need space. I have to work out what to do."

"Don't be too hasty in whatever you decide. It's a tough decision."

"He came back to me. Did I tell you?"

"No." I have no idea what she is talking about.

"You remember the weekend that Kat came over to Belfast? I was upset and I spent the weekend sleeping in the spare room. Michael told me just before he left last week, that he thought I knew then that he was having an affair. He thought I'd guessed and that was why I didn't want to share the bedroom with him and why I slept on the sofa. He said that's when he decided to end it all with this girl in Dublin and he asked for an internal transfer back to Belfast. How's that for irony?"

"Did you tell him about us?"

"No. But don't you understand? He thought that I had found out about his affair. But I wasn't even thinking about him. I was so upset that Kat had turned up in Belfast and she had reappeared in your life, and you'd ignored me that weekend and—"

"Maria, nothing happened. I booked her on the first flight the next morning. She isn't important to me. Since I met you, no-one has—"

"I know that now, Ellie." She pauses. "But I didn't know it then."

"You didn't suspect Michael was having an affair?"

"No, that's why it was such a shock when he told me. He told me all the details, like how he never came to Lily's school concert because he had to go back and see this girl in Dublin. You see, he missed her so much, Ellie. He can't live without her. Can't you see what this means? He missed his girlfriend more than he wanted to be with me or with Lily. She has a bigger hold over him than we do. He loves her—"

"Maria—"

"He loves her more than he loves us," her voice trembles. I wait while she blows her nose and she coughs to clear her throat. "I have to go now. Lily is out of the shower. I don't want her to see me upset."

"Maria, wait. Please call me anytime if you want to talk. I'm your friend more than anything else. You have to know that. Regardless of what has happened between us. I want to help you."

"Thank you, Ellie. I just don't know what I'll say to Mum, or to Pat."

"What about Connor? Do you think he knows? Didn't you say he and Michael were best friends?"

"Connor phoned me yesterday to see if we were all right. He must know about Michael's affair but he denied it when I asked him. He acted surprised."

"You'll have to tell your family the truth. It's not your fault."

"Mum will say it is. She believes it's a wife's job to keep her husband happy."

"What about a husband's duty to keep his wife and daughter happy? And safe, and cared for and—"

"She won't listen. I know she won't. She'll blame me. She told me enough times that I had started going out on my own and I was asking for trouble. Look, I've got to go, Ellie. It's my turn to shower."

"You're not a nun, Maria. We don't live in the dark ages."

"She'll say it was all my fault."

"Maria—"

"And she's right. It is all my fault."

That's when the line goes dead in my hand.

* * *

I had thought of getting a flight to London for the August bank holiday weekend to stay with Jenny, Richard and the boys but they've gone to stay with Richard's parents who live in Cornwall.

Dad and his new girlfriend Marta are on holiday in Italy and my mother is still with her hippy toy-boy in Thailand. I have nowhere else I want to go — except t0 Lanzarote and unfortunately — that's not an option.

I tidy up my desk and decide I will go to the gym and

spend the long weekend relaxing, sleeping and weeding Auntie Annie's garden. I'm planning my lonely few days ahead when John's head appears around my office door.

"Hi Ellie, I wonder if you would do me a favour?"

"Of course."

"Happy Days, you see, Simon has insisted we recruit someone new to handle the app development programme."

I nod. It had been my idea, at the last strategy meeting, to advertise our services for apps arguing that many ordinary people have great ideas and within a week we had received over twelve enquiries.

"We've had another six enquiries that Liam is following up," he says.

"That's great." My surprise and delight are both genuine.

"I'd like you to speak to the girl downstairs, Jessica Charles, I'm interviewing her at the moment. It's normally Simon's job, but he isn't here, again. I think he's meeting some businessmen from Dublin - or are they American? I'm not sure, anyway, I'd like a second opinion."

At his insistence, I follow him downstairs to his office wondering about Simon's meeting.

Jessica Charles is overweight and pretty. She wears heavy eye makeup and smiles with confidence. She also wears a rainbow coloured T-shirt with bright purple letters that says *Out and Proud*. Not the normal interview attire but I shake her hand and admire her openness.

When I scan read her résumé, I find out that Jessica Charles is more than qualified for the job. She is twenty-five. Her references are impeccable and she has the necessary skills and temperament to fit in with Stuart, Mark, Liam and Boys Aloud. We chat about inconsequential matters and she opens up quickly, hints that she's gay, relaxes and laughs easily. After twenty minutes I'm in no doubt that she will fit in well with our office policy and the guys in the techie lab and I wonder what John is playing at, did he ask me down here purely because she's gay?

I promise her we'll be in touch next week and we all shake hands, and she leaves. I have given her no indication that I am gay too. It's not relevant or important. There's no secret handshake or nod or special wink. It's business. It has to be the right person for the job.

"Thanks, Ellie," John says after she leaves his office. "I knew she had the talent and skill but I wasn't sure she would fit in."

"Why?" I try not to sound defensive.

"She's a bit glamorous, isn't she?"

"She's a bright girl with an attractive personality. What does glamour have to do with writing apps?"

"Nothing — I know." He puts his hands in his pockets and hitches his trousers up. "It's just that I don't want the boys distracted. Another pretty girl in the office might stop them from working or it might make them show-off but, to be honest, I really like her and I think she's the right girl for the job."

I smile. He mustn't have noticed the T-shirt, and I wonder if he's developed another crush already.

"Well, you're making the right decision, John," I agree. "She is the right person for the job and I think she will get on great with the team."

He looks surprised and he beams happily. "Happy Days, Ellie. Thank you. I'm pleased we've put our differences behind us. I think we work really well together, don't you? We're a good team."

"I do." I smile. It's only a small white lie.

179

Chapter Twelve

"Hi, Auntie Annie, it's great to hear from you." We have spoken a few times since she's been in Canada and I'm warmed and reassured by her happy voice at the end of the telephone. I miss her.

"I'm in the garden,' I explain and switch on the video and show her. "It's a beautiful evening here. I've mowed the lawn, weeded the flower bed, dead-headed everything that was wilting and planted trays of shrubs. Are you impressed?" Perspiration is dripping from my forehead and I wipe it with the back of my wrist, conscious of the mud on my fingers smearing across my cheek.

"You look hot."

"I'll take that as a compliment." I laugh.

"I've got some good news," she says, excitedly, so I hold my breath and screw my eyes up at the descending sun. "I've met someone," she adds.

I don't know what to say. In my head I'm mentally calculating her age. She is two years older than my mother, her sister, so she's sixty-one. I'd always assumed that she was past all that. I shake my head to rid the images of my Aunt and her new boyfriend in the throws of passion.

"Who is he?"

"I met him at the bridge social. His name is Gerard and he wants me to go to Seattle to meet his daughter." Her laughter is infectious.

"Is it serious then?"

"His daughter wants to meet me."

"She wants to check you out, more likely. Has he got money? Is she worried about your intentions or her inheritance?"

"He says, I will love her. She has four children."

"Goodness, I hope you're staying in a hotel then or it'll be very noisy."

"Gerard and I can be very quiet when we want to be." She giggles. She has misinterpreted me deliberately. "Oh, and guess what? He wants me to move in with him. And, I've said, yes."

"That's great," I say, but I'm thinking, that isn't so great. "But that's a long way from here. Won't you miss Belfast?" I ask.

"It's time to move on, Ellie. I've a new opportunity and a new life here and it's fabulous. Why don't you come out and join me? There's lots of eligible men here - and they're very good looking. It could be a lucky break for you too."

"I'll think about it," I lie.

"It'll mean I'll be selling my house. Not immediately, of course, but if everything all works out here, I'll come home and pack things up. You won't mind, will you? It's not as if you've decided to settle there or anything — it's just temporary, isn't it? It was just a place to go while you sorted yourself out, wasn't it?"

"It was," I reply. I don't add that it hasn't worked and that I haven't sorted myself out and that I'm in an even worse mess than I was after I left Kat. I can't begin to explain to Auntie Annie, who is thousands of miles away, that the feelings I have for Maria I have never felt for anyone else. Maria is special. We understand each other and I do know that if circumstances were different we would be happy together.

I was hoping Auntie Annie would be back soon. I'm lonely here especially now that Maria is away. I know I should be happy for her but seeing her happy, relaxed face and listening to her laughter makes me feel lonelier and sadder than before. After we hang up and as the evening wears on, I become increasingly morose.

It is almost dark and I have showered and eaten when Jenny calls me. The curtains are billowing in the breeze at the open window and the dying sunset catches the panes of glass showing them to be smeared with my hand prints where I have tried to reach out across the Lough.

"It's boiling here," Jenny complains. She sounds weary and tired. "The beaches are packed and, the boys and Richard are preparing a barbecue."

I imagine the vast Cornish beaches - the pretty coastal pathways and busy pubs. After catching up on their holiday news I tell her about Auntie Annie's new boyfriend Gerard and her trip to Seattle.

"So, isn't she going to live back in Belfast?" Jenny asks.

"Not at the moment. She's happy that I'm here looking after her house and paying the bills but—"

"What?"

"I wanted her to come home, Jenny. I miss her."

"You miss Auntie Annie?" she says incredulously.

"Well, okay, I miss the company."

"You need to get out more. Haven't you met anyone at the gym? What about your friend at work? The accounts woman you got friendly with?"

"Maria? She's on holiday with her daughter in Lanzarote."

"Ah, so you're pining for her. That's what's wrong with you and why you sound down in the dumps."

"It's not like that."

"Ellie, I've warned you. You're playing with fire."

Tears begin trickling down my cheek and I wipe them away. My head feels hot and heavy and a bout of nausea sweeps over me and I move out of the camera range.

"Ellie? Are you okay?"

"I'm fine."

Her voice softens, "You should have come back to England for a few days, caught up with some friends and had some fun. You're too alone over there. You need to come back to London and work over here again. You are out on a limb over there. You need to be with friends and family."

I am brushing away my tears. They won't stop falling.

"Ellie? Listen to me. I know you're upset. Why do you insist on staying there if you are not happy?"

"I am happy."

"You don't sound it. You're crying."

"I'll be fine."

She pauses, then I hear her take a deep breath. "Right, that's it. I'm coming over there. I'm coming to get you. I'll speak to Richard tonight. There will be enough room at Auntie Annie's if we all come over. We'll all come and get you. And we'll bring you back here, where you belong."

"Jenny—"

"Don't Jenny me, I'm sick of your nonsense. It's time for you to come home."

* * *

Stuart and Siobhan ask me to join them for dinner in Mickey Bleu's restaurant. It has an open kitchen with the longest grill I have ever seen.

Mickey Bleu is dressed regally in a white kaftan. She stands beside hot coals that are burnt orange and tinted with white ash, turning Cajun chicken, spicy beef and blackened fish. Waitresses carry plates with hot jacket potatoes and side orders of sour cream and crispy salad to tables.

The restaurant is a BYO so I have taken a chilled bottle of Sauvignon Blanc from my fridge and some non-alcoholic beer for me. After half an hour I can see that it won't be enough alcohol. Stuart is working his way solidly though a six pack of Bud and Siobhan has almost finished the bottle of wine. We're all pretending that she isn't leaving to go to London tomorrow to pursue her modelling career. They are both emotionally distraught and I'm caught in the middle of their drama.

Siobhan's hair is dyed black. Her eyeliner and eyes are painted black and her face is white like a Goth. Only her eyes are red from crying.

Stuart pretends he's not looking at her but each time we speak, and I am doing most of the talking, he gazes at her and when she looks back at him his eyes linger before he turns mournfully away.

I wish Maria was here at my side. If we were together I'm convinced that the evening would be easier for all of us. But we can never be together as lovers and would I be satisfied just to have her as my friend?

How can I get rid of these feelings for her? How can I stop them? It would be so much easier if I didn't feel — or think.

I blink tears and make an excuse to leave to buy more wine from the supermarket across the road and I pause at the bar.

"Lover's tiff?" Mickey Bleu says, nodding at the miserable couple sitting at my table.

"She's going to London. She has to choose between him and her career."

"Decisions — always decisions. No-one has it easy. If it's not love, it's marriage, or it's children or the lack of them…" She shakes her pristine silk turban and there's a dark glint in her knowing eyes.

"It's not easy," I agree, and just for a moment I have a niggling sensation that she knows something more, she's in tune with those around her. She feels compassion and I sense she understands suffering and I remember her story when we first met and the hurricane that affected her home island of Haiti.

I take my time browsing in the wine department and when I return to the table things are no better. Stuart is still sulking and Siobhan remains resolute and silent. Her eyes have taken on a steely determined glint so once we have eaten dinner, I make my excuses. They are still not speaking when I leave but it's as if they have no place else to go.

Instead of heading toward Holywood, I turn the car in the opposite direction and drive to Jordanstown remembering the morning I drove Maria home after our night together. We had held hands like teenagers, our bodies filled with warm caresses of our naked skin and our lips moist from the other's passion. Then, more recently, ten days ago when I collected them and taken them to the airport.

I drive slowly into their street as if I am a stalker and I feel guilty spying on their house. The blinds are drawn. There is no sign of life. I turn the car at the bottom of the road and register the street lamp under which we parked that morning where I suggested that we move abroad with Lily.

Maria had called it a dream.

I brush my eyes. My cheeks are wet with my tears and I thump the steering wheel and restart the engine.

"I'm a stupid bitch! Stupid! Stupid! Stupid! Una tonta, my father would say, Una tonta perdida!"

I put my foot on the accelerator narrowly missing a car driving manically toward me. It's a red Audi. It screeches to a halt and when I glance sideways I glimpse Michael glaring at me.

I drive home, fast, along the motorway vowing I will not go back across the Lough. I will never go to Maria's house. It's too upsetting. What was I thinking? Am I going crazy?

My mobile begins ringing as I walk in through my front door. I toss the keys on the kitchen counter and barely register the caller ID.

"You're not at home. I tried your landline. Can you speak?"

It's Maria's voice and I can't believe the coincidence. My heart soars. I know she understands me. I know she's thinking of me even if we are just friends.

"I've just got home." I dump my bag on the floor. "This must be telepathy. I was just thinking of you."

"Lily is with her friend and I wanted to speak privately to you."

"Oh, good." I feel I am alive again. My pulse is racing, my heart is pumping and my hands are shaking. I block the memory of Michael's angry face from my mind.

"There's something I have to tell you."

"Okay. Do you want me to call you back?"

"No, this will be quick."

I'm aware of the excited and upbeat tone of her voice and I

reach for the whiskey bottle and pour a small measure. I raise the glass to the ceiling in a mock toast wishing she were with me.

The whiskey hits the back of my throat and a warm wave of hope and desire scurries through my veins so I take another hearty gulp, wondering how I will phrase my reply.

I miss you too, Maria. I need you. I love you.

"Ellie, I can never be with you. I want you to understand this. We will never be together. I think it is only fair to tell you this now. I don't want you to build your hopes up and think that just because Michael has left that I'm about to fall into your arms and live happily ever after because it's not going to happen. Ellie? Are you there? Can you hear me?"

I am pouring another whiskey.

"Yes, Maria, I heard every word."

"I mean it. You're a lovely person and you've been a kind friend but that's it. There can never be anything else again, ever, between us."

"Okay."

"I can't - I mean, I don't want Lily to think, or to feel, or to know about — anything. Do you understand? She's too vulnerable. She couldn't cope with any more emotional traumas. She's not strong enough—"

"I understand, Maria. I told you before. There's no problem."

"We're just friends."

"Yes. Friends," I confirm.

"Good. I just wanted you to understand all this before I come home next week."

"I do," I reply, "I understand it very well, Maria. You have explained it all very nicely. Thank you."

* * *

At six thirty in the morning I'm on the treadmill in the gym. Perspiration trickles down my temples, my back and into my groins. I'm panting, straining and pushing myself hard. I pause the treadmill to gulp water, mop my face and then I continue running. My head is pounding and my arms are rhythmically driving my feet. I have music in my ears that I don't hear. I'm alone with only the pounding of my heart for company, angrily pumping the frustration from my heart, my soul and my head.

Thirty minutes later I am standing beside the water dispenser. The girl with black glasses who I recognise from the treadmill says, "I haven't quite worked up to your speed yet."

"It doesn't get any easier," I reply, sipping water. "I wish it did."

"No, it doesn't, but I dread to think what my weight would be like if I didn't bother — too much wine and chocolate." She smiles. She's skinny and I can't imagine her eating or drinking much at all.

Twenty minutes later I've showered and dressed and I'm drying my hair when the same girl appears in the mirror beside me.

"I don't wear makeup, only this." She holds up a cherry coloured stick that matches her lips. She looks at my neck in the mirror and says, "Wow, I love your stars. This is my star sign in Hindu."

She shows me a red tattoo on her bicep. We talk about body art and she tells me that when she was a student she went back-packing around India. As a student, I also went to Agra and Jaipur so we speak about the culture and the food with growing interest in each other. She's relaxed and easy to speak to and we laugh easily. We're ready to leave at the same time so we walk out into the car park together.

She drives a new white Seat 500 with a soft black roof which I admire but she whistles when she sees my old Mercedes.

"Maxie would love that."

"Maxie?"

"My partner, she would love a car like this." She runs her hand over the bonnet.

I smile and hold out my hand. "Ellie Bravo."

"Anna MacCarthy. I'm a nurse at the City Hospital." Her handshake is firm.

"I work in the Lisburn Road - marketing," I explain that it's an IT company.

"Maxie is a nurse too but on a different shift. Tonight we are both off and we're meeting up with friends in town for dinner. Why don't you join us if you haven't any plans?"

"I've no other plans and I can't think of a single reason why I shouldn't. Thank you." We swap contact details and she promises to text me later today. And, for the first time since Maria left for Lanzarote, I go into work with a smile on my face.

That evening we meet in a trendy restaurant in the Cathedral Quarter. One of the 'in' places to eat. The furniture is haphazard; a mixture of chairs and assorted tables, something of a cross between grandma's old fashioned living room and an uncomfortable school room. Colourful watering cans are suspended from the ceiling and an array of assorted teapots line the length of one wall and on the other are oddly-shaped mirrors and picture frames.

"It's shabby chic," Anna explains.

They introduce me to the table of girls. It is someone's birthday. I smile and wave feeling slight awkward as newcomer to the group realising I would never remember all their names.

Between them they tell me they have been together ten years and I can see that during that time they have morphed into each other. They wear similar striped T-shirts, blue jeans and rectangular black-rimmed glasses. They also have short curly hair.

"I work up at the City Hospital too," Maxie says. "Did Anna tell you she works in casualty?"

I shake my head. "That must be traumatic?"

"She says that going to the gym is the only thing that keeps her sane. Not that it's working. She obviously doesn't spend enough time up there working out. She's still a little crazy." She laughs and her smile is infectious.

After we've ordered the meal a girl called Suzie with cropped hair leans across the table and asks why I moved to Belfast. I try to keep the bitterness from my voice and gloss over the details of me splitting from Kat and how she gave my job to the company plonker. I tell them I am staying at my Auntie Annie's house in Holywood.

It seems to satisfy her curiosity and she nods. Her eyes are intense and I feel I'm scrutinised for my looks and my non-Northern Irish accent.

"I could never do that," says Maxie, "I could never begin again somewhere new. It would be like moving to a foreign country."

"You'll never have to," replies Anna, placing her hand on top of her girlfriend's arm. "We're staying here. We will always be together — forever — and I'm certainly not moving."

They both smile. It's a morph smile ringed with black glasses and I realise how lucky they are to have found someone they are totally in tune with and so obviously adore.

Suddenly there is a hand on my thigh. The girl sitting beside me Mary, leans in closer, I think she will ask me something but she doesn't speak instead she makes eye contact and reaches past me for the salt cellar.

"Sorry," she purrs, "but it was easier to reach than to have to ask."

Her hair smells of smoke and now I know why she disappears at regular intervals. I assume that Suzie with the tight smile and Mary are a couple.

A few minutes later a girl called Carla sitting on my right draws me into conversation but I'm not concentrating. All I see is her wide mouth, painted red lips and flared nostrils. Her hair is long, curly and unrestrained which makes her seem wild and reckless. She has an air of excitement about her and an aura of calm and controlled strength.

"I teach physical education at Strathern School. Do you know it?"

I shake my head but she continues speaking telling a story about a young talented student whom she coaches and I'm in no doubt that she's good at what she does. She commands attention and I notice that Mary, Suzie, Anna and Maxie watch in anticipation of her punchline. She has the attention of the table. They seem to hold her in high esteem and whenever she speaks they all stop to listen. I too am captivated. She is both fascinating and intimidating.

During the meal I eat with gusto. My chicken with cream spinach is delicious and it's great to have company but Carla only picks at a salad. She doesn't drink alcohol but we are already on the seventh bottle of wine and I am bathed in a glow of warmth and happiness fuelled by friendship. I have at last found some like-minded people with whom I can enjoy a meal, have an intelligent conversation and, who know I'm gay.

My attention wanders to Maria and I wonder how she would react if she met this group of women. How would she fit in? Would she be comfortable with gay girls or would she feel unsure or labelled?

And as the evening continues it also begins to prove to me that her theory is wrong. There are gay people in Belfast and it is tolerated here. She should get out more. Perhaps one day I may be able to introduce her to my new found friends.

In the street we all say goodnight and, just before I get in the taxi, Carla kisses my cheek and slips a note into my pocket with her phone number.

* * *

The following week I work out in the gym every morning. I chat briefly to Anna. She knows I'm single and she tells me, quite pointedly, that Carla is a genuine and lovely girl.

"She's on her own too, you know, and a girl like her shouldn't be alone and neither should you. Life is too short. Life is for sharing." We leave the changing room and I sling my bag over my shoulder choosing my words carefully.

"There is someone I have been with recently. She is very special but — she's married."

"Oh Ellie, I hope she's worth it. Married women are trouble. Most of the time they're just bloody curious, besides what if her husband finds out?"

"He's just left her — for a younger woman in Dublin — and

so she's in Lanzarote with her daughter."

She pauses at her car door and looks over the bonnet at me. "Seems as if you are bottling up lots of emotions inside, are you?"

"Um," I open my car door and give her a wry smile.

"You look like you need to talk. Come over for dinner and you can tell us about it. We probably won't be able to do very much but we're good listeners."

We say goodbye, smile and wave, get into our cars and go our separate ways — Anna to the City hospital and me to the office.

This morning I'm feeling positive. The euphoria of meeting new friends on Friday night has stayed with me. I could have a good social life here once I break out of my insular routine. Now that Maria will not be a part of my life I must get out and meet people. I must do more to socialise and develop a circle of friends.

Siobhan has gone to London and she hasn't yet been replaced. And it's mid-morning when Simon calls me into his office to go through paperwork and invoices that Maria has been handling.

"We need to get the money in and we can't do that if we don't invoice." His face is grey and his eyes are tired.

"We need a new receptionist and Maria needs an assistant," I reply. "She has been coping with all these new accounts and I don't know how she has managed it all."

"Have you heard from her?" he asks. "Is she okay?"

"Yes. She's struggling but I think she has done the right thing, going away." I can't meet his grey eyes that regard me carefully.

"You're a good friend, Ellie. Dominator could have been the

end for us. These past few weeks have been a nightmare and I don't know what I would have done without you. You've been professional and very dependable. I really appreciate it."

"Don't give me too many compliments Simon or I'll burst into tears or be looking for a pay rise." I grin.

We finish the last invoice and I close the file and stretch. I'm in a playful humour but my question is serious. We don't have the opportunity for many conversations and we rarely connect any more so I decide to push this to my advantage.

"What about Louise? How is she? I heard a very sad rumour and I hope that's all it is — a rumour?" He pulls on his nose and doesn't reply, so I continue, "I'm not going to ask anything, Simon. It's none of my business and I respect you, especially when John decided to broadcast my relationship with Kat, and you stood up for me. I just hope that you can both work things out, one way or another, just go carefully and think about the love that you share and don't be too hasty in any decisions."

He looks close to tears so I change the subject, taking advantage of this rare moment together when he doesn't have an excuse to rush off somewhere more important.

"Have you thought of selling the company?" I probe. It is a question that has been going around my head since Dominator infiltrated our system and this is the first opportunity I have had to ask him the question.

His eyes widen in surprise and he shakes his head vehemently. "No."

"Okay. So, have you thought any more about the Dominator? Are you worried it might happen again? If it was done by someone in the company then this could just be tip of the iceberg. It may also be a prelude to something bigger."

"No-one in the company would do that. And Stuart has

reassured me that it's all sorted out. They have built our software defences so that it won't happen again. There's nothing to worry about."

"It won't happen again with Dominator but someone else might create another worm — a more destructive one."

"I doubt that—"

"No-one thought it could happen this time."

It's been a tough—"

"We can't be complacent, Simon."

"I'm not complacent," he says loudly sitting up as if he wants to regain control of the conversation. He interlocks his fingers on the desk and leans forward. "Stuart is taking charge. He is looking at it."

I regard him carefully and speak deliberately quietly and slowly. "Now that Siobhan has left Stuart is in an emotionally vulnerable situation. His concentration is all over the place."

"Just because somcone is emotionally vulnerable doesn't mean they cannot do their job." Simon's eyes are grey steel like his voice.

We stare at each other not speaking for a few minutes. I can see he is resolute. I would like to get into a serious discussion about his long absences from the office and spell out how I've had to solve issues and make decisions without him, and I think of his secret meetings with American investors.

"There's something going on, Simon, isn't there?"

He's the first to turn away. He pulls his gaze from mine and stares out of the window and down into the street as if looking for inspiration.

It dawns on me then that we are all trying to manage our lives. We all have problems. Simon and Louise are on the brink of a divorce. John is divorced and develops secret crushes.

Stuart misses Siobhan. Maria's husband has walked out on her and she has had an affair with a female colleague. And then there's me, a gay, single woman with no roots, no future and no aims; a woman wandering through life.

Not all who wander are lost.

"What?" says Simon distractedly. "What's that you're saying about being lost?" He turns from the window and I know our connection is broken.

I don't reply. I have found Carla's phone number in my jacket pocket and it is burning my hand.

Chapter Thirteen

I'm invited to dinner in Anna and Maxie house. They live in a compact detached house in a small cul de sac. Their welcome is bubbly and infectious and, to my delight and consternation, Carla is also invited.

Anna has prepared guacamole and I sip white wine and dip carrots into the tasty garlic dip. Then, with barbecued steaks we switch to red wine. The conversation flows and we laugh and tease each other. The company is informal, funny and refreshingly honest.

"So, come on, spill your heart out," Anna says, opening more wine. "We're not working tomorrow and we want to help you."

"Well, I am working in the morning," I reply but hold out my glass for a refill. "And I feel suddenly shy. I'm not used to talking about my personal life."

Carla crosses her legs and looks at me expectantly. Her features are large but attractive and her big, enquiring eyes do not leave my face.

"Don't be, you are amongst friends." Maxie sips her wine. "We want to help and a problem shared is a problem magnified."

"Magnified?"

"Of course, because everyone has their opinion and if you didn't know what to do before then you definitely won't know what to do afterwards. It's even more confusing." She laughs.

"Ignore her. I give great advice. And, my counselling service is free to friends," Anna says.

"Sounds like the therapy you need. How can you resist?" Carla's smile is wide and encouraging.

So, in the comfort of their home, around the small dining table, I confess my love for Maria. I tell them how we first saw each other. I tell them about Lily and our trip to the cinema, dinner out, our shopping trip and the school concert. I skip the details on the love-making. Don't mention my jealous streak when I imagined Maria across the Lough but I do tell them about Michael and my damaged Harley. I keep it brief and I know I have their attention. They don't interrupt and when I end by telling them that Maria returns tomorrow from the Canary Islands. They sit in contemplative silence.

"Wow," says Anna eventually.

"Well, it's a no brainer," adds Maxie. "It'll never work. She's married and if her family lives up in West Belfast then they will have more prejudices than the average person. I should know, I'm a Catholic from there. I know what they're like. She would have to be a very strong woman to stand up to them."

"There's more tolerance now—" begins Carla but Anna interrupts.

"You won't win her over. She will never go against her family. Look what happened to Maxie — her family barely speak to her since we've been together and we're not invited to any family gatherings. I'm the devil in disguise — not only am I gay but I'm a protestant too."

"I love you Anna, and my family weren't going to stand in

my way. No one can tell me who I can and can't love and who can and can't be my friend. I will not be controlled like that or dictated to." Maxie reaches for her girlfriend's hand.

"You're very brave." Carla leans forward and pours wine into my glass. "I don't think I could do that Maxie, although I do admire you. My family don't know that I am gay nor do they know at school. I would be worried what they thought. The old labels of gay and lesbianism still exist especially in the PE department in schools and although we are supposed to teach equality and understanding. It isn't always as accepted as it is supposed to be."

"They have enough on their hands with cross community education and coping with religion." Anna laughs mirthlessly. "Let alone tackling the gay issues."

"So it would be hard for Maria's daughter, Lily, at school?" I ask.

Carla nods. "Definitely. Two female mothers - I think so, yes. Impossible."

"Nothing is not insurmountable. Everything is possible. I have proved that." Maxie squeezes Anna's hand and they morph into a unified smile but after this discussion, I already have my answer.

Maria is right.

Our situation is impossible.

* * *

I arrive early at the International Airport. The flight from Lanzarote is a few minutes late and I pace restlessly backwards and forwards as tanned passengers push over-laden trolleys, rattle bottles in yellow duty free bags and gaze around with happy familiarity at their surroundings.

Three weeks have passed since I dropped them that early morning. They were exhausted with emotion and I was sleep-deprived after Dominator had attacked our software system. We have repaired the damage and I have new gay friends. A lot has happened.

It's Lily who sees me first. She pushes through the crowds and throws her skinny arms around my neck kissing me hard on the cheek. The whites of her eyes flash brightly from behind her glasses, her hair is unruly and curlier, and she smells of salty sea and fresh air.

I pick her up. "You've got taller and heavier." I laugh and place her back on the floor where she continues to hang onto my arm.

Maria's soft brown velvet eyes shimmer like a sparkling sea of rich dark chocolate. She wears a simple yellow cotton blouse, white jeans and summer sandals. Her hair is clipped onto her head revealing her tanned, slim neck. Words fail me and I smile like an idiot as she leans forward and kisses my cheek. When her fingers linger in my hand a ripple quivers down my spine and I am confused. Does she know what effect she has on me?

"Ellie? Aren't I brown? Did you miss us?" Lily dances excitedly, rolling up the sleeves of her blouse to compare her arm with mine and I welcome her diversion. It saves me from having to look at Maria.

Driving home they chat happily about the hotel, the people they met, the excursions; the camels, the hot springs, the Timanfaya National Park, the boat trip to see dolphins and the markets where they bought T-shirts and costume jewellery.

I have bought them supplies of milk, bread, eggs and fruit

but they haven't eaten dinner and Maria suggests we stop to pick up a Chinese and take it back to her house.

When we arrive, she heads straight for the kitchen and throws open French doors that lead onto an untidy garden. Warm stale air from the house escapes and evaporates and cool air begins to circulate inside and I breathe a sigh of relief.

"That's better." She smiles encouragingly. "Let's eat in the garden."

She throws me a cloth and together we brush down the dusty terrace table and chairs. Lily brings mats and knives and forks and Maria disappears inside to fetch plates and wine.

We eat the takeaway as a picnic, outside in the cool air, under the dipping sun. And I'm aware that I'm not the only one who is happier sitting in the garden than in the house they shared with Michael.

We laugh and chat contentedly. I tell them how Stuart and Mark stopped Dominator and Liam's dynamic presentation in the hotel. I don't mention that Mark is trying to find out who the hacker could be. But I do tell them that Jenny, Richard and the boys are visiting me the following weekend. "They're staying with me in Auntie Annie's house and I am really looking forward to their visit. Matt and Jake are very excited." I don't add that Jenny wants to drag me back to London to live and work.

"How old are they?" Lily asks.

"Jake is twelve and Matt is ten. They are great fun and I hope you will meet them," I add uncertainly, not daring to look at Maria. I don't want to put her under unnecessary pressure to meet my family.

"That's cool. We could have a barbecue, couldn't we, Mum?" Lily is leaning with her arms around Maria's neck. She is weary and suddenly the excitement of being home seems to knock her out.

"Let's see nearer the time," I suggest diplomatically.

Lily yawns. She moves and leans against my chair casually draping her arm over my shoulder. Her finger tracing the stars on my neck. "I'm pleased you're here Ellie," she whispers. "I missed you."

"Me too." I pull her toward me and kiss her forehead.

"Time for bed," Maria says. "Come on sleepy."

Lily pulls a face but her eyes are drooping and she yawns again. "Night night, Ellie. I don't know what Mum would do if she didn't have you." She kisses my cheek with such intensity that I laugh and so I tickle her tummy gently making her loosen her grip. She giggles and squirms away from my grasp. "I don't know what I'd do without you, either," she adds.

Maria follows Lily upstairs and I sit for a few moments contemplating the garden and the memories they must have here as a family. It will not be easy for either of them to move on with their lives. I remember the pain from my own upbringing but it is easier not to think so I gather the empty boxes and throw the rubbish in the bin. I wash my hands and return to the garden trying not to imagine them eating around the table. I feel like an impostor, an usurper, who has stolen the crown of another king which is ridiculous. Michael left on his own accord and I'm certainly not taking his place. Maria has made that very clear.

The evening has turned chilly and I rub my arms.

"Lily's asleep already. She could barely brush her teeth she was so tired." Maria appears wearing a fleece. "I thought it would be harder coming home but it hasn't been that bad. That's one hurdle over with. It was lovely to sit outside tonight but it's cold now. Come on Ellie, let's go inside."

We close the French doors and Maria looks around the black and white kitchen as if it doesn't really belong to her. I perch on a stood at the island in the middle of the room knowing I must leave and go home.

"I looked upstairs and Michael has taken most of his things. It all looks a bit strange but to be honest he's hardly been here for the last nine months so it's not as if the house is empty without him. I'm used to putting Lily to bed on my own and sitting here watching television. We've led separate lives for so long…" her voice trails off and she folds her arms and leans back against the sink and I'm reminded of the kiss we shared in the office kitchen just before John burst in to tell me that Kat was downstairs. To change the subject, I ask,"Have you spoken to Michael?"

"He called a few times to speak to Lily. He says he wants to see her when she's back. Ironically, he'll probably end up spending more time with her now than he did when he was supposed to be living here."

"It's not going to be easy for you, or Lily." I think of his angry snarl when I drove past him in the road outside.

But Maria doesn't seem to be listening. Her eyes are the colour of warm chestnuts and I see the desire swelling in her eyes and butterflies rise in my stomach. A warm tingling sensation spreads down my arms and into my palms to the very tips of my fingers. I tilt my head to look at her more closely and I'm filled with a desire so intense that I want to take her in my arms. I want to hold her and make love to her. I want to feel her skin, suck her lips, taste her kiss and I am overwhelmed with love.

"I can't make any promises, Ellie."

"I understand Maria. I think it is best if I go. I left my car keys on the—" But Maria reaches out, takes my hand and clasps my fingers to her mouth. She places them against her lips and begins to nibble and lick them as she gazes into my eyes. She is sucking my fingers, her tongue probing between each one and she caresses the palm of my hand and my wrist.

"You can't go yet," she whispers. Her arm reaches behind me. Her lips nuzzle my neck and her tongue traces the outline of my stars and she takes my earlobe between her teeth. "I need you. And besides, you haven't told me how much you missed me."

"Lily's upstairs," my voice is barely a whisper. My resolve is crumbling I'm willing my body not to respond but desire is pulsating though me and I turn my cheek to inhale the freshness of her skin and my hand reaches to her breast.

"She's fast asleep and she won't wake up. We can go into the spare room."

I shake my head. "You're confused Maria. You're vulnerable. You're emotional coming home and you don't really know what or who you want."

My hand is inside her blouse and when I feel the softness of her skin my knees weaken. A shiver ripples though her body and a groan escapes her lips.

"Oh, yes I do," she purrs, her lips are on mine as she speaks. "I want you Ellie. I've missed you. I need you. Come and make love to me. Talk to me in Spanish, tell me how much you want me."

I can no longer resist and I'm wrapped in the softness of her lips. She is two separate women. She has two identities. Two personalities that compete with each other - one wanting me, the other resisting me. And I know that at this moment in time that is not Maria my friend speaking but Maria my lover. She is *The One*.

* * *

I have cleaned the house, made up the beds, shopped and stocked the fridge with wine and beer and I've prepared my special Tandoori chicken for dinner. It's the boys' favourite meal - and Spanish Cava is chilling in the ice bucket. Jenny, Richard and the boys arrive at seven and my step is as light as my heart at the thought of their company for the whole weekend. I haven't seen them for six months and it seems like an age.

I work out in the gym. Anna is not there as she is on night-shift this week at the hospital and I make a mental note to call her and Maxie and invite them for dinner the following week.

I go in search of Maria in her office. I want to make plans for them to meet my family over the weekend and I'm excited at the prospect.

She is wearing beaded pearl earrings and a simple gold wristwatch illuminates her tanned arm. I do not touch her. I do not think about kissing her or even allude to anything remotely romantic as I wait for her to finish her phone call.

Instead I reflect on the conversation we had after our love-making, two days ago, on her return from Lanzarote.

"There will never be anything between us. We can never have a permanent relationship. And we cannot be together — ever." Yes, I've heard it all before too, but here's the good part. She can't resist me. Presumably, I am kind and loving, a good friend and great fun but also sensual, sensitive, caring and deeply passionate. I think that's pretty good for a personal reference.

At least we are speaking and we're friends. This week she has settled back into office life and we even made time to eat a sandwich in the park yesterday lunch time, sitting in the sunshine on our favourite bench.

"I miss Lily's Friday visits," I say, when she hangs up the phone.

"Her ballet classes start again in September."

"September seems so far away. I can't begin to imagine where or what I will be doing," I reply, thinking of how Jenny will insist I return to London.

Maria gives me a puzzled look but says, "Michael wants Lily to go and stay with him in Dublin."

"Oh? How do you feel about that?"

"I can't stop her but I'm not thrilled about it either. I can't keep him away from her — he is her father — and she needs him. But the fact that she will be meeting his girlfriend bothers me. I can't bear the thought of another woman being friends with Lily or hugging her. But on the other hand I would hate her to be horrible to Lily." Her mouth turns down. "I tried to tell him it was too soon and that she needed more time. I even asked him to wait a while until he introduced his new girlfriend but he was furious."

"It is difficult. How does Lily feel?"

"She doesn't want to go."

"Does she have to go?"

"I think it's my duty to point out to her that she should go. I think she is only saying she doesn't want to go to be loyal to me. She's frightened of leaving me alone."

"That's understandable."

"What happened with you when your parents split up?"

"Mum was only too delighted to get rid of us in the summer. She sent us to Dad in Malaga so she could go off around Greece or Turkey or some lost island in Croatia with one of her young boyfriends."

"You didn't really have much emotional stability then?"

"I suppose I did." I stare out of the window. "They loved us. They both loved me and Jenny but they just fell out of love with each other. They were actually quite selfish and still are."

"Do you think your upbringing made you gay?"

I laugh, "Oh no. For that I had to download a recipe from the internet. You should try it sometime." Her eyes open wide and I laugh. "I'm joking, Maria. I've always known that I was gay. I was born this way. I was always drawn to girls and attractive women and the older I became, the more normal it felt. But it was just that you hid — or I did. Then I went to University in Madrid and realised it's not such a big deal. Maybe thirty or forty years ago it was, but times have changed, laws have changed, and there are equal rights and less stigma attached to being gay. Attitudes have changed in England too. And with the introduction of Civil Partnerships, and same-sex marriages it becomes more mainstream and it's definitely more acceptable. It's quite fashionable to be gay now, Maria. Most families have someone who swings the other way or isn't completely heterosexual. More people are out and proud. Look at the new girl downstairs. Jessica Charles who turned up for her interview wearing a rainbow T-shirt but poor John doesn't seem to have a clue. Because she's voluptuous and pretty he thinks she's straight but does it matter? Although, I suspect he has a crush on her." I smile at the memory.

"My family are stuck in a time-warp. They don't understand divorce let alone anyone being gay. They think it is normal to get married and stay married whether you are happy or not. But they're in shock. They haven't taken it well that Michael has left me."

Maria has brought me up to date with her family's attitude on her separation so I can't help teasing. "You didn't mention to them that you might be gay?"

"I'm not gay." Her eyes grow wide in denial.

"Ah."

"All I'm saying, Ellie, is that they are having trouble under-standing that Michael and I are separating. They don't believe in divorce."

"They'll be fine when they get used to the idea. It just takes time."

"I'm not holding my breath. They think it's all my fault that Michael has fallen in love and run off with a younger girl."

"They have to blame someone."

Maria contemplates me for a second and her eyes twinkle. "Have you ever thought you would like to get married or have a civil partnership?"

"Well now, Maria, is that a proposal?"

She laughs and shakes her head. "Not me, I'm married and never again. But are you frightened of commitment, Ellie?"

"It's not about commitment Maria. I'm frightened that once my partner says I do, she will find out what I'm really like and will fall out of love and leave me."

* * *

"Crawfordsburn National Park is one of my favourite places. I often walk through the forest trail or down onto the beach and take the footpath right toward the Irish Sea. Left takes you back toward Holywood and Belfast Lough," I explain to Jenny pointing.

On a clear day, like today, the coast of Scotland shimmers on the horizon, slow-moving tankers and cargo ships enter the Lough and planes fly in low to land at the City airport.

"I haven't been here for years," says Maria.

"Nor me. We came once as children but I don't really remember it," adds Jenny.

"Will we set up our picnic under the shade of this beech tree?" Richard calls.

"Great idea."

And very soon the air is filled with burning charcoal as he barbecues sausages, burgers and chicken wings.

Jenny pours wine for the adults and soft drinks for the children. Maria uncovers dishes of crispy salad, mayonnaise potatoes, packets of crisps and fresh rolls. It's like their maternal instincts have taken over and I feel redundant so I drift between supervising Richard cooking and wandering down to check on the children playing on the beach, content to be a part of the family but not an integral cog. Happy to listen and not to speak. Pleased to watch rather than participate.

Jake and Matt are both captivated by Lily. From the minute they met, they all made friends and chatted easily. Lily's confidence and natural ease has charmed the boys who like to push the boundaries. This appeals to Lily's sense of mischief. I watch them laughing and picking at broken shells and odd shaped stones. They perch on rocks and paddle ankle deep in the water. Sometimes splashing and, at other moments, they seem to speak effortlessly and quietly — as children do — locked in a world away from inquisitive adults and I wonder what they say to each other.

We eat a long and noisy lunch around a wooden trestle table then afterwards the boys and Lily venture back to the beach. They are giggling and daring, egging each other on, filled with summer naughtiness and it makes us laugh.

Occasionally I feel Maria's eyes on me and when I look up she holds my gaze and we share a warm smile. It gives me a snugly feeling in the base of my stomach and makes my fingers tingle. She looks happy. Her skin glows and her eyes shine. She laughs a lot and that's the most important thing for me.

Later in the afternoon Richard buys us fluffy ice creams. Jenny opens more wine and Maria talks about her separation. Michael's name is on her lips. But in a moment when we are not observed she reaches a hand under the table and I stroke her fingers. Her hand is on my thigh and I revel in the warmth of our love, remembering our recent passion and the intensity of our love-making.

Then suddenly, in the middle of this perfectly warm and glowing Sunday afternoon, I have a terrible premonition. Maria might meet another man. She might one day fall in love with someone who could be a father to Lily in a structured family environment. That would be acceptable to her family and it is what she wants.

I move away. My mouth is dry and I have a sudden urge to escape. I mumble an excuse, refuse to meet her questioning look and head down to the sea. Farther down the beach Lily, Jake and Matt's laughter floats on the breeze as they leap over shallow waves, pushing, daring and laughing.

Families are spread out in the sun basking on colourful towels with buckets and spades at their feet. Children build rugged sand castles that are partially crumbled from lapping waves. Babies with sturdy pink legs totter happily at the edge of the water. And for a moment I resent all these happy and domesticated families.

I will never be able to share my life with Maria as they do with their partners and children. Tears fill my eyes and I concentrate on the horizon and the heat-shimmering coast of Scotland.

Richard appears beside me and begins to skim stones across the water. "Are you okay?"

"It's a great place to live," I reply. It isn't what he means and we both know it.

"You know how much Jenny wants you to come home."

"Yes, she spent all day yesterday trying to convince me to come back to London."

"She's worried about you. And, we all miss you."

"I miss you all too but coming back to London isn't an option at the moment." I don't tell him that Maria's seduction technique on the night she arrived home from Lanzarote has completely bewitched me. I'm utterly in love with a woman who denies she's gay and who insists can never have a proper relationship with me.

"Are you going to continue living in Auntie Annie's house?"

I try to skim a flat stone but it plops to the bottom of the sea. "I'm not sure. I'm thinking of selling my London flat."

"It would be great if you could invest that money in property here. Housing is increasing in value and it would be good to get in at the bottom before it shoots sky high."

Sometimes I forget Richard is in finance.

"You can see the level of investment here already," he continues. "It's just a matter of time. You'll easily make a profit. If you don't leave it too late."

"It would make sense for me to buy something over here.

Besides it would be lovely to have my own things around me again. I left everything behind."

"You'll probably need a bigger place than the one you have in London though."

"Why?" I squint at him.

"Maria and Lily?"

I shake my head. "I don't know, Richard. I haven't been down that route. Her husband has only just left her."

"It's something you might have to think about."

"The whole situation is impossible. Fortunately, you and Jenny understand my lifestyle but her family wouldn't. She only told her mother this week that Michael has left her and she's furious. In fact the whole family have turned against her and blamed her saying it's all her fault for not keeping him happy. They don't believe in divorce and they are urging her to go and get him back."

"It's time they lived in the modern world."

"Tell them that."

"Divorce is commonplace and, there are also lots of gay couples living happily together. In California there are over forty-thousand children living with same sex couples. It's only narrow minded bigots you have to worry about, but then again, they're not worth worrying about anyway."

"Maria's family seem to come into that category. And, anyway, you seem to be well up on it all, Richard. Are you in touch with your sexuality?" I joke and stoop to select another flat pebble.

"You'd be very surprised at the people that I meet. Even a boring accountant becomes confidant to couples when they are looking for a loan or mortgage. I'm amazed at the amount of same sex couples there are, and same sex marriage. I think that by the time the boys are my age it will be the norm and no one will bat an eye lid."

"So how would you feel if one of your boys turned out gay? It's always a different matter then."

I watch him scrutinise the pebble he's holding before he flings his arm wide and casts it into the sea. He is a gentleman. Not some strutting Alpha-male or like John who tries unsuccessfully to be macho or Michael who wants to bed every woman. He's kind and caring and there isn't a vindictive bone in his body. He listens to understand. He speaks to make sense of what he hears, and he's compassionate and sensible. Jenny is a very lucky woman.

He shrugs. "My son will be no less of a man if he is gay. Every parent hopes for the best for their child and that's all we want for Matt and Jake. I want my sons to be happy and if it happens to be with another man then, what can I do about it? Don't get me wrong, society makes life easier for heterosexual couples but having met many gay people, I do understand their situation. It isn't always acceptable or easy but eventually attitudes will change."

"And what about children in same sex relationships? What about Lily? She will be tormented at school."

"In every walk of life we must stand up to bullies whoever we are and whatever the circumstances. Bullies are cowards and often emotionally stunted. Isn't it more important that Lily is loved by as many people as possible? It's up to Maria and her husband to explain their love. And if Maria is in love with a woman and wants to share her life with her, then she must explain that to Lily."

"You're speaking to the converted," I say. "Maria is from a staunch Catholic family who believe firmly in the bible and the concept of man, woman and marriage equals child and family, and in that order."

"Well, if that's true, then her family will already be dealing with divorce so maybe that's a step closer in the real world."

The sun dips behind a cloud and I shiver. I think of Maria's mother Brenda and a giant shadow is cast upon the beach and over my heart.

"Maria's family is important to her but I also realise how resentment, stubbornness and ignorance can be part of a family's indoctrination process," I say. "They would never accept me. And Maria will not put me before them. She cannot live without them and their endorsement of her life. They mean too much to her."

"Is that what you think?"

"Either that or she doesn't love me enough." The flat-stone I skim doesn't bounce and it plops immediately under the water.

* * *

A few days later, we are in the office kitchen finishing a lunch of tuna, mayonnaise and sweetcorn salad when Maria says to me, "Lily is increasingly difficult. She's even started to argue with Grandma Brenda and she's been very rude to everyone. She even swore at Connor's two boys last night when they changed the television channel."

I suppress a smile. "I would swear under those circumstances. Have you spoken to her about it?"

"I did last night. After she told Pat she hated them all."

"She's just hurting. It's a difficult time for her."

"I know, so I told her to invite Charlie over tonight for

dinner."

"Why not bring them over to me?" I say, and Maria looks surprised. "It will be a change of scene for them and besides Lily has always been curious to see where I live. Charlie will love it. So it's a good opportunity and it may help the situation."

Maria and I behave as friends, although occasions, our eyes hold each other's gaze and we share a loving smile or touch hands. Now she places her hand across the table and brushes my fingertips. "Thank you Ellie, you are so kind."

"I take it that's a yes, then?"

* * *

That evening I make a big show of preparing a barbecue. First, I throw cocktail sausages onto the grill then I marinade chicken in Cajun spices, add two red peppers, cloves of garlic and a generous douse of olive oil. In a separate dish I make a summer salad with chopped baby tomatoes, spring onions and small wedges of avocado. I add a handful of fresh coriander and juice from a whole lime.

Lily stands beside me mixing, stirring and poking the chicken into submission in the marinade and Charlie watches me make a salad dressing.

"It's one of my father's recipes: take one freshly squeezed orange, two cloves of garlic and a dash of olive oil," I tell them as I toss the ingredients into a bowl and stir.

Maria mixes gin and tonics but she is unusually quiet. She seems content to listen and watch us fooling around, singing to music, and our silly banter as we eat in the garden.

After dinner it turns chilly so I put on a *Harry Potter* DVD on in the lounge for the girls. They have seen it before but are happy to curl up on the big sofas with a cosy blanket over them and Maria and I sit outside, dressed in our fleeces and sip white wine.

"So? What's happened? What's wrong?" I ask.

"Is it that obvious?"

"It is to me, Maria. I do know you, remember? I am your friend."

She regards me carefully before she replies, "Sometimes I think you understand me better then I understand myself." She sighs. "Pat thinks I've let Michael down and that's why he has gone off with another woman and I should do more to get him back for Lily's sake. Then Pat and Mum ganged up on me again and when Connor came in I ended up having a blazing row with them all."

"Well, it isn't the first time they've said this to you. Why didn't you tell me earlier you were upset?"

"I can't come running to you every time something happens. I have to stand on my own feet. At least Joe is kind to me. He's been very thoughtful. He's great to speak to."

I know that Maria's eldest brother Joe is her favourite.

"I'm pleased he is supportive." I bite the skin at the end of my finger then stop. I am suddenly incensed at her insensitive family. "But what do they expect you to do, Maria? It was Michael who went off with someone else. He even invited her to a hotel with your money. But you would never have left him. You made no secret of that." To my shame my tone sounds bitter.

"Connor said that I haven't made much effort with my marriage in the past year or so. He must have spoken to Michael at some stage and Michael said it was my fault that he found someone else — someone younger."

"But what is it to do with him? Anyway, I suppose the good news is that I am not to blame. That would have been worse."

"You? Why would this have anything to do with you?"

"Just the obvious reason — or have you forgotten?"

She leans forward and hisses, "What happened between us has nothing to do with Michael leaving me. You need to know that Ellie. I was bored. I have been bored and fed up for years. It was only when you arrived that I finally found a sense of adventure."

"I led you astray."

"It could have been you or anyone."

"What? Great. Thanks. That makes me feel good." I stand and take a few paces around the garden. There's so much I want to say but more than that, I want her to say so much more to me. There seems to be a great chunk missing that she conveniently forgets. That I am *The One,* or that I make her feel special or the fact that she has never in her entire life made love to anyone like she does to me.

"Anyone?" I ask. "So, it could have been me or anyone?"

"I didn't mean that Ellie. I'm sorry. I'm vulnerable. I was in a stagnant marriage. My husband was never here. It might have happened at any time — perhaps with anyone. Don't take it personally. Just give me time, Ellie. It's this situation that isn't helping."

"I thought I was more important than that. I thought I was *The One.* I'm not a doormat, Maria, nor will my feelings be reduced to nothing. How silly of me. All this time I've been thinking that we had something very special. All your declarations of love now sound very, very hollow." I reach over the table and pick up my wine glass. I take it inside and I sit watching television with the girls until it's time for them to leave. I have nothing left to say.

* * *

I'm on automatic pilot over the next few days. I'm numb. I'm angry with myself realising my hopes and my expectations have now dissipated to nothing. I'm shocked with Maria and how cold she is toward me.

She blames her family for her complete inertia. When she loves me I feel special. I'm happy and filled with hope. This creates expectations and fuels my dreams but when her emotional shutters come down, I'm left grieving wondering who it is she loves. On the one hand, I am *The One* but on the other hand, she won't fight for me. I will never be first or even second in her life. I will be in a line of countless family members from whom she constantly seeks approval, endorsement and support. Does that make her a genuinely selfless mother or is she weak and fickle in her love?

Who is the real Maria? My friend or my lover?

There's a noticeable shift in our friendship. I'm hurt and she can do nothing to make me feel better. She is too busy coping with the problems in her own life. Our conversations are cordial but I'm frustrated and tired. I have to continually wait for Maria to show any warmth or affection toward me. Although she attempted an apology for what she said on Wednesday evening, I'm as helpless as a pawn in a complicated chess game.

On Friday afternoon, Lily phones me in the office from grandma Brenda's. She insists that I go over for dinner to their house and, as if to reinforce the idea, Maria stands beside me, smiling, at my desk and rubs my arm encouragingly.

It's the first intimate contact we have had and I'm both warmed and upset at the reaction Maria has on me. Goose-bumps break out on my skin and I want to take her in my arms but I know that if I make a move toward her she will turn away. Is that love? Or is she protecting herself and her emotions?

****

That evening at Maria's house I'm not angry but I am un-comfortable. Maria's conversation is friendly and safe. It consists of *Masterchef*, *Britain's Got Talent* and *Simon Cowell*, and popular songs on the radio and a new drama series on TV.

Lily shoves Lasagne into the oven, made earlier by Maria, with the aplomb and the smile of a magician carving a body in half. She is curtseying and bowing to our applause when the front door bell rings.

Maria leaves the room and I hear voices in the hallway.

Lily, who is leaning on a barstool at the island worktop with me, leaps up. "Auntie Pat, Auntie Pat," she calls and disappears, and I'm left in that awkward moment where I can hear everything but see nothing.

I hear Maria explaining my presence. "Ellie is a colleague. She works with me in the Marketing department."

Pat is heavily built with thick ankles and a double chin. Unlike Maria's rich dark hair Pat's is nondescript and mousey. It's tied in a pony-tail and she wears round Harry Potter glasses just like Lily's.

I know that Pat moved to a new job in the Civil Service

recently and, for some reason, I see her as a stereotypical bureaucrat at work, unhelpful and unfriendly.

When we're introduced, Pat barely takes her eyes from Lily. She doesn't hold out her hand or smile so I turn away and focus my attention on the garden. It's more interesting.

I sense that Maria is also uncomfortable and to make matters worse Lily insists Pat stays for dinner.

It is a meal that I cannot describe. Only to say it couldn't have been over quick enough. I have put my knife and fork together on my plate and I'm thinking of an excuse to leave when Connor, Kate and their two noisy and horrible children decide to pop in just to see how 'Maria is coping alone.'

Fortunately Lily takes the two noisy brats to watch TV in the lounge and although I want to go home, I'm torn between staying. They're all worried about Maria and I'm keen to listen to their advice.

"We only came over as we thought you were on your own and you'd like the company," Connor says, and regards me with frank disdain. "Didn't realise you would be socialising."

"She's separated - not in mourning," I joke.

"It's not too late win Michael back," says Pat, who ignores me. "You did something right once. You managed to attract him the first time."

My smile fades.

"Ma's distraught, she can barely show her face to the neighbours. Divorce would be the final straw for her," Connor says,"It's a shame you haven't been more thoughtful."

"Michael is so understanding, surely you can talk him around," adds Pat. "It's probably just a hiccup and he'll be home next week. You shouldn't have told Ma. You should have waited and tried a bit harder instead of flying off to

Lanzarote and sunning yourself. That's hardly going to win Michael over, is it?"

"Pat's got a point," Connor says. "It would have been best to stay quiet until you had chance to speak to him and he came home."

"He's a good man and he doesn't deserve all this. The family can't all go against him. He'll never feel comfortable again with us all. Besides, you know how much Ma loves him." Pat stirs the pot of emotion with the proverbial wooden spoon. "It's not fair if everyone starts ganging up on him."

To my annoyance Maria says nothing. She sips her tea while I try to make eye contact with her. I'm furious. I'm willing her to say something in her defence. But she doesn't. She stares meekly into her swirling tea. Why doesn't she stand up for herself?

"He's made a mistake," says Connor. "He knows it. He'll be back. You'll soon be back to normal. These things happen."

"You haven't been yourself since he left." Kate speaks for the first time, in tandem with her husband. "You need him. Perhaps you're depressed?"

"You should go to Dublin and fetch him back. Give him a good talking to. That's what I would do." Pat's glasses slide down her perspiring nose. "I'd get in my car, and confront that woman who has obviously led him astray and tell him just how much you need him. Tell him how you can't live without him and what damage this is all doing to Lily, let alone our Ma."

Pat isn't even married so I think this is rich advice coming from her. It's obvious she has a crush on Michael and I'm on the verge of suggesting that she should be the one gets in her car and goes and keeps him for herself, when she says she has spoken to their eldest brother.

"Even Joe thinks that you could do more, he said—" Maria's eyes darken. She holds up the palm of her hand and replies in a very soft yet clear voice. "I have spoken to Joe. I know this is tough on Lily, and it is hard on Ma and all of you, but to be honest, I'm not sure if I want Michael back. Things will never be the same. Not one of you have considered how I'm feeling in all of this and you're determined that it is all my fault. Well, let me tell you. My marriage is over."

"Hallelujah," I sing loudly, and my slow hand clapping fills the room startling them all. I can't help myself. My smile stretches across my face as three furious faces stare at me with something akin to hatred.

* * *

After the disastrous evening at Maria's on Friday night with her well-meaning but odious siblings, I spend the weekend partying. It's not as if I am included in Maria's life. She never asks what I'm doing or what my plans are. She just seems to think I'm available as and when she needs me. It's my own fault. I've been too readily available and there's only so much I can take. There's only so much goodness inside me and when I get pushed too far I become a rebel.

Things must change.

I meet Anna, Maxie and Carla for dinner in town on Saturday night where I drink copious amounts of red wine and get very drunk. Afterward, we go on to a trendy club and I am so enamoured with my new friends that I invite them all to Sunday lunch the following day in Auntie Annie's house.

It seems a good idea at the time and Saturday night flows

into a Sunday lunch barbecue in my garden. Anna, Maxie and Carla help me shop, cook and clean up. We all drink far too much and laugh loudly. It is hot and sunny and we dance in bare feet on the grass as if we're teenagers and our parents have left us alone at home. Suzie with the tight smile and Mary are definitely a couple. There are a few single people, and Dave and Roger who have been together for seven years. As the evening wears on we chat quietly with rugs around our shoulders swapping stories, anecdotes and jokes, and I finally feel like I belong. I have a warm snugly feeling; I'm making friends, having fun and finally fitting in with my new life.

On Monday morning, I venture into the office kitchen in search of caffeine. My shoulders are sore, my head aches and my mouth is like sandpaper.

"You look rough." Maria regards me carefully. She pours coffee and holds out a mug. "Where have you been?"

"Thanks." I take the coffee and I don't look at her. I sip it carefully aware that my eyes are red and sore. "I was out with friends. It was a bit of a weekend. I suppose I got a bit carried away."

"Oh? Who with? I didn't think you knew anyone up here."

"I met a girl at the gym when you were away."

"Did you?"

I smile at the frown on her face. "Anna - she's a nurse at the city hospital. She introduced me to her girlfriend, Maxie, and some other friends and I've been out with them a few times. We were out on Saturday night and in a moment of complete madness in the club, on Saturday night, I invited a roomful of people to a barbecue at home yesterday." I shake my head and giggle at the memory. "I lost count of how many people turned up in the end — probably a dozen."

Maria stares at me. Her eyes are not smiling and her voice is terse. "That must have been fun."

"It was."

The phoning begins ringing in her office and she leaves to answer it but not before I see a flicker of doubt, concern, or was it jealousy in her eyes?

Good. It's a small triumph but unfortunately it doesn't make me feel better.

It's a very slow and long day and I feel ill.

Simon is out of the office.

Ray is sick.

Liam is on holiday.

John is on a day off, and Stuart is sulking. He misses Siobhan and when he tells me she's having a brilliant time in London he doesn't smile.

It's Monday and we're all miserable. All caught up the emotions of our small worlds.

At lunchtime, I am startled when Louise pops her head around my door and suggests lunch in Mauds. Eager to escape the confines of my four office walls I jump at the chance but then sitting in the cafe I listen for an hour as she tells me her problems.

"Simon is so stubborn," she says with a mouthful of a prawn sandwich. "I can't seem to get through to him. A family is important to me and he just doesn't understand. We're talking about divorce. I can't live my life like this —I don't feel complete..."

She continues her monologue about wanting children but I'm only half listening. I'm fed up. Between Maria and Michael and her family's advice. And now Simon and Louise, children or no children, I've had enough of married couples and I feel blessed to be gay and single and even hungover.

After lunch, I stroll through the park on my own. I stop at our favourite bench where Maria and I have shared sandwiches and discussed the pros and cons of living happily ever after and I feel a pang of sadness. My life is like a chess game and it appears to have arrived at stalemate. I have no solutions and no answers. Even flirting with the gorgeous Carla at my barbecue didn't inspire me. It's Maria who continues to occupy my heart.

I'm tired and fed up when I get to my office. All I want to do is flop in the seat and close my eyes but someone is already sitting at my desk.

Lily has a scowl on her face. Her eyes are dark and she looks tired and angry.

"That chair suits you," I say, slouching in the visitors chair opposite her. "You can have it. You can do my work too because I can't be bothered."

She places her chin in her hand and looks serious. I think she is about to cry. "I'm not happy."

Join the club, I want to say, but out of my mouth come the words. "Want to tell me why?"

"What if I don't like her?"

I contemplate her question carefully. I remember Lily is due to visit Michael and his new girlfriend but I am not sure when. "I'm sure you will like her. Try to remember that she is probably just as nervous about meeting you. And, she is probably hoping that you will like her a lot."

"Do you think?" Lily pushes her round glasses back onto her nose and I nod gravely. "Mum says I have to go and stay with them - this weekend…"

"Don't be so glum about it. You might even enjoy yourself."

"I won't like her. I know I won't."

"Try not to be prejudge her. Keep an open mind and an open heart. She may be very nice and very kind."

"She hasn't been kind to Mum."

"Perhaps not but that is up to your Mum and her. Their situation is different to yours. You have to judge someone on how they treat you. You cannot fight your mother's battles, nor would she want you to."

"Grandma Brenda says she's a…hussy."

"Yes, well…" I try not to smile. "You will find that everyone will have their own opinions. You love your father, just remember that, and he loves you. So focus on your relationship with him. If you feel a sense of conflict or you're uneasy about something then you must be honest and speak to him, or to your Mum, or both of them. Try and give them chance to explain things so that you will understand the situation better and feel more comfortable. It's going to be difficult for everyone."

She nods seriously. "But it's not my fault."

I lean across the desk. "No. It definitely isn't your fault. It's just life and relationships. Will you promise to try and keep an open mind and an open heart?"

"I suppose…"

"Good."

"What about you?"

"Me?"

"Yeah. That's what I want to speak to you about. Mum will be so lonely on her own. I've never left her before. Will you look after her for me while I'm gone?"

"I will, if she will let me," I reply honestly.

Chapter Fourteen

Simon has begun his disappearing act again. Although I feel sorry for his personal situation I'm frustrated as I'm left to open up new negotiations, hoover up the details of new contracts and sort out ongoing problems. Secretly, a part of me wonders if he's selling the company. Perhaps he's arranging some complicated deal with foreign investors and doing some big deal behind our backs. Rumour has it that he's in America again and that Louise has gone with him.

John and Jessica are both in my office and we're going through all the app contracts that have been signed and a list of pending contracts. We're also preparing new targets for a marketing strategy. He is happy with Jessica Charles. He has told me on numerous occasions that she is capable and hard working and, more importantly, she has earned respect in the techie lab. I like her because she's smart and positive - she never says a job can't be done and I respect her for that. I suspect his crush on her is on-going and I feel rather sorry that he pursues girls out of his league. He appears to have transferred his fickle affection from Maria, to me and now to Jessica as lonely, single men are often wont to do.

Jessica seems not to notice. She's dressed in her white lab coat and has long painted nails, different rainbow colours, and she takes notes diligently of her tasks in the coming weeks. Following every decision, comment and conclusion John says, "Happy Days," and it takes me a while to realise he actually doesn't bother me any more.

Maria was right when she said all those months ago that John was like a puppy underneath because when he's relaxed he has that enthusiastic and naive quality about him.

Once the meeting is over and Jessica has gone downstairs, he leans across the table and glances over his shoulder before he speaks, as if there is someone lurking in the corridor who may hear him, and he says, "She also plays pool."

"That's great. You did well recruiting her. She's a team player," I reply.

He nods in satisfaction then says, "Do you think Simon's having an affair?"

I shake my head in mock admonishment and exasperation at his line of thought. "Well, if he is, John, it has nothing to do with us."

"It's just that he's been hanging around at Mickey Bleu's. They seem very good friends."

"How do you know that?" I pretend I'm not taking him seriously and I flick through = papers on my desk but my mind gathers speed.

"Can I be honest?" he says, checking again there is no-one lurking in the doorway.

"Of course."

"Well, I know that we haven't always seen eye to eye Ellie, but that was in the past. It's just that I'm worried about the company and what's going to happen in the future."

Now he has my full attention and I stop what I'm doing. I try not to look at his bulging tummy hanging over his waist band or at the shiny sheen of perspiration above his top lip. There is a tang of stale tobacco from his mouth and I lean away from him but I don't take my eyes from his. I want him to trust me and to tell me what he knows.

"He's been going to the Mickey's Deli nearly every night."

"So? Maybe he's hungry. If he and Louise are not getting on, then it's somewhere for him to go and eat. It passes a few hours before going home."

"He stays until closing and the other night he waited for Mickey to finish work and they drove off in his car."

"How do you know all this?"

"I just happened to be in town and I saw him — I saw them."

"So?" I am not even going to ask him if he is stalking Simon. He removes his hands from his pockets and leans his elbows on the desk. "I think they are having an affair."

"Have you met Emmanuel?"

"Who?"

"Mickey Bleu's husband. They have two beautiful children. They are perfectly happy. Just because someone gets in a car with someone else doesn't mean they are meeting in secret or having an affair."

"I'm aware of that," he says patiently. "But what if he's got some other motive? She knows a lot of people in America. Investors and companies, people with a lot of money and influence. Perhaps he wants to sell Bizweb to one of those investors."

"Perhaps the world is flat." I stand up to end this meeting. "I cannot live in a world of, what if this, or what if that, John. What's to be is to be - end of story. If he is having an affair or if he is selling the company then there isn't much you or I can do about it, can we?"

He stands up and with his hands in his trouser pockets and his white shirt and skewed tie, he reminds me of a naughty schoolboy.

"I won't let him sell the company," he says. "I've worked too dammed hard. All these years down the drain for nothing? Just for him to sell it off and for me to be replaced by someone younger and more energetic — with an American accent. It's not going to happen. I'll stop him. I will. He isn't going to sell everything that I've worked so hard to build up. It's been blood sweat and tears. It even cost me my marriage. I've nothing left to lose and I'm not losing Bizweb."

I rub the back of my neck. I have an increasingly bad headache. "Well then, speak to Simon. Wait until he gets back to the office and then tell him how you feel."

After John leaves, I begin thinking that one way of sabotaging the sale of the company would be to create a virus or a worm, like Dominator, and a feeling of unease settles over me. I wonder to what lengths John will go to have his own way and to stop the sale of the company. I'm also concerned that John is following Simon and spying on Mickey Bleu. It all seems very sinister.

* * *

Later in the week, we're drinking coffee in Maria's office. She is on the verge of tears. Her bottom lip quivers as she struggles to maintain control and she pushes her hand through her hair, pulling it into a twisted bun and securing it in a bulldog clip.

"He wouldn't come into the house. He just stood on the doorstep like a stranger and waited for Lily. He had on a new shirt and jacket that I haven't seen before, and his hair is cut

230

shorter. He stood there like a soldier on duty at Checkpoint Charlie."

I move away from the window to stand beside her. I reach out and rub her shoulders gently feeling the knotted tension under her skin.

"Lily didn't want to go with him at all. She didn't want to meet her — to meet his you know — girlfriend. I don't even know what to call her. I feel I've forced Lily into it. She will be so miserable."

"You didn't force her but you did have to make it look as if you didn't mind too much. It is something you are going to have to get used to. It was the right thing to do."

I drop my hand and she looks tearfully up at me. "The thought of another woman looking after Lily for a week infuriates me. Why a whole week? He's never spent so long with her before. She's mine."

"I understand that but she also belongs to Michael."

"What does he know?"

"He's her father. It will give them time to get to know each other and get closer. Every child needs their father too."

She shakes her head as if this motion will empty her tear filled eyes. "That's the repayment I get is it? All these years of marriage and all I get is to be a single mother. And he will get closer to Lily because we are no longer together. He will spoil her for a week then leave me to cope with bringing her up the rest of the time. It will be easier for him with another woman. They will take over. They will do girlie things together and…"

"It doesn't seem fair Maria but that's the way life is some-times."

"What if Lily likes them? What if she likes staying with them and wants to spend more time with them than with me? I don't mean this summer but next year or the year after. What if she wants to go and live with them?"

"Don't start paying the 'what if' game, Maria. It won't do you any good. It will be a long and difficult road for you these next few months, perhaps even years, but you must do the best thing possible for you and Lily, and you must be strong. You must also try to start a new life and to have fun."

"This morning, after Lily left, it was like the core of my life has been sucked out of me and I have been left to shrivel up to nothing. I've never been without her. I wandered through the house, through all the rooms feeling their emptiness knowing the soul has gone from them. The house feels different. It is different. It's empty. I'm empty without her." She rubs her eyes and stretches her neck and continues, "Sorry Ellie, I always dump my emotions on you. I do appreciate it. Thanks for being here for me. I wish I was brave like you."

The phone in my room rings and as I leave her office she says, "I'm going to have to speak to Simon with all this new business there is so much work here now. I'm finding it hard to keep on top of things."

"You need an assistant," I agree. "Hang on in there, Maria. We will get everything sorted. Everything will work out in the end. We need to speak to Simon about a good few things."

I spend a few hours dealing with the urgent business on my desk and shift anything remotely unimportant or pending to one side for next week. Then I spend the next hour trawling through the internet. It is almost three-thirty when I go back into Maria's office and when she looks up her eyes are red-rimmed either from crying or from working.

"Right. Come on. We're going. We're leaving early and getting out of here."

"Going where?"

"I've made a reservation in a small hotel in Donegal and we're getting out of here right now. Come on, turn your computer off."

"I can't."

"Can't what? Turn off your computer? Then I'll do it." I reach over but before I reach the button she has done it.

"I can't go anywhere," she protests.

"Why not?" I fling my arms wide open. "Sorry? Is there something you haven't told me? Like, you have an exciting date tonight or there's something important on your agenda for this weekend?"

She shakes her head. "Just Mum. I said we would go shopping together. I can't take off just like that." She clicks her fingers.

"Yes, you can." I stand with my hands on my hips doing my best to look sexy and provocative.

"You have to be honest with your Mum and tell her you've had a better offer. Come on. Chop chop! We need to get home and pack an overnight bag. It's about time you discovered one of the joys of being a single Mum. It's called freedom."

"What about Lily?"

"Lily isn't here. She's in Dublin. Besides we'll be back on Sunday night and Lily isn't home until next week."

"What about my mother?" She looks at me with brown excited eyes.

"Well, she's DEFINITELY not coming with us. Come on, hurry up or I won't wait for you..."

* * *

Donegal is a dream. We book into a small hotel in the beautiful St. John's Point. We arrive in time for a walk along the sandy beach then talk for hours in the gourmet restaurant with big windows and views overlooking the curved bay. We watch the Atlantic Ocean's tumbling waves crash gently against the shore as we eat fresh turbot and drink chilled Chablis from crystal goblets. We laugh and talk with ease and familiarity. We are excited, happy and relaxed. I'm with Maria my lover and not Maria my friend.

Later, we retire to our room and make love with gentle tenderness and wild passion, satisfying our senses and filling our soul. Maria is *The One* for me and I know that at this moment she feels the same about me.

Afterward she snuggles into me and I lie awake relishing her soft snoring and inhale the natural and unique scent of her skin. It is musky, sweet and warm. And, as she sleeps in my arms, I think of the impossibility of our situation. It's the reality of life that comes between our relationship; attitudes, prejudices and stubbornness and I feel as doomed as Romeo and Juliet.

In the morning, after a lazy breakfast, we walk barefoot in the sand. The summer heatwave is trailing off and the air is fresh, relaxing and rejuvenating. The cold Atlantic waves tickle my toes and salt from the sea breeze settles on my lips. My skin grows darker, I have my father's Mediterranean olive colouring and I tan easily. The sun has made Maria's cheeks pink and I find new freckles dotted across the tip of her nose.

"I feel free and at peace," she says, when I reach out to hold her hand and we pause to admire the rugged countryside where fields of strong horses, grazing cows and wandering sheep live contentedly, and she rests her head against my shoulder. We climb the hill and watch huge waves rising up and crashing to the shore on the rocks below, and we stand transfixed as the fishing boats unravel their orange nets and begin to unload their haul in the local harbour.

Maria sends a text to Lily. They have spoken together on the phone and exchanged photographs, and I know that although we're having fun, Lily is never far from her mind. She watches the fishermen as she speaks. "I feel the distance between Belfast to Donegal has given me a sense of perspective. A new way to look at my situation and it has revived my spirit. Thank you, Ellie. It's been therapeutic. It's strange to have no responsibility and no-one expecting me to do anything for them. I've always had to do things for others whether it's been Michael, Mum or Lily. Not that I mind doing anything for Lily but for the first time I'm beginning to feel that I can be me. I can have my own identity. Do you understand that?"

"You need to have your own life Maria. You must make a future for yourself and be your own person." And for some reason, I feel an unexplained and unexpected surge of hope.

* * *

After breakfast, the next day, we decide to take the longer and more scenic route back to Belfast. We stop for lunch in a pretty pub and it is while we are sitting in the garden at a wooden table, drinking chilled lager that Maria says to me, "I'm going to have to put the house on the market."

"So soon? Is there no way that you can stay there?"

"I can't afford a house that size and Michael won't support me any more than he has to. He will pay toward Lily but not for me to live in the house. I can't afford to pay for the mortgage and the bills on my salary."

I stare across the lawn to where a small boy sits playing with a plastic dinosaur. He makes unusual, guttural, sounds and runs it across the top of the table splashing its feet in spilt beer.

"There's something I haven't told you," she adds and takes a deep breath. My heart skips a beat and my mind races. "I told Joe about you."

"Joe? Your favourite brother? What did you say to him?"

"I didn't tell him about us. I just said that my friend at work was gay."

"Why?"

"I wanted to test his reaction."

"And? What did he say?"

"Nothing."

"That's a point in my favour then."

She ignores my sarcasm. "He asked, if Lily and I would move in with him. He thinks it's a good idea. He wants to move out of his flat and he says we could get somewhere together. He's been wanting to buy a bigger place for a while with a garden and he wants to buy a dog. He can't afford it on his own. He also said that he will be a father figure for Lily."

The invisible silence weighs between us tucking a blanket of reality around my thoughts. Maria's life is separate to mine. I'm not included in her future plans.

"And what do you think?"

"It's an option, Ellie. You know that Lily is my priority and I want to give her the best life possible. He's very good with her and they get on well and laugh lots."

"I have another option for you." The sun is beating on my face and I feel my cheeks redden. "You and Lily could—"

She holds up the palm of her hand. "Don't say it, Ellie. Please don't ask us to move in with you. That isn't an option and I'd hate to have to turn you down."

* * *

A week after our weekend in Donegal, Stuart is smiling again. Siobhan is in Belfast and back at work. It's Monday morning and I'm in the reception making photocopies and asking her what went wrong with her modelling experience in London.

"It was glamour modelling," Siobhan replies. Her hair is dyed jet black, her nails are pink and her smokey eyes painted green. "So I decided I'd better come home."

"Seedy Soho," I joke.

"Worse. I feel so silly."

"You did the right thing to come back. You must be careful."

She's looking over my shoulder and her mouth falls open. "Michael? Hi! What a surprise. I'll call Maria and let her know you are here."

Michael stares at me. He doesn't speak but his eyes are challenging. He's working his jaw as if he's controlling his temper. "I'm going to get you," he hisses. "You're messing with the wrong man."

Maria hurries down the stairs and she stops mid-stride but then she fixes her eyes on Michael.

"Is Lily alright? Where is she?"

"She's fine. I dropped her at your Mum's house. I want to speak to you — privately."

"I wanted you to bring Lily to the office. I want to see her. That was our arrangement you can't just change it. I didn't want her going to Grandma's until I've seen her."

"We need to talk, Maria," he insists, looking suddenly uncomfortable, conscious of me and Siobhan watching them. "Can we go somewhere?"

"Let's go across the road," Maria says opening the door, "to the park."

I watch from the window as they cross the road. They're a good-looking couple. They walk with ease and in pace with each other. They appear so natural that they could be lovers. A sense of unease spreads though me and my heart somersaults and, I realise I'm jealous.

* * *

What happened next? Well, I wasn't there. So I'll tell it to you as Maria told it to me afterwards as we sat drinking coffee in Maud's.

She said:

Although it's warm, my body is shivering and shaking inside my skin. Not because Michael seems different. He has a new haircut that makes him look more youthful but he walks faster. His stride is long and purposeful and the tiredness and stress around his eyes has gone.

When we sit on the bench in the sunshine. It's our bench. The one where we always sit. Where we spoke about living happily ever after. I remember all the times we've eaten our lunch here but I'm uneasy. I feel you beside me but I'm frightened that Michael will also feel your presence.

He is angry. I can tell. His jaw grinds and his chin is set at an angle that I know means trouble. I wonder if it's to do with Lily or my mother, so I challenge him first.

"Why did you change our arrangement? I wanted Lily to

come to the office." I knew that you had missed her, Ellie. She wanted to see you and I am so angry with him. "Who do you think you are, changing our plans? It's so typical of you to do what you want without thought or regard for anyone else." And it dawns on me, he has been doing exactly what he wants to do throughout our whole marriage. He has been completely selfish. Whether it was playing golf, disappearing for weekends to Dublin, or not taking Lily or I out. He has always pleased himself.

He places his arms on his knees twisting his index finger as he speaks. I notice that he has removed his wedding band. "Look, I'm going to keep this brief, Maria. We're separated and I'm filing for a divorce but I will object to Lily being influenced by a lesbian who wants to become a father figure to Lily. I will go to court for custody—"

"What?"

"I mean it. I don't want that type of woman involved with my daughter. God knows what sort of long-term effect it will have on Lily and what she will learn."

"Michael what are you talking about?"

"Ellie is gay. Don't pretend you don't know."

"That's none of your business, Michael. It's no concern of yours or anyone else's." But I am wondering how he knows and my heart is racing.

"It is my concern, especially if she's spending time with my daughter. Then it becomes my problem."

I panic but my anger grows. "How dare you interfere with my life? Who are you to sit and judge anyone? Besides, Ellie is a very kind and good person and, even if she were gay, it would be no concern of yours. My friends and colleagues have every right to be Lily's friends too."

"I don't want a dyke influencing my daughter."

"Ellie is my friend and her sexuality isn't an issue, and neither is the sexuality of any other friends I have. It doesn't matter if they are gay, bisexual, transsexual or anything else so long as they are decent people. Who are you to say what friends I can and can't have? What happens if I meet a man and start dating? Are you going to object to each one of them? Are you going to be interrogating Lily about the suitability of all my new boyfriends and lovers?"

"You won't date again. You won't get a lover."

"Why not?"

"What about Lily?"

"It didn't stop you."

"That's not the point. You're her mother."

"That doesn't mean I can't fall in love with anyone else or that I can't experience love or happiness or I'll never make love to anyone else. Michael I'm thirty-five. I might even have another child."

He rises angrily to his feet and stands glaring down at me. "That's ridiculous."

"It's not as ridiculous as you. Thinking you can choose my friends or have any influence over who Lily likes or doesn't like. She's very sensible and thank goodness she's not bigoted and arrogant like her father. Ellie is Lily's friend. She has been very kind to her during these past months when - I can honestly say - herfatherhasn'tputLilyfirstonce."

"You're sleeping with her, aren't you?"

"No."

"You are."

"It's none of your business."

"You can't have a relationship with her."

"I'll have a relationship with whoever I like."

"If you are, I'll sue you for custody of Lily."

I stand up and glare into his eyes. "Grow up, Michael. In case you've forgotten, you're the one who walked out. You'll never get custody of Lily and if you did, she would hate you forever. Is that what you want?" I taunt him with a confident smile. "Besides, equality rules Michael. Civil Partnerships are all the rage now. It's quite fashionable to be gay. It's legal here in Northern Ireland or hadn't you heard?"

He grits his teeth. His fingers are clenched into fists. "If you think I'm angry now, this is nothing, Maria, I can get much worse and it won't be nice or pleasant. You don't know how far I will to go to stop you from being with her. You will never be together. I will destroy you both. And Lily will be with me. You will be left with nothing."

* * *

Lily has spent the past two days with Maria's family. Grandma Brenda, Pat, Connor and his family, and tomorrow Joe is taking them into the country, horse-riding.

Tonight it is my turn and to celebrate her return we eat in an Italian restaurant.

"No fatted calf, " I say. "But pizza is a great option."

"Fat calf?"

I explain to her that it's like the re-run of the prodigal son and explain the parable and compare her situation with that of the two brothers in the New Testament. Where the eldest son returns home after wasting his fortune and is welcomed with open arms by his father, much to the disgust of the younger brother who has worked and saved diligently.

"Do you think I'll ever have a little brother?" she asks and Maria shrugs. "I hope not, I like being an only child."

It's still early and it's warm outside so after our meal we head to the beach and catch the last rays of the evening sun. We sit beside the sea watching the waves lap against the shore as the Ferry glides toward the dock. On the grass, on the beach and on the small pathway there are couples, families and lovers who are walking dogs, flying kites and like us eating ice creams.

The spire at Jordanstown rises above the village and there are tilted red-sails participating in a regatta at Carrickfergus.

Maria's takes a call on her mobile. "Hi Pat," she winks at me and walks away talking into her phone leaving Lily and I sitting on the small wall gazing at the water.

"Can you do this?" I bite the bottom end of my cone and suck the ice cream out from underneath.

Lily giggles and copies me. She has been reticent about her time to Dublin and I work on the assumption that if someone wants you to know something, they'll tell you. So I don't ask about her trip and instead I tell her about our weekend in Donegal.

She swallows the last of her cone and I pass her a tissue. She rubs her hands clean and sits kicking her heels against the wall. "Will you bring me there one day?" she asks.

"If you like or we can go somewhere else on holiday."

"We went on the sightseeing bus around Dublin and we saw deer in Phoenix Park."

"How lovely."

"I like Dublin," she says, and tells me about a trip to the cinema. But she doesn't mention Michael's new partner. I guess she will when she is ready.

Maria returns to us and we walk for a while along the coastal path.

This time my mobile rings and I stop to answer it. They walk on ahead and find an empty bench where they sit and wait for me.

It is Mark Bowman. He is still at work. His Scottish accent rings in my ear. "Are you in the office on Monday, Ellie? I will have news about the hacker. I'm going to find him. I'm almost there," he drawls.

"I'll need proof," I reply. "It will have to be watertight. No mistakes."

"You'll have it next week."

"I'll be there."

"You'd better give it some thought what you are going to do."

"I will." I promise him.

I hang up. My mind is racing. I haven't spoken to Maria yet about the hacker. Even though I've hinted that Simon is behaving strangely. I haven't told her that John thinks he is having an affair or worse, that he is looking for investors and is thinking of selling the company to American investors and that John will go to any lengths to stop him.

Lily sits swinging her legs with Maria's arm draped over her shoulder. Their feline bodies move comfortably as they lean against each other chatting quietly. I'm happy to watch them and as I approach, Maria is speaking, "Daddy and I had a chat on Wednesday after he dropped you off at Grandma's. When you were in Dublin with him did you mention to Daddy that you thought Ellie might be gay?"

I stop a few yards behind where they sit.

A dog barks and a man with a small boy releases a kite with

a long, yellow and green tail. It flies high into the sky and the boy squeals and skips after it.

"I think…" Lily pushes her glasses onto her nose. "Maybe sort of…"

Maria strokes Lily's curly hair. "What did you say to Daddy? You can tell me. I'm not angry. I just need to know."

"He asked me, if you and Ellie went out looking for boyfriends and I giggled. I think he was worried that you might meet someone like Charlie's mother did, and have another baby, and he seemed so sad. He'd been so kind to me and I didn't want him to be upset. I said that you wouldn't do that, you know — go out looking for boyfriends, as Ellie likes women."

The kite soars above my head and a child screams.

"And what makes you think that?" Maria asks gently.

"Jake and Matt told me. They told me that day when we had a picnic and we were on the beach. They said that they missed Ellie living in London and it was all because Ellie's ex-girlfriend went off with someone else and Ellie was sad and she came to live here."

"Oh?" Maria pauses. "And how do you feel about that?"

I feel like an eavesdropper but I can't move. I am like a garden statue.

"Sad for Ellie, but she's got us now, hasn't she?" Lily leans her head on Maria's shoulder. "It wasn't a secret, was it?"

"No, but there's no reason to tell anyone else."

"I probably shouldn't have told Daddy, should I?"

Maria hugs her close. "Well, it is none of his business, is it?"

Lily shakes her head in agreement.

"Do you mind that Ellie's my friend?

"No." Lily sits up straight. "She's my friend too and she

makes you happy. You only laugh when you're with her."

"Yes, Ellie is your friend too."

"She won't be angry with me for telling Daddy?"

"She will understand."

I wander away to where kids are swinging on swings, sliding on slides and getting dizzy on the roundabout. I know how they all feel. I too feel disoriented. Everything is out of control and my head is spinning.

Chapter Fifteen

There's a dead magpie on the bonnet of my car. Its neck has been twisted and its gut ripped open, and the blood is smeared across the window screen. I check the Harley is safe and untouched in the garage and go back inside the house. I put on plastic gloves get a bag, cleaning fluid and a cloth. The lifeless and bloody weight in my hand is still warm. There is no evidence of how it happened.

"I can't make it out," I say to Anna, in the gym changing room. I pull my T-shirt over my head. "It's a mystery as to where it came from. It's as if it fell out of the sky apart from someone had cut its belly open."

"Who would have done that?"

"Maria's husband Michael is very angry. He's threatened Maria. And I think it was him that trashed my Harley a few months ago. He knows I'm gay." I climb on the back of my motorbike. "I couldn't bring myself to drive the Mercedes this morning."

"Well, be very careful. He sounds a nasty piece of work. You never know what lengths people will go to up here."

"Should I be worried?"

"You should be cautious. You never know what friends he has and how far he is likely to go to keep you and Maria apart."

"He can't control us. He can't govern our lives."

"He thinks he can and that is what makes him dangerous. We are going to France next week. Come with us. Carla may come too. It will do you good to have a break abroad. And you never know. Carla is a lovely girl and she's still single. She waiting for the right woman to come along…"

"I'll think about it." I reply with a smile. "You're very kind to ask me and I do appreciate it but maybe I have to be here for Maria and Lily right now. I think they need me," I say these words even though I haven't seen Maria at all over the weekend. She devoted her time to Lily. They wanted mother and daughter quality time together, plus of course, a trip to Grandma Brenda's and an excursion with Pat to the north coast.

"You're not exactly a part of their lives Ellie. You need to think about yourself."

I'm still mulling over our conversation when I'm in the office kitchen. I stir coffee while Maria tells me about her conversation with Lily on the beach last Friday evening and I react as if I hadn't overheard them and I shrug.

"It isn't Lily's fault. It is the truth. I am gay. I can't be angry with her for telling the truth. Does it bother you that Lily and Michael know?"

"We're friends, Ellie. It's like you said. You are you. And what I said to Michael was true. I can have any friend I want."

"And us?"

She shakes her head. "You know the answer to that."

"There was a dead magpie on my car bonnet this morning. Its stomach was ripped open and blood smeared across the window."

She shakes her head in disbelief. "An accident."

"Only if you believe it to be."

"It couldn't have been Michael. He wouldn't do such a thing." She is defensive of him and so I change the subject.

"Auntie Annie telephoned again at the weekend. She's definitely moving to America. Her trip to Seattle went well and she had the seal of approval from Gerard's daughter. They've found a perfect condo and she's staying out there. She said she's probably coming back next month to pack up and sell her house."

Maria looks at me thoughtfully before replying, "It looks like we'll both be homeless then." And she leaves the kitchen without a backward glance.

At lunchtime I ride the Harley like an angry stallion down the coast to Donaghadee. I need space. I need fresh air and I need to sort myself out. I stand staring across the sea to Scotland inhaling salty air and wiping my tears of anger and frustration. I'm wasting my time. Maria doesn't love me. She's messing me around. All her declarations of love seem to disintegrate when we live in the real world and it's disconcerting. Even if we were ever together how could I live with this fluctuation of her emotions, this pendulum of feelings? One day she loves me, one day she doesn't. One day she wants me, the next day she doesn't. One day she needs me, the next…

I drive quickly overtaking cars with no regard and a 4X4 suddenly swerves out in front of me and I'm so close to the driver's window, I see his ashen face. In a nano second I register his shock and I wobble precariously and swear loudly gaining my balance. It's a sharp lesson learned and I slow my speed.

I make a detour and call into the restaurant to see Mickey

Bleu. The conversation with John has been going around in my head and although I don't think for one minute Simon is having an affair, the part about her knowing influential and wealthy investors in America has peaked my curiosity.

Mickey is friendly. Her eyes shine like large hazelnuts and her laugh is as deep and as rumbling as the Atlantic. She's busy and she skilfully evades my probing questions. Instead she directs the conversation toward Emmanuel and the girls and invites me for dinner to her house later in the week. Feeling none the wiser and putting my investigative skills on hold I return to the office disgruntled, unsettled and out-manoeuvred.

In between phone calls, I flick balls of tiny rolled paper into my crash helmet. I'm thinking I might give the tenants in my apartment in London their notice. I could be back in England in a month or so and start a new job in October. I would easily find work. Not with Proctor and Gowan but in another firm. Perhaps even an IT company.

I avoid Maria. I work late, reviewing and editing a project for a retail outlet in the House of Fraser commercial centre. But my mind is elsewhere. This job has been a lifeline for me and I'm stronger now to return to London. If I leave Belfast then I must design an exit strategy so that when I do go, the company will be taken care of. Even if Simon sells the company it would be beneficial for him to have a detailed business plan for the future. And it is not as if John or anyone else is going to produce one. Besides, it's the least I could do.

I'm thinking of the practical details of moving back to London and I am thinking of my conversation with Jenny and telling her I'm coming home when Mark Bowman appears in my office.

His face is flushed with excitement and his Glaswegian accent is thicker than ever. "Do you want to know something?"

"What?"

"John told me to stop. He told me not to keep trying to find the hacker but I couldn't. It really annoyed me to think someone would do that. To think that someone we worked with would do that to us."

My skin prickles with anticipation. "Do you know who did it?"

"I've traced the source. Now I am just finding the codes and trying to match them so the proof is solid."

"It sounds complicated. Can you do that?"

"I hope so."

"You definitely think it's someone from this company?"

"I'd lay money on it — and that's a Scotsman speaking." He beams happily.

"Should we call the police?"

"It would stop them from doing it again."

"You will have definite proof?"

"Yes."

"When?"

"Whenever these codes match with the passwords."

"So, I have a little more time to work out what to do," I say aloud and Mark nods contentedly like a toy dog in the back window of a moving car.

* * *

Later that evening I am about to go to bed when my phone rings.

"I know people," he says. "I am not having it. You have

250

seriously pissed me off. You will have nothing to do with Lily or with Maria. Do you understand me?"

"Don't threaten me, Michael."

"I am seriously pissed off. And when I get angry I do bad things."

"You don't scare me."

"You have no idea what you are doing, you feckin' dyke."

"You cannot bully me."

"Don't mess with me or you will know about it. You have no idea what you are getting into."

"You can't intimidate me."

"I won't have to - my friend, Steve, is keeping his eye on you. Don't be alone in the dark."

"I'll call the police."

He laughs. "And what'll they do? They couldn't do anything the last time, could they?"

"So you did trash my bike."

"You led me on. But next time it's for real."

"And the magpie?"

"It's what will happen to you."

"Get lost Michael. You're an emotionally stunted, control-freak. You need to get a life."

"Go near my wife and daughter and it's the last thing you do. It's time you went back to England. I'm not telling you again. These boys don't mess around. One word from me and your life is over. You have no idea what goes on here but you will find out if you insist on staying. You will disappear — permanently—"

I hang up.

* * *

Anna and Maxie are going camping with their two dogs, Bumble and Rumble, and Carla.

I join them for a drink in town before they go.

"A holiday would do you good," Carla insists and I'm aware of her leg brushing mine."You need to have some fun."

"A hot tent in the middle of the French countryside, isn't my type of holiday," I reply with a smile. "I do need a little more luxury."

"We'll have the dogs and we can take long walks," insists Anna.

"And the bikes, there are some lovely trails we can go on," says Maxie.

They morph smile at me.

"Er, no thanks - I'll just hold out for a better offer."

"You're wasting your time waiting for Maria," says Carla. "She doesn't appreciate you."

"She has to put Lily first." I reply testily.

"Yes but she's playing with you. She blows hot and cold. She doesn't love you if she can treat you like this."

"More drinks?" They're telling me things I don't want to hear. Across the other side of the bar are two rough-looking guys. One has a shaved head the other colourful tattoos up his arms and across his neck. They're staring unblinking at me.

"You deserve better than Maria." Carla stands beside me. Her features are large and her forehead broad. Her lips are wide and painted red and her mouth is dangerously close to mine. "You need someone who values you, someone who cares for you and knows how to treat you properly." She is flirting heavily.

"Maria values me. We are good friends." I pay the barman and lean away from Carla's persistent and intensive gaze.

The two thugs continue watching me.

"It isn't a good friend that you want though, is it? You want a lover. You need someone who will please you." Carla holds my elbow.

The shorter, stockier bald guy picks up his pint. His gaze doesn't waver and I stare back.

"You have to live, Ellie. Didn't you tell us that you came to Belfast to get away from your problems and start a new life? And now you are embroiled in a whole set of new problems with a married woman. You haven't even given yourself chance to sort yourself out or to find out what you want—"

"I have, Carla. I've met Maria."

"She has Lily."

"I know that. But Maria is *The One*. She understands me. She's the girl I have only ever dreamed of — she's special and I love her."

"Bah." Carla turns away. She walks over to the table where Anna and Maxie are watching and waiting for us.

The tattooed thug rubs his forearm across his mouth wiping beer from his lips and I wonder if one of them is called Steve.

"Are you two arguing?" asks Anna, as I sit down beside her.

"Ellie believes that Maria is *The One* and that there is no-one else — and it's rubbish," replies Carla.

"Why is it rubbish?" Maxie takes a sip of her wine.

"Because she's on the rebound anyone can see that."

"Maria and I have a connection. We've had it since the first time we saw each other when her husband almost knocked me off my bike on my first day at work. We get on brilliantly and..."

"And?" Anna leans forward. "What?"

"She is amazing. I have never made love to anyone like I

have to Maria. She is special."

"Oh puke," Carla says. "You have no idea have you? She is playing with you and you deserve more than that."

What they say makes sense but it doesn't stop me from wanting to be with Maria more than anything in my life. I miss her constantly. I'm lonely without her.

It is dark when we leave the pub. Although it is normally a busy road there is no traffic and it all happens very quickly.

Smash and grab. My face. Carla's bag.

His fist is hard. My head is ringing with pain. He's well-muscled and strong. His tattoos are a kaleidoscope of colour and he swears at me in a heavy thick accent. "Fokkin bitch!"

I pull his T-shirt and won't let go. He drags me along the road. I seize him by the neck and try to punch him. He pulls away so I kick him in hard in the crotch.

"Ah!" he screams, "Fokkin lesbo!" He doubles over then lunges his body through the open-door of a waiting car. Its engine is running and it moves immediately, so I kick it shut trapping his leg that still hangs outside. I hear him scream as the car roars through red traffic lights.

It's over in seconds, leaving only the sound of their screeching tyres and I'm left with a bloodied nose and bruised eye and, after realising my wounds aren't life threatening, Carla is angry at having to replace her stolen credit cards and driver's license.

Annie and Maxie relate the version of events to the police and I tell them about the two guys in the bar who had been watching me.

"CCTV?" I ask hopefully, having described them in detail.

The young policeman who looks like he has just finished school and barely shaves, shakes his head. "We've been having problems with them recently but we will check."

"They were watching us in the bar," I say. "Someone might remember them or know them?"

"We'll check."

The next day Maria is concerned when she sees my face. I tell her about the attack in Belfast and she's horrified. So then I tell her about my Harley and Michael's threatening phone call just a few days before.

"That's ridiculous. It couldn't have anything to do with him. Michael isn't like that. He's angry but he wouldn't do anything like this. He's not violent. I know you don't like him Ellie but there's no need to pretend he could have anything to do with this…" her voice trails off.

"He mentioned a guy from a dodgy part of west Belfast. He was one of the guys in the pub I'm sure of it," I insist. "I also woke up to a dead magpie on my car last week - remember?"

Maria looks at me as if I am making things up.

"Well, at least you know. If I ever disappear look for a thug called Steve."

* * *

Today is the 19th of August. It is my birthday and I'm thirty-four. The bruise on my face has turned from purple to yellow and my swollen eye is almost open again. The thought of a luxury break does entice me but when I think of Anna, Maxie and Carla in the heat in a stifling tent. I'm pleased I turned down their kind offer.

I know that the weekend I spent with Maria in Donegal was as close to a holiday as I will get this year. It was almost perfect but it has left me feeling lonely and sad.

Just before eleven o'clock Maria bursts into my office and she's shaking with anger.

"He's phoned Mum," she says, wiping her eyes,"And he's told her."

"What?" I move toward her but she pushes me away.

"He's told her everything. That you're a lesbian and that we're having an affair."

"But he doesn't know, Maria. He's only guessing—"

"Well, he's told her anyway. He said that's why he's gone off with Kate and that I left him no alternative. I neglected him. He told Mum it was because he found out I was a lesbian and I wouldn't sleep with him. And that I ruined our marriage. Mum is furious. She is also very upset." Maria sinks into the chair and I watch her with detached shock. "Mum is mortified. She's been onto Father Donnelly and he wants to talk to me and she's told Pat and Connor and Joe. She's hysterical. She can't believe this is happening to her and she says it's making her ill. She's frightened the neighbours will find out."

"Well they will, if she keeps telling everyone. It's not going to be much of a secret in her local community, is it?"

"Stop it, Ellie. Stop being so flippant. Don't you understand what this means? Michael will do anything to take Lily away from me. He wants her to live with him. I'm convinced of it. He's trying to put everyone against me. He wants my family to be on his side. He's trying to put them all against me."

"He's a misogynistic bully. He's always tried to control you and now he hasn't got what he wants and his ego is in tatters, he's vindictive and now he's gone running to your mother with a tittle-tattle-tale of how you don't love him any more. He's pathetic but dangerous. But you must stand up to him, Maria. You must stand up to them all."

"He's going to take Lily away from me." She holds her head in her hands.

"Ah Maria, don't cry. Come on. He can't do this. You have to be stronger than him. We won't let him. We can sort this all out. We just need to explain—"

"How many times do I have to tell you? There is no *we* and there is no *us*. And there never will be. You just don't understand what it's like Ellie. You have no idea what I am going though. I could lose my family. I will lose my daughter."

"Maria — I want to help."

She jumps up and holds up the palm of her hand. "Then just stay away from me, Ellie. I can't deal with all this at the moment. It is just too much. I can't risk it."

In the afternoon my father telephones and sings, Cumpleaños Feliz. I promise him I will go to Malaga after the summer when it is cooler and we will celebrate my birthday and eat fish in Pedregalejo, in his favourite restaurant beside the sea. He's happy with Marta and I speak to her briefly. She sounds happy and fun and they're obviously in love and I feel a pang of envy.

He doesn't ask me about my love-life or if I am happy. He doesn't ask what I am doing today either. He's caught up in his own world and his own life.

I don't expect to hear from my mother. With the time difference between Thailand and Belfast she probably won't know what day it is until the weekend and then it will be too late to sound genuine or sincere.

Normally her first question to me is — are you still with that girl? She means Kat. So, at least this year, if she calls, she'll have some good news when I tell her I am single again.

Simon has done his disappearing act and the rumour, spread

by John, is that he's in America. John also tells me that Louise is with him which means they may not be getting a divorce, but - he thinks - they maybe meeting investors to finance the business. Simon may be merging the company with a parent US based company. Presumably - John believes - it is Mickey Bleu who has arranged all this.

Which tells me one very obvious thing, John doesn't have a clue.

By mid-afternoon I am flicking screwed up paper balls into my half-filled coffee cup and I'm deliberating what to say to Maria. I flick another rolled-ball. I could go into her office now and be dramatic and tell her I'm moving back to London. Or I could tell her it's my birthday and make her feel guilty so that she changes whatever plans she has. Maybe she and Lily can spoil me and get a cake with candles? But is this the type of relationship I want?

I'm learning that I cannot make someone into someone they are not. Maria will never be able to put me first and I have always known this. She will prioritise Lily. But it isn't just that. It's also the fact that Maria blows hot and cold. She doesn't know what or who she wants, and until she does, she expects me to hang around and be at her beck and call.

It's all about how Maria treats me. Carla is right. I deserve more than this.

I touch my sore face gently with my fingertips.

I am worth more.

I need someone special in my life to support me too.

I need Maria to fight to keep me.

It's almost five o'clock and the thought of my birthday evening at home alone fills me with dread. I ignore Maria in her office and head downstairs to the techie lab.

"Anyone on for a party tonight or have you all got exciting dates and something better to do?" I call out. Heads look up - momentarily distracted from their computers and programming. "Anyone want to come for dinner, play pool and have lots to drink? I'm paying."

I'm greeted with a burst of applause and cheers by Boys Aloud. Siobhan puts her arm around Stuart. "Great idea. We all need a party - especially midweek."

John comes out of his office hitching up his trousers. "Don't play pool with Jessica. You'll only lose."

"I like a challenge," I call back. "Who's choosing the teams?"

Liam has grown a goatee. He is tanned from his holiday in Greece and looks very like a pirate in the Caribbean. He salutes me. His eyes are twinkling when he says. "Your bruising is going down Ellie. You even look quite respectable again. Just don't get into any more fights."

Ray, the quiet boy grins. "I'm always in a party mood."

The boy band are bantering with Jessica and Mark is slow-clapping and whistling. Within minutes we are making plans where to go, what to eat, and who is on what team for playing pool.

"I'll be with Jessica," I say. "We will whitewash you all."

"You'll need me on your side," John says. "You won't win without me."

"That's the girlies side, John," teases Mark.

"No way," Stuart joins in. "Jessica is with us."

So this is how we banter and choose the teams. After five minutes John takes me to one side. His brow is creased in a frown. "The company isn't paying for this, is it Ellie?" he whispers.

"No — I am."

He looks at me strangely and I smile back conscious that he is looking at my battered face and he feels sorry for me.

Maria comes down the stairs. She must hear the commotion in the lab and so she puts her head around the door. "What's happening here? What's all the excitement?"

"Ellie's had a great idea. We're having a mid-week party," Siobhan replies. "We're going for burgers then a game of pool. Are you coming with us Maria?"

Maria's eyes meet mine and my heart skips a beat. "I can't," she says. "Lily is waiting for me. Maybe some other time."

It's at this moment that I know my future is sealed. I will ask the tenants to leave my apartment in London. I will tell Jenny I'm coming home and I will finish the business plan to move the Bizweb Solutions forward in my absence.

My decision is made.

That evening, I invite the team to dinner at Mickey Bleu's restaurant. We eat excellent burgers and salad with garlic dressing and drink full-bodied wine. It is only after I've had too much to drink that I blurt out that it is my birthday. Then, it's as if the team is coasting into the evening but once they have cause to celebrate, there is no stopping them. I become the focus of their attention which is embarrassing, their jokes even worse. But they make me laugh. They are affectionate with me and I had forgotten such kindness existed. I feel overwhelmed at their happy attitude.

Mickey Blue produces a chocolate sponge cake with a single pink candle and invites us to several bottles of Prosecco so by the time we arrive at the pool hall, I am flying high. Living the moment.

Tomorrow begins another day - and another year. I'm going home. Back to London.

* * *

I don't know if Maria knew it was my birthday or if she heard about the party I don't go into her office and I avoid the kitchen. She's in the same category for me now as Simon. I can't be bothered with either of them. I'm tired and hungover and it's mid-morning when I'm sitting in the window of Mauds, on my own, eating a smoked salmon bagel when Mark Bowman appears as we arranged.

"I know who it is," he says, sliding into the seat opposite me.

A trickle of dread slinks down my spine especially when I think of the fun we had last night. "I can't believe that someone would do this, Mark. Please tell me it's not an inside job. Please tell me it isn't one of the team. Please tell me they weren't with us last night."

He eyes turn cloudy and he shakes his head. "It's not good news."

"Do you have evidence?"

"Yes."

"Could you be mistaken?"

He shakes his head and pulls a wad of papers from the inside of his pocket. He places them on the table. They're marked with yellow and blue high-lighter pens, and he explains the patterns. The dates, times and logins.

There is no doubt. I see it with my own eyes.

"Whose login is it?" I ask and when he tells me my heart sinks and I put my head in my hands. Half an hour later I return to the office and walk up the stairs, I'm digesting the information about the office traitor.

Maria stands in the doorway. "Ellie?" I stare at her. "Are you okay?"

"Fine," I lie.

"I'm really sorry - about last night - Siobhan just told me. I didn't know. Why didn't you tell me it was your birthday?"

I look at her blankly. "It wasn't important. Besides you were busy anyway."

"You might have said something to me. We're not strangers." There is uncertainty in her eyes and a patchwork of creased tiny lines on her forehead.

"That is rich coming from you." She recoils at my words. Her body seems to shrink against the wall but I can't stop. "Strangers? You'd know all about that. You seem to think that you can come in and out of my life whenever you like with no regard to my feelings. You please yourself; when it suits you or when it doesn't suit you. When you want to be with me or not. You blow hot and cold. One minute you say you need me and you want to be with me and the next you behave as if I am no-one. I know I'm not important to you. I know you can't have me in your life. I know I will be spending another lonely weekend on my own. I know Michael has told your mother you're gay and we had a relationship and I know how this hurts you. But the fact that you deny me — you deny me — the right of being a person and of having been your lover, hurts me too. I accept that you can't cope with being gay that you have feelings for me but I would help or do anything to support you. But you've made it very, very clear to me Maria about how you feel. I understand the person that you truly are. So, please don't accuse me of being a stranger — or blame me when you feel bad—"

"Ellie—"

"I've had enough Maria. I too, have a life and feelings. I need and deserve more. I would like to be in a loving relationship with someone who cares about me. And I can see that it will definitely, definitely, not be with you."

She is holding her hand to her throat. Her brown eyes are swimming and floating in tears, and she turns and pushes her way into the office kitchen and slams the door.

I don't follow. I don't do anything. I stand for a minute listening to her banging cupboards and slamming doors then I go into my office and stand at the window regretting my outburst. A few minutes later I hear her quick footsteps going down the stairs.

I turn at the sound of her leaving and it is then that I see two neatly wrapped birthday presents sitting on my desk.

* * *

I spend a sleepless night tossing and turning, thinking of Maria. It's Saturday morning and I could lie in bed but at seven o'clock I'm showered and dressed. I go to the beach and walk across the rocks leaving wet footprints in the sand. My hands dug firmly into my jacket pocket.

I don't notice heavy clouds forming across the Lough or as the sky turns misty and purple, persistent rain falls. Dog walkers and joggers run for cover but I don't. Instead, I stand and let the rain beat against my face. It dribbles down my collar and onto my neck leaving my clothes plastered to my body but I don't care. I spread my arms wide and cast my face toward the heavens like Christ on the Cross. Hoping for redemption and cleansing until I realise that my tears are falling in torrents on my cheeks.

After this unnecessary drama, I feel ridiculous so I go home. I take a long, hot shower and dry myself. I spray *Paco Rabanne* generously and wrap a cotton dressing gown around my naked body and I make coffee and stand at the window looking across the Lough.

I'm thinking about Dominator and the Hacker. Why?

I consider John's accusations and theories. I think of Simon's long absences from the office. He should be home again this weekend and I need to speak to him first thing on Monday morning. My mind teems with memories. The company anniversary party in Jazz bar. My birthday. Jessica playing pool with Boys Aloud. Siobhan and Stuart in a passionate embrace. Maria in Donegal. Anna and Maxie with Carla on holiday in France. And my father with Marta in Malaga. I need to get away. Back to London. I need to get out. I must leave. Just Go!

My mobile rings.

"Ellie? I'm sorry to bother you — but, Mum's been taken ill," Maria says. "They think it's a stroke. I'm on my way to the hospital. Lily is with me but I don't want her in the hospital. The rest of the family are on their way. Charlie is on holiday with her family and, well, besides all that. Lily says she wants to be with you. I'm sorry, can you—" She is tripping over her words and I am almost dressed before she hangs up.

"I'm on my way."

She needs me. Is Brenda ill because of the news Michael told her? Is it that traumatic?

I meet them outside the hospital and Lily hugs me tightly. They both look sad and frightened.

"Lily can stay as long as she likes," I say. "Phone us later. Let me know if there's anything or just come over to mine when you can and…"

"Thanks Ellie." She turns to leave but then, as an afterthought, kisses us both quickly before she disappears into a sea of hospital visitors.

At home, Lily and I light the fire. We hold bread on forks over the flames to make toast and spread the slices with thick butter and marmite.

We watch a DVD - it's an American High School musical that enthrals Lily. We sing along to the songs and when I deliberately sing out of tune or muddle the words she shrieks with laughter.

In the evening, Lily takes a bath then snuggles up against me and falls asleep. I relish the warmth of her small warm body and think of the fragility of her world and I'm amazed at the wave of protection I feel toward the little person snuggled into me and I imagine having my own family.

At the sound of the doorbell, Lily wakes up. She rubs her eyes and looks at her surroundings in surprise so I ruffle her hair and smile at her troubled face.

"Is that mummy?"

"I guess so. Let's go and see."

We both rise at the same time. Just as the sound of breaking glass fills the room and a hurtling ball of flames explodes in our eyes.

Lily screams.

The sofa explodes into a gush of fire and smoke fills the room, a bright flashing inferno dances before me.

"Lily," I shout. I reach out and in the confusion I slip on the upturned coffee table and I fall choking. My face is burning.

"Lily?" I cover my cheeks with my arm and grope into the smokey darkness. My hand finds her arm and I pull her to me but she doesn't move. I bend down and pick up her motionless body. I cough. I spit. I kick furniture from my path. I'm blinded. My eyes are streaming. Guided only by my sense of direction and the memory of the room layout I move quickly, choking, my eyes stinging. My pace falters and I'm disorientated blocked by things I can't define in my path. I kick a door. I see light and an arm grabs me. Voices fill my ears but I won't let Lily go. I can't see and I'm fighting them off until someone says, "We're here to help. The ambulance is on its way." It's my neighbour's voice.

I release Lily, lay her on the ground and rub smoke from my eyes.

"She's not moving," I shout. My throat is dry. My voice raspy. She's lifeless. I lock my hands and push down on her chest. I lean over her and blow air into her lungs. I try to get a rhythm but it is only when I see blue flashing lights and feel a restraining hand on my arm do I let her go. I sink back on my heels and fall into darkness.

When I come around there's confusion and commotion. My head is filled with white noise. The driveway busy with people, uniforms and shadows. A young girl kneels beside me, she's a paramedic intent on covering my mouth with a mask but I push her hand away and sit up.

"Maria?" I gasp confused as she leans over me. "What are you doing…?" But my voice is only a croak. I struggle to my feet, looking at the body on the stretcher beside me but Maria holds my arm.

"I called you from the car to tell you I was on my way. Then I saw the ambulance and the police cars."

"Where's Lily?"

"She will be okay. They're taking her in the ambulance now to hospital. I'm going with her but I want to make sure you're okay."

No-one stops me when I lean over and I touch Lily's cheek. Her eyes flick open and she gives me a tired smile before closing her eyes again. Maria's arm is around my waist holding me up.

"She looks so vulnerable without her Harry Potter glasses," I say.

The ambulance driver smiles. "Are you coming with us? We need to look at those burns you have."

I look over at Auntie Annie's house and shake my head. "Is the fire is out?"

"The neighbour and his two sons," Maria explains, "They were just coming home and saw flames. They came immediately and turned on the hose from the garden and managed to douse the flames."

"I must fix the window. I can't leave it unsafe. Poor Auntie Annie. You go with Lily," I say to Maria. "I need to sort things here."

She kisses me. "Thank you," she whispers.

I spend the next few hours speaking to two detectives. They are in plain-clothes and I tell them everything; about Michael's threats, my damaged Harley, the dead magpie, and finally Steve and his friends and their assault outside the pub. My words are a torrent. A floodgate of relief, a tidal wave of accusations and I wonder how much they believe of my story.

"It's as well you reacted so quickly this evening or it could have been devastating," says the skinny one with stooped shoulders wearing jeans.

"They think they are above the law," I reply.

The older one's brow creases in concern. "Perhaps before but it's not so easy to hide now."

After they have gone I begin tiding the house.

My ginger-haired neighbour Derek and his two teenage sons help me to board up the window with some wood from the shed.

"I'll get a new pane in the morning. I'll never be able to thank you enough," I say.

"I couldn't believe it when I saw the flames and someone running away. The boys called police and ambulance while I got the hose. The living room is a mess but you were lucky, Ellie."

"The sofas are burnt. The walls are black. The coffee table and lamps are toasted but it doesn't matter. You risked your lives to help us. Thank you so much."

They behave with modesty leaving me feeling humble and emotional at their kindness. With promises that I will call on them if I need anything they leave and, by the time my jobs are done, I am exhausted. I put vaseline on the burns on my face, arms and hands. They're sore but not life damaging and I drink a whiskey to stop my body from shaking. And when Maria phones me from the hospital she tells me she's staying the night with Lily.

* * *

It takes several day to scour the walls with bleach and I purchase two new sofas, new coffee tables and lamps, and everywhere smells of fresh paint.

It is midweek when Lily, who spent only one night in hospital, says she wants to spend an evening with me while Maria is at the hospital visiting Brenda. She admires the painting and the new furniture and we cook dinner and watch a film.

"You're safe," I tell her. "The police will protect us."

"Your burns looks sore."

"They're fine. We're both fine now, aren't we?"

"Yup." She smiles and snuggles against me and all thoughts of the fire are banished from our minds.

Much later, when Maria arrives she wraps Lily in a big hug and adds a kiss to her forehead. "Nice pyjamas."

"Ellie gave them to me. I had a bath and she sprayed some *Paco Rabanne* on me." Lily stretches in satisfaction. "Can I buy some?"

"Um. You do smell gorgeous." Maria presses her nose to Lily's neck. There are dark circles around her eyes, her irises are large and black and they glisten with worry.

"How's your mother?" I ask.

"She's a little better. The specialist is coming around again tomorrow so I'll see him in the morning."

"Can I stay with you again tomorrow, Ellie?" Lily looks excitedly at me. "What will we do? Let's do something exciting."

"Like what?"

"We could go house hunting," she says. "I might find one for us, Mum, mightn't I?"

But Maria has laid her head back against the sofa and is snoring softly.

"Come on, time for bed, Lily. Let's leave your Mum for a few minutes and I'll make her something to eat when she wakes up."

I take Lily to the spare room, the bedroom she declared that she just loves, and I settle her down with a book. I kiss her goodnight and tell her Maria will join her in an hour after she's rested.

When I go downstairs Maria stirs.

"I guess you haven't eaten all evening," I say. "You're exhausted. I'll make you something. You need to eat to keep your strength up."

She follows me into the kitchen and watches silently as I prepare a salad.

"Tea or wine?"

"Wine, please," she replies.

As I slice cheese and chop lettuce I'm thinking about the Sunday afternoon she came to this house after the storm and of how we made love. Then I am reminded of the night, after the company party back in June when she came home with me and the tenderness and passion we felt and how it all seemed so right.

I still smell Channel on her skin. I remember the softness of her kiss. I imagine the caress of her hands. We know we shared something so special - it is inexplicable to anyone else.

She is my soul-mate.

We take the salad and wine and sit in front of the fire chatting quietly as she eats.

"I told Connor what you said about Michael's threats. Connor knows Steve too. They worked together on the same construction site for a while. So we've nothing to worry about. He's promised me that he will sort it. The family is very upset about what happened. He won't let anyone threaten us. After all, Lily is his niece."

"And the police?"

She shrugs. "I'll let Connor handle it." After she eats she leans her head against my shoulder and I hold her in my arms as she describes Brenda and her condition in more detail. "Joe wants to meet you. He wants to thank you for saving Lily's life."

I hold her close and stroke her hair. She's almost asleep and when we go upstairs and I kiss her goodnight and tuck her in bed beside her sleeping daughter.

* * *

It's the start of the new school term. The air has turned cooler and the summer is over. Maria goes backwards and forward to the hospital and she is busy ferrying Lily to and from school, and I am once again relegated to the least important person. I have scant attention from Maria only crumbs from her table of affection. Although Maria hasn't said anything to me I can guess that she feels responsible for Brenda's stroke. When Michael phoned and told her that Maria and I were having an affair she was fraught and upset. I know Maria believes it was the catalyst to her illness. The damage has been done. It is irreversible and permanent.

On Wednesday morning Mark wastes no time in cornering me in my office.

"Simon is back. You're back. We have to act. We must do something. I'm just worried in case our hacker has another surprise in store for us."

I sigh heavily, gaze out of the window and eventually I nod my head. "Yes, you're right. It is time." I had been putting off the inevitable and it takes me a few minutes to gather my thoughts before I go to Simon's office.

He's sitting gazing out of the window lost in thought. It seems he has more important things on his mind but Bizweb Solutions is his Company, and his responsibility, besides I'm leaving next week so it's about time he took the helm and sorted things out. I've had enough. I'm determined. I'm going back to London.

His grey eyes smile with tiredness yet there is a hint of something else. Is it excitement? Happiness? He begins pacing the room. His grey floppy hair falls into his eyes and he appears more energetic, more revived, as if he's been charged with excited energy.

He says,"Look Ellie, there have been a lot of changes since you joined us last March and I've been meaning to speak to you for some time. You've done such a good job. I can't begin to tell you. You are brilliant. You're more than a skilled marketing executive. You're an entrepreneur in your own right with fantastic business acumen. I've given this matter careful consideration and I do hope that you will say, yes," he pauses. "I hope you will help me grow the company to its full potential. You see, my life is about to change. I can't say more at this stage only that the past few months have been a nightmare and without your support here in the office and as a friend, I don't know what I would have done." He has tears in his eyes. "I want to come to some sort of arrangement with you. Shares or directorship, so that you will stay—"

"Wait Simon, I'm not staying in Belfast. It — it's nothing to do with the company. It's personal. I'm leaving. I have my own plans for the future. But please don't let's talk about this now. We have a more serious problem in the company that we have to sort out immediately." I watch the smile fade from his face and I continue speaking, "Mark came to me. He wanted to find out who the hacker was. He wanted permission to track down the person who planted Dominator and did all the damage to the company."

"And?"

"John didn't want him to waste his time but we need to know Simon. I had to find out who would willingly want to damage this company or who would benefit from it."

"Yes of course, but no-one came to me. No-one has spoken to me about it."

"You haven't been here, Simon. The company is growing. Our business is increasing and it needs someone at the helm to take charge and to make decisions. You're the founder of the company, Simon. The leadership of this company is your job and your responsibility. You have a duty to your staff. But one thing at a time. More importantly, Mark has found the hacker and he has the proof. He knows who it is."

"My goodness," Simon says. "Who?"

"If we let him off with just a warning I'm afraid he will probably laugh in our faces. He may leave the company and go somewhere else and wreak havoc again. Or he may look for notoriety or control or for whatever it was he was seeking the last time. Another business might not be as lucky as ours. They might not escape as relatively unscathed as we did. We were fortunate that we were active in our damage limitation."

"Yes, that lunch you and Liam held in the hotel saved us. It restored our reputation."

I nod in agreement. "We were extremely lucky. It could have been much worse. The company could have gone under. You would have lost your business and the staff would have lost their jobs. It is up to you, as the owner, and us the management team, to protect our staff and make them feel safe."

"What do you suggest, Ellie?"

"I think we should sort everything out once and for all. Let's call John upstairs.

He comes into Simon's office hitching up his trousers and I

decide I will buy him a pair of braces before I go. He'd taken a few days leave and has only returned to work today and I mean, it's a Friday, who takes time off and returns to work for one day? Who would be bothered? This man is a complete enigma to me but right now, I have more important things on my mind.

Simon is staring out of the window. He's miles away with a small smile on his face. What is he thinking? Investors? Money? A company sell out? A lover?

They're all too much for me, far too complicated. A new job in London will seem like paradise, a walk in the park, compared to this bunch.

"Mark traced the hacker," I say to John.

"I told him not to bother. He's been so busy."

"He made time," I reply.

John shifts uncomfortably. "Happy Days."

How can the head of sales who is supposed to be witty charming and effusive say the same thing all the time? His eyes dart nervously from me to Simon and back to me again. There is a trace of perspiration across his top lip.

"We have proof," I continue.

"Happy D—" He must see my expression because he coughs, removes his hands from his pocket and sits up with a serious frown on his face. "So?"

"What do you think we should do?" I ask him.

He looks from me to Simon. "It's a crime. We have to tell the police," he says.

"Good. I agree with you," I reply.

He smiles at me. I mean, the guy actually smiles at me like I am a million dollars or like I've given him a present of a diamond Rolex watch.

"I've waited a long time for you to say that to me, Ellie," he says, "we finally agree. We're a good team. We think the same."

"Then I am going to leave you to handle it all. He's a member of your team. So I expect you to deal with it and organise suitable cover for his work once he is gone." I'm not doing another thing for anyone. It's time they all began doing things for themselves.

A flicker of doubt crosses his forehead and he glances uncertainly at Simon. "One of the team? Who is it?"

"Don't worry!" Simon slaps him on the shoulder.

He takes the folder of evidence from my desk. "I'll be with you, John. We'll do it together. It's about time we stepped up to the plate as they say in America. It's about time we gave Ellie a break and took responsibility for what's going on in this office."

John nods uncertainly. "Who is it?"

Simon looks at me.

"This is your ball game, Simon, as they say in America."

"It was Liam," Simon says.

John's mouth falls open. "Liam? Why?"

"You'll have to ask him but I'm guessing he wanted the prestige of smoothing out the problem and being in charge of damage limitation. He certainly rose to the occasion in the hotel. He was brilliant. He got all the kudos. It was our biggest contract and he was their hero."

* * *

I leave them to the task in hand and return home to an empty house with an empty heart. I cannot continue living like this. It's torture.

I telephone Maria and stand gazing out of the window, across the Lough, at the church spire of Jordanstown, it's a view I know from memory and one that I will remember when I return to England.

"It was Liam," I say, "Simon and John are dealing with it now. They will call the police."

Her sharp intake of breath reminds me of her vivid expressions. Her cheekbones, her soft skin and melting-chocolate-coloured eyes. I rub my own eyes. What is to be — and what is not to be — perhaps there are no happy endings. Romeo and Juliet.

"What did you say — what's ending?"

"Nothing," I reply.

"Lily wants you to come over for dinner tomorrow night. She's cooking."

I want to ask her if it is what she wants. I never seem to know what Maria wants. But then I think that she doesn't know herself what she wants. Perhaps we've never known or understood each other. People who supposedly fall in love and love each other, and believe that their partner is *The One* - don't behave like this. They don't hurt their partner — no matter what happens.

"That would be lovely," I say. It will be the perfect opportunity for me to tell them both that I am leaving and that I am going back to London.

Chapter Sixteen

On Saturday night I gel my hair so it is unruly and messy. I wear an olive green blouse with khaki trousers and high heels then decide to ride the Harley, so I change into my biker's boots and my red leather jacket.

I ride down the motorway past the City airport that is busy with black cabs lined up waiting for disembarking passengers. The yellow Harland and Woolf cranes dominate the skyline and there's a cruise ship just beyond the ferry port, and I'm reminded of the day I arrived on the ferry, and the snow covered hill they call Napoleon's Nose and the flurry of snowflakes that landed on my cheeks.

I'd been sad then but now I'm infinitely worse. I'm a pinball being ricochet from one emotional disaster to another personal crisis. I'm destined to be a wanderer.

When I arrive they are in the kitchen and Maria pops a champagne cork and is disappointed when I won't touch a drop.

"I've come on the bike."

"You can stay over." She smiles.

I shake my head and turn away but not before I notice deep brown flecks in her eyes and small laughter lines at the corner of her sensuous mouth.

"Yeah, we've a spare room," agrees Lily. "We can have a sleep-over." She places a butcher's apron over her head and ties it at her small waist then she kneels at the counter on a stool and begins to mix the meat and onions for the hamburgers.

To keep my mind from wandering I tell them about my meeting with John and Simon, and how Mark tracked the Dominator back to Liam.

"But why would he do something like that? He had every-thing going for him and now he will end up with a criminal record."

"Simon won't press charges - I think he just wants Liam to wake up to the reality and the responsibility of the huge damage he could have caused. The company could have gone under. Everyone could have been left without work. It could have been disastrous."

"Mummy, do you still have a job?"

"Yes, darling."

"It doesn't make sense, that a guy who had it all only wanted his cheap moment of fame as the hero in the hotel and to the detriment of the company and his co-workers. I honestly don't understand why he did it. But who would know what anyone thinks or what anyone wants or what anyone's intentions are? I've given up trying to work anyone out."

"That sounds very bitter." Maria frowns at me and I deliberately ignore her watchful eyes that follow me as I pace restlessly around the kitchen with a bottle of non-alcoholic beer swinging in my hand.

Lily runs from the room to fetch a painting that she drew at school for me and while we wait for her, I gaze out at the garden. It's almost dark and the sky is a purple hue. I remember when they came home from Lanzarote and the passionate night I spent with Maria in the spare room, leaving before Lily woke the next morning. It had felt so right together. We had the same rhythm. The same pattern of loving and giving and it was one that I knew, I would never feel again.

"Michael is in the bad books with Mum." Maria smiles and tosses chips into the fryer. "He hasn't even telephoned her to see how she is. She's really put out. He hasn't even bothered sending her flowers. Imagine her perfect, soon to be ex son-in-law, hasn't even sent a card and she's very hurt. I think he might have fallen off the proverbial pedestal. And Connor is also very angry with Michael. They're not speaking now."

I don't turn from the window and she speaks quietly and quickly before Lily returns.

"He will get what is due to him, Ellie. He is controlling and manipulative and one day his next girlfriend will realise it. She won't be as stupid as me. She won't put up with it and he will grow into a lonely old man."

"I doubt that Maria. Some people never get what they deserve in this life."

"Judgement day comes to us all, Ellie."

Lily returns to the room and throws a painting on the counter. "It's a picture of you in the kitchen," she explains pointing at the stick figure with a blue and yellow apron.

"I think I look gorgeous but I'm obviously not eating enough."

Lily giggles.

Maria is leaning against the kitchen sink, her arms folded and she is smiling and sipping champagne watching us both. Across the room our eyes meet and linger until I turn away but not before I've seen the question in her eyes asking me, what's wrong?

With the expertise of a circus entertainer Lily begins a running commentary as if she is a famous chef on television. "Now mix fine herbs and chopped onions to the minced meat in the bowl. Stir vigorously for three minutes then pat neatly into shape squashing them flat and bash them hard." Lily pounds the meat and laughs.

I take a deep breath. I'll tell them now. I'll tell them I am leaving next Friday. In six days' time and get it over with.

Lily washes salad and decorates it with jagged tomato, slices of cucumber and diced avocado. When the burgers are cooked and the chips are crisp and brown she lays the feast in front of us with a flourish of her hands. She accepts our applause with a small bow and I realise that I've missed my moment to say anything.

It will have to be after dinner now. I'll definitely tell them then.

Half an hour later Maria has stacked the dishwasher and Lily is tucking into chocolate ice cream and I am sipping coffee when she says, "I met a friend of yours in the hospital yesterday."

"Mine?"

"Yes, Maxie. She said her friend Anna met you in the gym a while ago and that you had been out with them a few times. She seems to know you quite well."

"They are nurses, but I had forgotten they work in the City Hospital. I hadn't connected them at all to your Mum being in there. They must be back from France."

"Maxie is lovely. She's a good nurse, very kind and funny, too."

"Her partner Anna, comes to my gym. That's where we met. I'll give them a ring." I make a mental note to call them before

I go back to London next week.

"She said that they had been over to your house for a barbecue."

"Yes." I laugh at the memory. "That was the mad spontaneous party one Sunday lunchtime. I had been out on Saturday night and invited everyone over. Then I had a manic hangover in the office on the Monday."

"I remember. I made you coffee. She also mentioned a girl called Carla?"

"She went with them on holiday. She's a school teacher."

Maria raises an eyebrow and waits for me to elaborate. I don't tell her that Carla slipped me her phone number on our first meeting and that I only met her a few times and nothing happened.

"Maxie said they asked you to go on holiday but you wouldn't go with them."

"They did but I didn't fancy a camping holiday in France."

Maria stares at me and I return her solid gaze. "I had no idea you were that friendly with them."

I shrug. "How would you?"

Lily spoons ice cream into her mouth and there is a streak of chocolate on her chin.

"Charlie's mother is going to have a baby boy and she showed me a picture of it in her tummy?"

"She must be very excited," I reply, encouragingly, and Maria gives me a withering look.

"It was yuk! I don't want you to have any more children mummy."

There is a lump stuck firmly in my throat making my eyes water. Does Maria want another child? Does she remember how happy she was with Michael when Lily was born? Doubts and insecurities flood into my mind. I love them both so much but I must tell them I'm leaving. I will never be a part of their life in the way that I want to be. It will kill me to continue living and loving them like this. On a friendship only basis. It is not enough. Nor will it ever be.

It is now or never.

I must get this over and so I tell them.

I open my mouth and I drop my bombshell.

* * *

On Monday morning, I wait for Simon to finish a series of phone calls. His office door has been firmly closed most of the morning, now I knock and enter. He's ensconced in his own world in whatever business deal he is arranging or planning and I'm irritated with his lack of attention to his staff and to his business.

Now that I have told Maria and Lily, the worst is over. I'm in a hurry to leave but I sit down and cross my legs, I can see he wants to say something to me first so I wait to hear about American investors, a company investment or another scheme he's thought up. He is clearly agitated and excited. He runs his hand through his hair and checks his watch.

"Louise is flying into Dublin as we speak," he says.

"Louise?"

"Yes, I've got the most amazing news, Ellie. You'll never believe it." His cheeks are gaunt but his eyes are alive and vibrant. "We've adopted twins."

"What?"

"I know! I know! It was the last thing you would expect, right? But you and Louise talked me into it — and Mickey

Bleu — she's been amazing," he speaks excitedly, "They're from Haiti. Their parents died in the cholera outbreak, after an earthquake. A little boy Webster and a girl called Tatiana. They are four years old and they are beautiful."

"Oh my G—"

"We can't believe it. Mickey and Emmanuel have been fantastic. They made phone calls and they've introduced us to the right people. They set up appointments for us in America and on the island. They've arranged everything. And now we've set up a foundation in Haiti. The Louise Tavner School to help educate all those poor children. It's taken time, and a lot of money, but it's been worth it. We spent a few days with the twins in America to acclimatise and get all their documents sorted, then I came on home ahead of them all, you know, to organise things.

"Louise has just landed with the children in Dublin airport." He checks his phone again. "They should be home in a few hours and we're going to take them home and later this evening they will meet their grandparents. My parents are driving up from Sligo and Louise's parents are coming to stay from Enniskillen, so we will all be together. We will be a proper family at last."

"That's fantastic Simon." I stand up and give him a hug. His eyes are rimmed with tears and I can see the strain that he must have been though in the past months and the happiness that now fills his heart.

"I'm sorry, Ellie. I know I've been difficult and I know that I've been absent from the office. We've spent months going for fertility treatment in Germany and America but..." He shakes his head. "This is by far the best thing that has happened. We're thrilled and Louise is so happy." He stands up and moves to the window and looks down into the street. "We are so lucky. Imagine how our lives will change."

I smile. I'm genuinely pleased but I cannot, nor will not, be detracted from the purpose of my visit to his office. I must tell him now. Or my plans will go out of the window. I must stay focused on what is important to me. "I have some news too, Simon."

He looks at me and smiles optimistically.

"I'm leaving. I'm going back to London. I'm leaving on Friday."

His jaw drops. "You can't. Not this Friday? I'm changing the structure of the company, Ellie. It's what we talked about. It's what we discussed. I want you to become a Director."

"We didn't discuss it, Simon."

"But it is what you want, isn't it? You've worked so hard and you've turned the company around. We're a team Ellie, all of us; you, me, John and Maria and the techies downstairs. We've never been so successful and it's all down to you."

I toss my carefully prepared three-year business plan onto his desk.

"This will help you, Simon. This gives a clear indication of growth areas, key accounts, sales orientation and competition plus a marketing budget and strategy for the next three years. It's all in there. It will help you. It's everything you need."

"But, Ellie you can't leave. I need you. The company needs you. John and Maria will be lost without you. Besides, I'll need to take more time out of the office and be with my new family. I won't have time to—"

"Yes, you will. Believe me Simon, in a few weeks' time, you will need an excuse to leave the house and take refuge here in your office. It will be your sanctuary. It will be the only place you will be able to find peace and quiet."

* * *

When I return home, I switch on the television and Steve's face stares defiantly from the screen. It is an old photograph. Distorted and faded from when he was arrested during a July parade several years ago. I would recognise him anywhere, the tattoos and his sneering smile. I remember his cold eyes staring at me across the bar and calling me a 'Fokking Lesbo' when I kicked him in the balls and he hurled himself in the car. I turn up the sound. *"Police are investigating the murder of missing man Steven McGrath whose body was found yesterday..."*

* * *

My last day in the office is over. I glance around the room satisfied I've tidied everything. It seems a long time ago that I arrived here. Seven months ago I escaped London and ran away from one life to find sanctuary but instead, I found true love and heartbreak in Belfast. Now I am returning home.

I remember that March morning, my first day at work on my Harley when I saw Maria how my heart skipped a beat when our eyes locked across the street. She was beautiful. Standing on the pavement and staring at me with open curiosity and interest.

Had it been love at first sight?

I remember sitting at my desk flicking paper balls into my crash helmet and meeting Lily for the first time and the Easter story I told her, I think I had loved her from that first moment.

But I will not be distracted by emotion.

Maria left early. Her office door is closed. I resist the impulse to open it and engrave the image of where she will continue to sit and work, long after I have left.

I must move on. It's time for me to go.

Since I told Maria and Lily that I was leaving, we haven't spoken. Maria has avoided contact with me as I have avoided her. I turn off the office light and close the door for the final time.

When we arrive at Mickey Bleu's restaurant there is a big sign on the door saying, Private Function.

"Won't that affect business?" Stuart asks, as we walk inside.

"The more you can't have something, the more you want it. They'll be queuing in the street tomorrow night," Siobhan replies, she now has pink hair and sky blue nails.

"I know what you mean." I turn away from their shared kiss and the love in their eyes.

Mickey's changed the layout of the restaurant. There are two long tables in the centre of the room covered with white and yellow linen cloths, glittering cutlery and matching napkins fan out of shining crystal goblets.

"Are you having a laugh, Mickey? I don't know this many people," I say.

"You'd be surprised. Are you sure you're doing the right thing, Ellie? It's such a shock. I don't want you to leave." She clasps me in a hug. I cannot answer her. There is something lodged in my throat.

The techie crew arrive from the office, Mark Bowman, Ray the shy one, Jessica the demon pool player and my Boys Aloud; Steve, Adam, Jeff and Mike.

Liam is not here. He was the hacker and is now in police custody but I miss him. It seems such a waste. He was such a valuable and fun member of the team.

John is wearing a new set of red and green braces that I gave him this afternoon. He shuffles toward Mickey. His eyes full of affection and I guess it will be another unrequited love.

"Another crush," Siobhan mouths at me and we both grin.

Music from the loud-speakers play Katie Melua's song, *I Will Be There.*

Don't ever be lonely, remember I'll always care.

Wherever you may be, remember I will be there.

I swallow before gathering my emotions and my resolution. "You're going because you have to. There is nothing for you here. There is no future," I mumble.

The atmosphere is subdued and I think of the night of my birthday, the last celebration we had a few weeks ago and the banter and the laughter. Maria had not been a part of that night and I wonder if she will appear this evening.

"This is a party," I call aloud. "Try and look a bit happier. You'll be pleased to see the back of me." I slap John on the shoulder and throw my arm over Jessica's shoulder.

"We'll miss you, Ellie" he says, sincerely.

"Feck off!" I reply, in my best Irish accent. But suddenly Maria's words come into mind. In that first week she had said that John was harmless and he was like a puppy underneath. How right she is. I've grown quite fond of this weird-man, I would never meet anyone like him again and I smile.

"I'm pleased that we became good colleagues who could work together," he says. He playfully puckers his lips and plants a big kiss on my cheek. "If only you were straight. We could have been more than work colleagues. You don't know what you are missing."

"That's the best offer I've had for a long time, John. Thank you. I'm flattered." I laugh.

"Stop flirting, John. That girl is mine," Marks calls.

Jessica is holding my hand that is still draped across her neck. "You're my role model. It won't be the same in the office without you, Ellie. I wish you weren't leaving."

I untangle myself and take her hand. Her nails are painted rainbow colours. "I love your nails Jessica. You always have great taste always so colourful." She turns away but not before she wipes her damp eyes with a green nail.

All the techie guys know that Jessica is gay but John hasn't twigged on yet. It's a secret that everyone is happy to keep from him — at Jessica's instigation — just to watch his reaction to certain conversations. It's office banter and familiarity that goes on in offices world-wide and I revel in the camaraderie.

I hand around more drinks and Ray gives an embarrassed cough when I kiss his cheek. I feel uncharacteristically tactile but it seems the most natural thing to do. I hadn't realised how close I had become to the team and how much they all mean to me.

Emmanuel arrives with Cassandra and Flore and the children are soon busy offering bowls of crisps and a spicy dip. When they offer me food I smile but I can't eat. I have a large lump wedged in my throat and I feel sick.

I push my hair up and out at the back, so my neck is cool. It gives me something to do and I am conscious of maintaining my composure. I breathe deeply, the aroma of *Paco Rabanne* from my wrists comforts me in this uncomfortable situation and I inhale deeply and slowly, regulating and controlling my rapid heartbeat while I sip sparkling water.

The door opens and Simon, Louise and their two newly-adopted children arrive to cries of delight. Webster and

Titania are twins and they're beautiful. Webster is dressed in long blue shorts and T-shirt and Titania wears pink. They have big brown trusting eyes, short tight curly hair and wary smiles. They regard me cautiously and I hold out my hand for a high-five but they are shy and cling to Louise and Simon.

Louise is beaming and she kisses my cheek. "I can't believe you're leaving, Ellie. Just when everything will settle down."

I force a smile.

"I got a few things wrong, didn't I?" John says in my ear. "It wasn't an affair, or a divorce, or American investors — it was just a couple of kids."

"Don't worry. We all get things wrong, John. It's learning from our mistakes that count."

"Ellie," I turn at the sound of my name and I am enveloped in a big hug from Anna, then a slap on the shoulder from Maxie.

"Oh my, gosh. What a lovely surprise! What are you doing here? Have you nowhere else better to be?" I joke, conscious that I haven't seen them since they came back from France.

"Maria invited us," Maxie says by way of explanation. "I've got to know her over the past few days. She's a really great person and her Mum is on the mend. She's a lovely old dear."

"That was never my impression," I mumble.

"Were you going to leave without saying goodbye?" Anna asks. "You will have to see Carla before you go. She's devastated you're leaving."

"You should have come to France with us. We missed you. Carla was lonely. It would have been more fun with you there. She wouldn't come tonight, though. She said she was heartbroken you were leaving and you hadn't phoned to say goodbye," Maxie talks quickly.

I push my spiked hair from my face and pour bubbles of

sparking Cava into fluted glasses — any task that will keep me busy and not thinking.

"I hope we'll stay friends. I know we haven't seen much of you, Ellie, but when we do meet up, we always have great fun and I'll miss you at the gym." Anna laughs. "You always kept me on my toes. I'm going to train harder like you—"

The door opens.

Lily's pupils are large behind her black glasses and her nose is red. She looks vulnerable, small and sad. She leans against Maria's waist and holds her mother's hand. The cocky confident little girl seems to have been replaced by an insecure child and I'm conscious that Michael is not the only one who has abandoned her.

Maria looks equally as tired and bewildered. She appears daunted by the amount people and I dare not speak to them so I'm pleased when Louise gathers them into her family group. It's not long before Maria is holding Webster in her arms and Lily is speaking to Titania.

There are twenty-two people here and I'm aware that not this many people gathered for drinks when I left Proctor and Gowan in London. The irony of my situation doesn't escape me.

Suddenly, I feel that I'm outside myself. A stranger playing a part. Merely a role in my insignificant life that has suddenly become centre stage and I'm the focus of attention. My life takes on its new rhythm. My fanciful mind and my senses are combined and I'm propelled by an invisible force that sweeps through me, buffeting this surreal and unrealistic scene that I must play-out. I am an actor. A player merely acting out my final scene. My farewell speech. My goodbye. I imagine the evening panning out, what I will say and my life ahead of me.

I might as well get it over with.

I clear my throat and tap my glass and take a deep breath. "I think it is probably best if I make a short speech before dinner, so I won't slur my words and I won't be heckled—"

"Don't you believe it," shouts Simon.

"Want to bet a Scotsman?" calls Mark. "I can heckle anytime."

I smile. I focus. I concentrate and I hold up my shaking hand.

"Firstly, I want to thank the Techie team, Stuart and Mark, Ray and Boys Aloud - Steve, Adam, Jeff and Mike. And of course our glamorous receptionist Siobhan, and also our new edition — demon pool player — Jessica."

A cheer goes up from my right. "Without them, the last seven months would have been pretty tame and boring but with them it has been challenging, exciting and fun. You have all been a pleasure to work with and I love you all." A louder cheer goes up.

"Mum, tell her," hisses Lily, who is standing on my left.

I raise my voice. "We've made headway in our business development." Another cheer goes up. "And we've gained lots of new and exciting clients, some of whom have become friends for life. The success of Mickey Bleu's restaurant is due to the dedication and fantastic personality of this beautiful woman and her amazing husband Emmanuel whom we all know is the real strength behind this powerful woman."

The laughter and cheers grows louder. Emmanuel waves a hand in acknowledgment. Mickey calls out. "He's my rock."

"Mum, you've got to say something," Lily's voice gathers speed.

"Mickey Bleu, you have been an inspiration to us all, and

as a result of all your endeavours behind the scene, you have helped create a very happy family." I wave toward Simon where Webster cowers behind his long legs and a smiling Louise holds a puzzled Titania in her arms.

There is more stomping and applauding.

"Mum, tell Ellie we don't want her to go," shouts Lily above the noise.

"We don't want you to go," John chants. "We don't want you to go, Ellie."

Focus! Concentrate! I smile, raise my hands and call for hush.

Is this happening?

"When I first came here, I was lonely, but over the months I've been lucky to have met these lovely girls." I open my arms to my gay friends. "Anna and Maxie whom you will all get to know this evening, they are great fun, kind and giving, and have been hugely supportive."

There is banging on the tables and cheering. The noise is deafening. I bite my lip. Focus!

"MUM! DO SOMETHING!"

I take a sip of Cava. My throat is dry. The bubbles bring tears to my eyes.

Concentrate.

"Simon," my voice wavers and I swallow before I continue. "Simon, without you, or John or Maria, I—"

"MUM!" Lily pushes away from her mother and stomps forward with her hand on her hips and stands directly in front of me. She pushes her glasses up onto her nose and shakes her unruly curly hair.

"YOU CAN'T LEAVE!" she shouts up at me. "MUM LOVES YOU AND I LOVE YOU!"

The whole restaurant explodes into life, whistling, calling and cheering.

"You tell her Lily!"

"We all love you."

"Go Lily!"

"Don't take any excuses!"

"Why do you want to leave your friends?"

"We love you."

"MUM–" Lily shouts.

But it's noisy. I can't think. My cheeks are suddenly wet. Everything is happening in slow motion and I'm a puppet, not in charge of my limbs, and this is not really happening to me. I have no control. I glance around the room and see snapshots; images in slow motion, faces with moving mouths, smiling, laughing and eyes all filled with sadness and bewilderment.

Mickey Bleu is clapping. Simon laughing. Louise is cheering. Anna calls out and Maxie wipes her eyes. The techie boys are whistling and catcalling and clapping.

I must focus. I must finish what I want to say then I can go. I can run and get away from here. I can leave.

"MUM TELL HER!"

Maria catches Lily's arm and pulls her away.

Relieved, I clear my throat and I reach for my glass but then Maria is beside me. She places her cool palm against my hot cheek and turns my face to hers. Her brown eyes question me with a slow beautiful smile and she leans, very slowly forward, and she kisses me gently on the mouth and instinctively my lips part.

I respond. I can't help myself. When we separate I can't take my eyes from her face.

"Please don't ask me to say it in front of everyone," she

whispers, "Please, Ellie." Maria presses her forehead against mine and our noses touch. She speaks so quietly but I hear every word. "Please don't go, Ellie. I want to be with you and so does Lily. We want to share our life with you." She trails a fingernail across the star tattoos under my ear. "I love you."

She's never said she loves me before and her arms are around my neck and I realise we are laughing and that she smells of *Channel* and I know just how much I love her.

"You are *The One*," she says, "I can't let you go."

Lily prods Maria's bottom with her hand. "Tell her my idea, Mum. Go on. Hurry up, tell her now."

When Maria's lips touch my earlobe it causes my skin to gather in goosebumps. "Lily thinks we should buy Auntie Annie's house together."

I smile and pull Lily into our hug relishing the love between the three of us. This special moment is filled with so much love and I'm overwhelmed with emotion. It's more than I could have dreamed.

It's the end of the evening. My party is over. Reality returns and my sanity is reinstalled.

Outside the stars glisten in the night-sky and I gun the engine of the Harley, remembering the day I arrived here.

Sun and showers, tears and tantrums, lovers and losers. Samson and Goliath are an omen. Are they a symbol of my colourful past or a painter's canvas and the opportunity to obliterate the pain and shame of my previous life?

Maria leans out of the taxi window. Her smile is radiant. "See you at home?"

Lily leans across her and shouts, "We'll race you."

I smile. This is me now and they are my life.

THE END

295

Janet Pywell's Books

Contemporary love stories:
Ellie Bravo
Someone Else's Dream

Short Stories:
Red Shoes and Other Short Stories
Bedtime Reads

Ronda George Thrillers:
The Concealers
The Influencers
The Manipulators
The Ronda George Thriller Boxset - books 1-3

Mikky dos Santos Thrillers:
Golden Icon – *The Prequel*
Masterpiece
Book of Hours
Stolen Script
Faking Game
Truthful Lies
Broken Windows

Boxsets

Volume 1 – Masterpiece, Book of Hours & Stolen Script
Volume 2 – Faking Game, Truthful Lies & Broken Windows

For more information visit:
   website: www. janetpywellauthor.wordpress.com

All books are available online and can be ordered through major book stores.

If you enjoy my books then please **do leave a review** from wherever you purchased the book. Your opinion is important to me. A few words will do. I read them all. It also helps other readers to find my work.

Thank you.

About the Author

Author Janet Pywell's storytelling is as mesmerizing and complex as her characters.

Janet's latest novel, a contemporary love story, *Someone Else's Dream* is a heart-warming, uplifting, feel-good novel about courage, integrity and friendship.

In the Mikky dos Santos international crime thriller series - art forger, artist and photographer Mikky is a uniquely lovable female: a tough, tattooed, yet vulnerable protagonist who will steal your heart. Each book is a stand-alone exciting action-adventure novel, set in three uniquely different countries/ locations.

In the first series of domestic crime thrillers, Ronda George is a kickboxing *Masterchef*. After ten years in the British Army assigned to some of the world's most dangerous places, Ronda is enlisted by Inspector Joachin García Abascal to infiltrate the murky underworld of greed, corruption and betrayal.

These books are a must-read for devotees of complex female sleuths - a female James Bond.

Janet has a background in travel and tourism and she writes

using her knowledge of foreign places gained from living abroad and travelling extensively. She currently lives on the Kent coast.

You can connect with me on:

- https://janetpywellauthor.wordpress.com
- https://twitter.com/JanPywellAuthor
- https://www.facebook.com/JanetPywell7227
- https://www.subscribepage.com/someone-elses-dream
- https://www.instagram.com/janetpywellauthor
- https://www.subscribepage.com/the_novel_mentor

Subscribe to my newsletter:

- https://www.subscribepage.com/someone-elses-dream